PRETTY
dependable

Lacey Black

Pretty Dependable

Pine Village Series, book 2

USA Today Bestselling Author

Lacey Black

Lacey Black

Pretty Dependable
Pine Village Series, book 2

Copyright © 2023 Lacey Black

Cover Design by Y'all. That Graphic.
Photographer Sara Eirew

Editing by Kara Hildebrand

Proofreading by Sandra Shipman, Joanne Thompson, and Karen Hrdlicka

Format by Brenda Wright, Formatting Done Wright

IBSN-13: 978-1-951829-42-1

Lacey Black

CHAPTER
one

Ellie

"Mom, I'm home."

A smile spreads across my lips as I pull the chicken out of the oven and set it on the stove top. I could have told him I knew he was home. My seventeen-year-old sounds like a herd of elephants coming up the stairs, but I keep that comment to myself. Instead, I spin around to greet him as he steps through the door at the top of the steps. "How was practice?" I ask the moment he breaches the threshold.

"Coach was a hard-ass," he states, barely able to get the words out before he chuckles.

That's when I spot the reason he's giggling.

His coach, Thomas Dexter—or TD as his friends refer to him as—is hot on his heels, entering my small kitchen space and consuming it with his broad, muscular body. I've known TD practically my whole life. We were in the same class throughout school and hung in the same circles. For a while, I wondered what it would be like to be his girl, but life had a way of throwing you a curveball. Since high school, we've remained friends, with my sole focus being on raising my son.

"You haven't seen hard-ass yet," he quips before adding, "something smells amazing," giving me a heart-stopping grin.

I shake my head and try to get rid of the girlish butterflies that take flight every time he sends one of his smiles my way. "Your stomach knows when dinner's ready. I made enough. Grab a plate," I tell him, unable to fight my own grin.

"I don't want to impose," he replies. It's the same song and dance we engage in often. He knows I make enough food for my growing seventeen-year-old son, as well as him. It's one of the ways I can thank him for all the help he gives me with Brody.

Not only is TD the head high school football coach, he's also a full-time police officer for our small town. Nestled along the Wisconsin/Minnesota border, Pine Village, Wisconsin is home to three thousand residents who don't mind the bitter cold winters and extra fluffy snow that seems to stretch on for months and months. For me, it wasn't so much I enjoyed my small-town upbringing and longed to stay here, but never had an opportunity to escape it. When you find yourself pregnant at seventeen and your parents basically throwing you out on your ass, you do what you have to. That meant finishing my last year of high school, working at the diner at night, and living in the small apartment above the business, trying not to get sick on the stench of deep-fried foods hanging in the air.

"What do you want to drink, Coach?" Brody hollers, pulling me out of my own head.

"Water, please." TD moves to the cabinet and pulls three plates down and places them on the small table, before stepping over to where I stand at the stove and retrieving three forks. "Seriously, smells amazing, El." His voice is like smooth honey on a warm biscuit and makes my mouth water.

A blush creeps up my neck, and I quickly turn my attention to the pan of chicken to hide my reaction.

"Mom, can I have a Coke?"

"You should probably stick with water or Gatorade after practice," I state, knowing that's what TD recommends.

"Yeah, you're right," he replies with a decisive nod before grabbing a glass and filling it with bottled water.

Once we've sat down at the table, I give my son my attention and dish out the chicken and potatoes. "How was practice?"

"Good. I had a touchdown on a sweet pass from Dorian," he tells me proudly, smiling from ear to ear as he cuts into his smothered chicken breast.

"It was a sweet pass and catch," TD chimes in, holding out his fist for a bump.

I shake my head, a soft smile spreading across my lips, enjoying their camaraderie. I'll never be able to repay TD for the friendship and guidance he gives my son. He's been a part of his life since he was little in some respect, but their bond has only grown since Brody started high school and decided to play football. I know my son looks at TD as a friend as well as a father figure, and TD doesn't seem to mind filling that role. That's something I'll never take for granted.

The entire meal is spent the way most of them are. Brody and TD talk football, and I don't mind. At this point in the evening, I'm perfectly content sitting back and listening. In fact, it's nice not to be forced into small talk. Not that I don't enjoy it, but when you do it all day long at work, I find joy in just sitting back and hearing about their day.

As the meal comes to an end, Brody hops up to start the cleanup. He's incredibly helpful around the apartment, especially with my sometimes unpredictable work schedule. As the manager of Frannie's Diner downstairs, I'm the one who gets called in when someone no-shows, is sick, or we get busy and need an extra set of hands. I don't mind, really. It's what I've done since I was seventeen years old. I love my job, even if I go home at the end of every day exhausted, my feet killing me, and smelling like I was dipped in grease.

"How was your day?" TD asks when we're left alone at the table.

"It was good," I assure him, giving him a pleasant smile.

He studies me like always. Honestly, it's a little unnerving. No one reads me the way he does, despite whatever front I put on for the world to see. TD can see past it, and usually calls me out.

Tonight, I wonder what he sees when he looks at me. Does he see the exhaustion? The extra wrinkles around my tired eyes from working five in the morning until three or four in the afternoon? Then coming upstairs to clean, do laundry, and get dinner on the stove. I wonder if he knows I lie awake at night worrying about Brody, not because something's wrong, but simply because he's my everything, and I fear I've somehow left him unprepared for the big bad world he's going to face one day soon. I give him every extra second I have in the day, but sometimes, it still feels like it's not enough.

I was never this much of a worrywart growing up. I actually had a pretty normal childhood. My father is a minister and my mother a schoolteacher. I had friends, played a few sports, and participated in after-school clubs and activities. When I was seventeen, I made a mistake. One my parents couldn't forgive me for, and when I wouldn't give up my unplanned teenage pregnancy, they sent me packing to deal with the results of my careless decisions all on my own.

That's when Frannie stepped up in more ways than one.

Not only did she ensure I had a place of employment, but a roof over my head. She rented me the available two-bedroom apartment above the diner for practically nothing, and I've been a devoted employee and friend ever since.

"I heard Saul made meatloaf today," TD says, referring to Frannie's brother's famous bacon-wrapped meatloaf. It's a staple and the reason our Fridays are so busy.

"He did."

"I missed it," he tsks, shaking his head. "We had an ATV accident out at Bluff Preserves."

"Everyone okay?"

"They will be. Driver has a broken leg, and the passenger a broken hand and gnarly arm contusions. Both were wearing helmets, fortunately."

My hand instantly covers my heart. "From here?"

TD shakes his head. "No, tourists. Supposed to be here for three days. Unfortunately, they'll be spending them at the hospital."

Bluff Preserves National Park is a one-hundred forty-thousand-acre park for anyone who loves the outdoors. With snowmobiling in the winter and fishing and boating in the summer, it's the perfect weekend getaway if that's your thing. It's part of the reason the diner is as busy as it is. While there's cabins, campgrounds, and small houses around the lake, visitors often make their way into town for shopping, meals, and medical assistance.

"I'm glad they're going to be okay."

He watches me from across the table.

"Mom, can I go call Matt? We wanted to run through a few of the plays from practice tonight," Brody says when the dirty dishes are stacked next to the sink.

"Of course," I tell him.

Before he darts off to his bedroom to call his best friend, he pauses in the doorway and gives TD his attention. "Thanks for the ride home, Coach."

"You're welcome, Brody. I'll see you at weightlifting in the morning."

My son smiles. "I'll be there." Then, he's gone, off to talk football with his closest friend.

"He seems ready for school to start," TD says, taking a drink of his water and keeping his chocolate brown eyes locked on me.

"I think so. He's excited for his senior year." Even though I smile at the thought, my heart hammers a little harder in my chest.

How can my baby boy be a senior in high school already?

"Hard to believe," he states. "It feels like he was just learning how to ride his bike in the back parking lot."

I snort a laugh, recalling the particular birthday TD's referring to. I rented one of the pavilions at the park for an end of June birthday party for an eager almost seven-year-old. I saved every tip I received for weeks to be able to purchase that Spider-Man bicycle, knowing it would be the highlight of his day.

Then, the brakes went out on my car, and I wrecked on my way to the big box store to make my purchase. There wasn't a lot of damage, but it was enough. I had a choice to make. The bike my son had his heart set on or fix my car during the heat of summer. Considering I had to drive him to daycare every day, I knew my car was my priority. I cried and cried, hating the thought of letting my son down on his birthday.

Little did I know, TD, and our other friends, Hallie, Ava, and Logan, went in together and purchase Brody the Spider-Man bike he had his heart set on. Not only that, but they threw in a matching helmet, knee pads, and elbow pads too. As much as Brody wanted to ride that bike, he refused because all his little friends didn't have a bike to ride at that moment. So, he waited patiently until we got home.

The moment we pulled into the parking lot, he asked TD and Logan to help him learn to ride that bike. For an hour, he rode circles around the lot of the diner, which was, thankfully, nearly empty. It turned out to be the best birthday he ever had, all smiles with a wide toothless grin, and I've never forgotten what they did for me and my son.

"It's going so fast," I concede, trying not to think about the fact I have a senior in high school. It hasn't been easy, but Brody and I have been a team since day one. There have been plenty of missteps on my part, but I never gave up. Not one single second, even when the pressures of parenthood—and at a very young age—threatened to pull me under.

His large, warm hand reaches across the table and wraps around mine, causing my heartbeat to skip. "You're doing an amazing job, El. Don't ever doubt it. Not for one second."

I gaze up into his dark eyes and feel a flood of emotions wash over me. No one can draw them out like TD can. Every uncertainty I've ever experienced when it comes to being a single mother is dashed away by the confident gleam in his eyes and the reassuring smile on his lips.

"Thank you," I whisper, forcing a smile so I don't cry. "I have a great tribe helping me."

Throwing me a cheeky grin, he quips, "We are pretty awesome."

A bubble of laughter slips from my lips easily and freely. "You all are. I couldn't have done this without you all."

"Bullshit. You could have and would have done whatever necessary, El. We're all grateful to be along for the ride."

That flutter in my belly returns as he holds my gaze for several seconds. Clearing my throat once more, I break the tension with, "Look at us. It's getting heavy in here."

"That's what friends are for. We help carry the load when it gets heavy." Standing, I realize it's that time of night when he heads home to his own place. "You need anything before I head out?"

Shaking my head, I turn my attention to the dishes ready to be cleaned and put away. "I'm just going to wash these and then read a little before bed. Four a.m. will be here before I know it."

One corner of his completely kissable mouth curls up. "I'll take your word for it." Glancing to the sink, he adds, "You sure you don't want help?"

I swat at his arm, doing everything I can to keep our interaction friendly. "No way."

"I don't mind. You did feed me. Again."

"Because I appreciate all your help with Brody. Thank you again for dropping him off."

He rubs his flat stomach; the one where hard abs hide beneath his Pine Village Football T-shirt. "I'd do it in a heartbeat any day, but you know I'd never turn down a homecooked meal like that. I'm a growing boy."

And cue the blush.

A parade of dirty images filters shamelessly through my head, and I push them away as quickly as possible, praying my red cheeks don't give away the state of my dirty mind. I can only imagine a man like TD...*growing*.

"You're gonna be growing out if you're not careful." I slam my mouth shut, wishing I'd just shut the hell up right about now. That's also when my eyes completely betray me and drop to the crotch of his athletic shorts.

Jesus, Ellie! Stop staring at your friend's groin!

If he notices my eyes fixated on his thighs, he doesn't let on. Thankfully. How embarrassing would that be? After decades of friendship, I could ruin it with one ill-timed glance at his...stuff. Not that I haven't stolen hooded looks behind sunglasses or whatnot, but I've never been as brazen as to basically stare at the goods right in front of him while he's watching me.

"I think I'll be all right," he replies, pulling me out of my naughty head and back to the conversation. "I'll just workout extra this week, because there's no way I'm giving up your food."

Smiling, I reply, "You do that. Sneak one in for me while you're at it."

Because I am *not* someone who works out. At all. I don't do yoga or hit any sort of gym, and if I'm ever running, you better run too because something's probably chasing me.

"Will do. Thanks again for dinner, El," he says, leaning forward and placing his lips against my forehead. He started doing that sweet gesture way back when we were friends in high school. I try not to read into it, but it's difficult when your heart skips a beat and your underused girly bits get all excited.

"You're welcome. Drive safe."

He heads for the door and releases the lock. There's one at the top of the stairs, as well as the base of them, and TD has been a big advocate of making sure I keep them both locked when we're home. Not that I've ever had to worry about safety in Pine Village.

Not a lot happens as far as crime in this small town, but as the town's police officer, he's always pushing me to lock up and keep safe.

"Night. Lock up behind me," he says, holding my gaze one last time before stepping out of the apartment and pulling the door closed.

I listen as his heavy feet carry him down the stairs, knowing he'll throw the lock on the bottom door as he exits the building. There's another set of stairs in the hallway, but those are never used. They lead down to a closed-off storage area in the diner, only to be used in case of emergency.

Finally, I exhale the breath I didn't even realize I was holding and throw the lock on the door. A bark of laughter spills from Brody's room, as well as the faint hum of conversation. Smiling, I turn my attention to the stack of dirty dishes and start filling up the sink, trying to push all thoughts of TD from my mind. The last thing I need is to get all caught up in my feelings over someone who has me safely and securely tucked in the friend zone.

I need him too much to ever jeopardize our friendship by entertaining thoughts of something more.

TD and I are friends, and that's all we'll ever be.

I'm okay with that.

Sometimes, I just have to tell my heart to get on board with it too.

CHAPTER
Two

TD

The door is barely closed behind me when I hear the knock. "It's open," I holler, knowing who's on the opposite side.

"Wild Friday night, I see," Logan, my closest friend, says as he steps through the back entry.

"Yep." Grabbing a bottle from the fridge, I hold it up for him.

Nodding, he takes the beer and twists off the top, while I pull a second one from the fridge and lean against the counter. "Wanna sit outside? It's pretty nice out," he suggests, already moving toward the door.

I follow behind and plop into one of the pub chairs at the table on my back deck before taking my first drink of cold brew. "Why aren't you out tonight?"

He sighs. "I met Marcus at Shiner's for a pizza and beer, but when Shay showed up, I got the hell out of there," he says, referring to his ex-wife.

Shay is a major thorn in my friend's side. Not only are they divorced, but she's part owner in his family's hardware business, thanks to Logan's dad. He left his business to the couple when he got sick and passed away, and now that they're no longer together, Shay refuses to sell her half. She knows dick about lumber—at least in the literal sense—but sees this as an opportunity to make my friend's life hell on a daily basis.

It's fucked up.

"How's Marcus?" I ask, changing the subject to another friend instead of the ex-wife. Marcus was another classmate of ours in school and is the mechanic and tow truck driver for our small town. He started in the garage, turning wrenches and changing oil, and eventually had the opportunity to purchase the business about five years ago. He puts everything into it, devoting more hours than any one human should, but has built one hell of a reputation and business over the years.

"Good. Busy. Said he was out today at Bluff Preserves with you."

I nod. "Yeah. It was a mess. Didn't get to chat much with him while he cleaned up the accident," I say, referring to the ATV he took care of for us.

"That's what he said." After a few long seconds, he asks, "How was practice?"

"Went well. I think we're ready for our first game next Friday," I tell him, kicking my feet up on the table in front of me. "Our O-line is young, but our QB, running back, and receivers are all seniors with experience."

"How's Brody?"

"He's great. Really coming into his own as a team leader and my number one receiver this season. He should get lots of playing time," I state.

"And Ellie?"

My heart does that weird little flutter every time she's mentioned. It's been happening for years, but I refuse to focus on the reason. "She looked a little worn out tonight. I know she pulled a double yesterday and opened again this morning."

When he doesn't reply, I look his way, only to find a not-so-subtle smile on his face.

"What?" I snap, already knowing what's coming.

"Nothing," he insists, taking a drink from his bottle. "Well, just one thing," he adds. "When are you going to admit you're in love with her?"

I sigh and shake my head. "Don't."

"No, really. You two have been friends forever. Neither of you date, and I'm pretty sure it's because you both like each other. Take the leap."

"It's not that easy," I concede, squirming in my chair a little. I hate talking about my feelings, especially when they involve Ellie. "We're friends."

He snorts. "Friends who want to bang."

"Stop," I practically growl at him.

"All I'm saying is," he starts, but I cut him off.

"I know what you're saying. You've been saying it for years. Not going to happen. I cherish my friendship with her too much to risk hurting her." I need her in my life. No way will I ruin what we have because I tried to date her. I've seen it too often in this small town. When the relationship goes south, the original friendship never survives. I won't let that happen to us.

"So, you just keep her tucked in the friend zone?"

"Yeah."

"That's fucked up."

Turning to face my friend, I can't help but ask, "Yeah? How come you haven't asked Hallie out yet?"

Even as the night falls around us, I can see the tips of his ears turn red. "Why would I ask her out? She hates me."

"Foreplay," I point out, taking a long pull from my beer.

"Dating her would be like trying to baptize a cat."

I can't help but laugh. "She is a feisty one," I derive, unable to hide my smile. The truth is, Hallie Rhodes is a pistol, and she loves to push Logan's buttons for fun. Hallie was another classmate of ours and is considered a friend in our small circle. Her older brother, Gabe, is one of the town physicians, as is her best friend, Blair. Gabe and Blair are dating now and living together in the house Gabe has been remodeling.

"Feisty isn't the right word. She's hostile at best."

"But only toward you, which is why I consider it foreplay. Her students and the parents love her." Hallie is the preschool teacher in town, always with a friendly, pleasant smile on her face. Well, unless Logan is around. Then, she turns snarky and shows her fangs like a feral cat.

"Last time I saw her, she 'accidentally' whacked me on the back of the head with a two-by-four."

A bark of laughter erupts from my gut.

"Stop laughing. That shit hurt," he mutters, rubbing the spot on the back of his head as if the mere thought of it brought back the pain. "Let's not talk about Hallie."

"Wait, why was she buying a two-by-four?" I find myself asking. Hallie isn't exactly a wood smith, and if she needs something done at her condo, she'd ask for help.

"For pleasure? To use as a torture device in her house of pain?"

Now he has me rolling, my stomach hurting from laughter.

"You're not my friend anymore," he murmurs, finishing off his beer and setting the empty on the deck.

"You love me." Clearing my throat, I decide to switch back to the one subject he hates talking about. "Any luck yet on buying Shay out?"

He just turns and stares at me.

His ex-wife refuses to sell, and no one can figure out why. It's not like she has anything positive to give to the business. Her biggest contribution was to set up social media accounts and maintain them during business hours. Oh, and let's not forget the implementation of color-coded polo shirts specific for the day of the week. That one actually makes me laugh. Anyone who knows Logan understands he doesn't give a shit about style and refuses to follow any of her color-coded bullshit. He wears a company T-shirt every day in whatever color he chooses, telling their employees to do the same.

Shay Johnson loves to stick it to Logan and happily spends her days doing just that.

"She wants to talk about the holiday party," he mutters, crossing his arms over his chest.

My eyebrows draw skyward. "In August?"

"Apparently, you have to book the good places in advance," he replies with a disgusted snort. "What good places? We always have the company party at Shiner's Sports Bar."

"Everyone loves Shiner's," I concede, knowing it's one of the hot spots in town. It's a big sports bar with tons of televisions on the wall, good food and spirits, and games. We're talking some arcade games, a few holes of mini golf, Skee-Ball, billiards, and more.

"Who doesn't love Skee-Ball?" Logan asks, shaking his head in disgust. "Shay thinks we need to rent out the steak house. Not that I'm against supporting Kameron, but my employees are more of the sports bar type of guys." Kameron was a few years older than us in school and returned to his hometown after culinary school to open a touch of fine dining in our small community. It's an amazing place with a variety of gourmet dinner options, but it's not the place you go when you're looking for cheap or quick.

I'm more of a Shiner's guy myself, and I know Logan is too.

"I like darts," I state unnecessarily.

He silently stews for a few minutes, and I just let him be. Sometimes, it's best just to be quiet while he works through his thoughts. Finally, after a few quiet moments, he asks, "Think Green Bay will go all the way this year?"

I snort and gaze up at the stars. He knows I hate the Packers, despite being from Wisconsin. The Colts are where it's at, where my loyalties lie. Yeah, I love the game of football, so I'll watch any team play, but if I have the choice of rooting for the Packers or their opponent, it's not the green and yellow I choose.

We spend the next thirty minutes talking football and baseball before it's time for my friend to slip back over to his own house. He lives on the block behind me, three doors down, so it's convenient for us to walk back and forth when the mood strikes.

"You working tomorrow?" he asks, tossing his empty beer bottle in the outside recycling receptacle.

"No, I'm off. Thought about wetting a line after team lifting and walk-through."

He nods. "Let me know if you want some company. The hardware store closes at noon, so I'm free after that."

"Will do," I reply, collecting my own empty bottle and throwing mine in the recycling too.

"Later," Logan hollers, disappearing into the backyard.

Once I'm inside and my trash is thrown away, I kick off my athletic shoes and head for the laundry room. There's always a load to wash, and tonight is no different. I toss towels and washcloths into the machine and grab a bottle of water from the fridge as I pass. My evenings are usually spent reviewing plays and working on the next week's goals or filling out paperwork I hadn't gotten to yet for the day job.

I flip on the television and grab my bag, pulling out the workout schedule for the next few days and make a few tweaks. My team is scheduled for lifting three days a week before practice and I love to add in a few fun elements, when possible, to keep things on the lighter side. One thing I discovered about high school kids is they rarely take things as seriously as we'd like, and their attention span can be pretty short. So throwing in some fun exercises every now and again does us all good.

At ten o'clock, my phone rings. Smiling, I reach for the device and tap the screen without confirming my suspicion. I'm ninety-nine-percent certain I know who it is. She calls like clockwork, always around this time of night, after she's put her kids to bed.

"How's my favorite sister?"

"She's good. Drinking a glass of wine on the back deck and watching a storm roll in. How's my favorite little brother?"

I drop my ink pen and kick my feet up onto the coffee table to get comfortable. "Not too bad."

"No hot date? It's Friday night, you know."

Grinning, I slide my left arm behind my head and lean against the couch cushion. "If I was on a hot date, I wouldn't be answering your call."

"Good to know," she mumbles, "and let's get back to the part about it being Friday night and you're at home. Why are you there?"

"Because this is where I live," I deadpan, the corner of my mouth curling upward.

"Yes, I know, smart-ass, but you won't meet a woman sitting on your couch."

Sighing, I realize too late I should have let the call go to voice mail. "Why did you call again? Just to give me a hard time?"

"Always. That's my job as your big sister."

"How are my nephews?" I ask, looking for a subject change.

"Rowdy," she insists, taking a deep breath. "Hagen has basketball camp this week, and Rogan is taking swim lessons."

My nephews are nine and six and packed full of energy. They definitely keep my sister, Loree, and her husband, Kenton, on their toes. The more activities they keep them involved in, the better it is for their sanity, or so they say.

"Bring them back to Pine Village soon. I'll take them fishing at Bluff Preserves," I offer, recalling how we fished and camped last summer for a weekend. The boys loved it.

"I've already talked to Kenton about planning a trip home soon. Is there a time that works best?"

"Fall is football season," I remind her, even though I know she's well aware. Once school starts next week and the first game hits Friday night, my life belongs to the grid iron. Six days a week, I'll be at the school, my ass on the sidelines with my team.

"I thought the boys would like to see a game."

"That'd be pretty cool, but you know how it is. The weather will start to get cold sooner rather than later." I don't mind the cold Wisconsin weather, but I know my sister does. That's why she moved to Arizona after college with Kenton. He was offered a job out west and they jumped at the opportunity to relocate.

"Our blood is much too thin for the likes of your winters, which is why we're looking into first of September."

Shocked, I find myself asking, "Wow, really?"

Loree chuckles through the phone line. "Yes, really. The boys have a five-day break over Labor Day weekend for teacher planning, and we're tossing around the idea of coming to see you. I'll have to check on cabins in the area, but if we can find one available on short notice, I think it's a done deal."

"I got your cabin. Logan still has the one on the lake and no longer uses it for a seasonal rental," I tell my sister.

"We'll rent it," she insists. "Why don't you make sure it's available before I book flights."

"Done, but I'm certain it'll be fine. He only uses it when he's trying to hide from his ex-wife and looking to fish in peace," I say. My sister has heard all about Logan and Shay's marriage, as well as their divorce. Nothing I told her was a secret, especially when Logan's dad died and left the business to both of them. If Mr. Johnson knew his son and wife would be divorced in less than a year after he passed, I'm sure he wouldn't have added her name to everything.

Fortunately for Logan, the cabin was his grandfather's and left to him long before he and Shay married. Otherwise, I'm sure she would have clawed her talons into that too and refused to let go.

"Why doesn't he use it for a rental anymore? I thought it brought good money in," she asks curiously.

"A couple of bad tenants destroyed some of the original shit in there that was his grandpa's, and he was just done. The money was nice, but not necessary. Plus, Shay was trying to get half of the income in alimony, so he just pulled it from the rental company overseeing it. Now, he just uses it for personal use, which extends to a few friends."

"Well, make sure it's okay for us to use it, and if it is, I'll book flights. Ideally, we'd come in early afternoon that Friday and leave Monday sometime."

"I'll call him as soon as we hang up. I'm really happy you're coming, Lor."

"Me too. Now we just need to work on getting you to Arizona," she says.

"Yeah, yeah. Maybe around the holidays," I state, even though I'm not certain that would work either. Winter is just as busy with tourists as it is in the summer months, and my day job can get busy.

"I'm holding you to it," she insists, a smile evident in her voice. "Go call Logan and let me know. I can get the ball rolling on this end. Oh, and Thomas? If it's not available, that's okay too. I can check into rentals."

"It's available, Loree," I counter, my words dripping with annoyance. First, because she called me by my birth name, and second because I've told her multiple times it is.

"Don't be a brat, little brother."

"I've got you by a solid seven inches in height and probably seventy-five pounds, *little* sister," I tease, knowing it'll drive her nuts. She's always been a tiny thing, despite being three years older than my thirty-five years. When it came to our genes, she definitely favors our petite mother, while I'm built like my dad and uncles and stand at six two, weighing about two fifteen.

"Don't sass me," she states.

Laughing, I reply, "Fine. I'll call Logan and text you."

"Thank you. Love you, brat."

"Love you too. Get ready to buy those tickets."

She's chuckling as I hang up and quickly tap my best friend's name.

"'Lo?"

"Hey, sorry to call so late, but any chance the cabin is available for Lor and her family over Labor Day weekend?"

"Of course."

"Sounds like Friday through Monday."

"No problem. It's there. Just tell me what you need me to stock it with," he replies.

"I can handle that part."

"I'll go out beforehand and make sure it's ready for them," he insists.

"Appreciate it, man."

"Don't mention it. Happy to hear they're coming for a visit."

"Me too. I'll text her so she can grab airline tickets."

"Sounds good. Later," he says before hanging up the phone.

I fire off a quick message to my sister, confirming the fact the cabin is theirs for the visit, and toss my phone onto the couch beside me. I'm excited to have my sister, brother-in-law, and nephews here for a short time. Too bad we couldn't get our parents here too, but with my grandparents aging, they've been in Florida for the last couple of years to help take care of my mom's dad.

Maybe next time, with a little more notice, we can make that happen.

Until then, I'll enjoy spoiling my nephews and squeezing in as much fishing and hanging with them at the cabin as possible.

Definitely something to look forward to.

CHAPTER Three

Ellie

"Order up!"

I spin around and head for the window to collect food. Sundays are always busy, especially the after-church lunch crowd, and today is no exception. It's just after two in the afternoon and the diner is showing no signs of slowing down. I'm not going to complain, though. Tips are usually really good on days like today, which is why I don't mind working them. Plus, we're a server short tonight, so I'll be hanging around for the dinner rush too.

Slipping the plates onto my tray, I hoist it up on my shoulder, ignoring the pull between my shoulder blades. Lifting trays of food can be taxing on the body, especially the back. My shoulders carry the brunt of the weight, but my lower back definitely feels the strain.

"BLT club with fries," I say, setting the first plate down in front of a woman who works at the bank. "And a patty melt with onion rings for you," I add, placing the second meal down in front of her husband. "Can I get you anything else? Refills?"

"No, we're good, Ellie. Thank you," she replies, grabbing the ketchup bottle already sitting on the table.

"I'll be back to check on you in a few minutes," I tell them, turning and scanning the mostly full diner. I walk quickly behind the counter and refill a pitcher of cold iced water, the bell chiming over the door as I spin back around. I'm about to tell whoever is entering to find any open table, but the words stall on my lips when I spot my son and his best friend, Matt.

"Hey, Mom," Brody says as they approach, holding a basketball.

"Good afternoon, boys. What are you two up to?" I ask, offering a big smile.

"Gonna head down to the park and shoot some hoops. Just wanted to tell you," Brody says. Even though he's seventeen, he's still very considerate when it comes to letting me know when and where he's going to be, which I greatly appreciate. I'm sure he knows how much I worry, even if he's about to start his senior year of high school and nearing adulthood.

"Sounds like fun. You boys be careful," I tell them, earning me two cheeky grins.

"We will, Miss D," Matt hollers as they head out to walk the block and a half down to the park.

"They're such good boys," Mrs. Voight, the high school English teacher, says as I pause to refill her water.

"They are. Both work jobs, play sports, and are on the honor roll," I state proudly, even though I'm certain Mrs. Voight is well aware.

"You're doing it right, dear. Always remember that," she says quietly, reaching out and placing her aged hand on top of mine.

My throat is thick with the onslaught of emotion. "Thank you."

She smiles before returning her attention to her Cobb salad and older sister, Edna. Both ladies have been widows for a few years now and enjoy a mid-Sunday meal together at the diner after their church activities are complete. Mrs. Voight probably should have retired years ago but is still very active and loves to teach. She's been at it for nearly fifty years now, teaching me in high school way back when too. She's a gem of a lady, and I'm happy she's still so involved in both the school and town.

The afternoon passes into early evening, and before I know it, it's time for me to clock out. I might be the manager, but I'm covering a shift for a high school girl who came down with a summer bug. That means I'm out of here early, which is welcomed, because my back, shoulders, and feet are killing me.

Just as I drop my apron into the bin to be washed, I hear the bell over the door sound once more. "Hey, Mom," Brody hollers, entering the eatery with his football coach hot on his heels.

"Hi, are you finished playing ball?"

"Yep," he replies, tossing the ball back and straight into TD's gut. "Matt had to be home earlier, and Coach was running through the park, so he stopped and played with me for a while."

"The kid's gotta killer jump shot," TD mutters, as Brody slides into a booth. "He beat me twice, and his reward is dinner."

"We can head upstairs," I tell them. "I just clocked out."

"No way," TD insists. "You've been working all day. Sit down and let me buy you both dinner."

I'm hesitant, mostly because all I want to do is kick off my shoes and put my feet up. Plus, I hate the idea of TD buying me dinner when I'm perfectly capable of throwing together something upstairs. But I can tell by the determined glint in his gorgeous brown eyes, he's not going to listen to any excuse I have, which is why I end up sliding into the booth closest to me, across from my son. I expect TD to move into the bench with Brody, since Brody left him plenty of room, but am surprised when my friend joins me on my side.

TD fills the seat with his broad shoulders and muscular body, so it doesn't surprise me his leg brushes against mine. What I wasn't expecting was the warmth flooding my veins and the butterflies in my stomach at the slightest touch. I imagine the hair on his leg sliding against my smooth skin, which causes my body to flush with desire. Something I try to fight, but it never fails to hit me when he's near.

"I could slide around onto the other side. Give you more space," I tell TD, even though I like the feel of his leg pressed to mine.

"You're fine," he insists, throwing his arm over the back of the booth. I can feel the heat of his body, which causes a new wave of goosebumps to pepper my flesh. "How was work?"

"Busy," I state, realizing I should get up and grab three glasses of water.

Before I can ask TD to slide out for a moment, Vivian approaches our table. "Hey, guys. What can I get you to drink?" she asks, placing three menus on the table.

"I can get our orders," I insist.

"No way. You're off the clock. Sit back and let me take care of it," the young woman states with a polite smile.

"Sprite," Brody orders, reaching for the menu he probably has memorized.

I wait for TD to put in his drink request, but when he just gazes at me, waiting, I go ahead and speak. "Ice water, please."

"And I'll have iced tea." TD takes a menu and slides it in front of me. When I don't open it, he just chuckles. "I guess I should have realized you don't need one of those."

"I've had it memorized since I was seventeen," I state proudly. A few menu items have changed over the years, and the daily specials are always evolving, but for the most part, Frannie's Diner is the same as it was back when I first started working here eighteen years ago.

Our drinks are placed on the table and orders taken. I opted for the grilled chicken salad with raspberry vinaigrette dressing, while both boys opted for something a little heartier and ordered the all-you-can-eat fried chicken special with mashed potatoes and gravy and rolls.

When TD glances over and catches my smile, he asks, "What?"

"Nothing," I insist, shaking my head. "I just don't know where you two put all the food you eat."

He gives me that cocky grin I've always loved and rubs his flat stomach.

"We burn a lot of calories, right, TD? I mean, Coach?" my son says between sips of his soft drink.

"We sure do, buddy. And you can call me TD when we're in a social setting like this, remember?"

Brody nods, and there's no missing the affection he has for his football coach and friend. "I know, but I don't want to make the mistake of calling you by your real name in front of the team."

TD grins back at my son. "I understand."

"Besides, his real name isn't TD," I state, fighting the smile.

Even though I keep my gaze locked on my son, I can feel TD's the moment he looks my way. "We're not going there, Ellie," TD grumbles, and I finally lose it and snicker.

"Why don't you like your real name?" Brody asks curiously, giving the man beside me his complete attention.

"It's not that I don't like it, per se, it's just so formal and old school. My teachers used to call me Thomas when I was little, and I hated it. Worse, they'd call me Tom or Tommy."

I continue to laugh, closing my eyes and keeping my face cast down.

"Tommy," Brody says, as if trying that name on for size. "You don't look like a Tommy or a Tom. Tom's are old and Tommy's are young."

"Thanks?" TD replies, that one word coming out a question.

"I just mean you're TD, not Thomas or Tom. It's a cool name and fits you," Brody vows with a decisive head nod.

I find myself with my elbow on the table, leaning my head against my hand as I watch their exchange. It quickly goes from discussing TD's birth name to football and the first day of school. My son hangs on TD's every word, listening quietly and absorbing any and all information our friend shares.

I've always noticed that about these two. Brody just soaks it all in with curious eyes and his big soft heart. There aren't many times I get sucked into a pity party where Brody's father—or the sperm donor—is concerned, but there are plenty of moments I'm grateful for the men established in his life.

Like now.

I remain somewhat silent as we eat our food, enjoying the relaxing atmosphere and comfortable conversation between the other two at the table. The fuller my stomach gets, the more exhausted I start to feel, and my shoulders and feet really begin to ache. I need a hot shower and to put my feet up, pronto.

Maybe a bowl of cherry chip ice cream, if there's any left.

"What's wrong?"

I glance over and find TD's dark gaze locked on me. It's the first time I realize Brody's gone. "Where'd he go?"

"To the restroom. What's the matter with you?" His eyes are full of concern.

"Nothing," I insist, as usual. Even if something *is* wrong, I'm not big on sharing. There's always someone dealing with something much worse than me, so what's the point of complaining?

His eyes narrow just a bit, and softly, he instructs, "Try again."

I paste on a smile. "I'm just tired. My shoulders tend to get a little sore at the end of a long shift," I reply with an uncomfortable shrug.

"That's why you keep tensing and shifting in your seat," he deduces, turning toward me. "Face the wall."

"What?" I ask, confused as to what he's asking.

"The wall. Face it."

I slowly turn, trying to figure out why he's instructing me to do this, when I feel his big, warm hands wrap around my shoulders and squeeze. "Holy shit," I whisper, gasping as a mix of pleasure and pain moves through me.

His chuckles hit my ears at the same time his warm breath tickles the back of my neck. Using his hands, he gently massages my muscles, kneading the knots until they slowly release and relax. My eyes are closed, and my head has fallen forward as the pure magic of his hands washes over me.

"You're really tense and tight," he murmurs softly in his sexy, deep timbre that makes my core clench with need.

"That happens," I whisper, hoping my voice isn't as raw and gravelly as it feels.

"Well, you need more massages. Any time you want my hands, just let me know."

My mouth goes Sahara dry.

Any time you want my hands...

If he only knew.

"What's wrong, Mom?"

I'm pulled out of my thoughts and slowly turn to face my son, who's sliding back into the booth. "Nothing. My shoulders were hurting, so TD tried to help work out some of the tension."

He nods in understanding, turning his attention to the man beside me. "That happens a lot. She's always rubbing her shoulders at the end of the day. Her feet hurt her too."

My eyes narrow at my son. "Traitor," I mutter before risking a quick glance to my left. "It's nothing. Usually a hot shower is the cure-all for a server like me."

A hot shower, some ibuprofen, and a good night's sleep, but who's keeping track.

TD makes a humming sound as he pulls his wallet from his shorts. Vivian drops off the bill and collects our dirty dishes, but before I can insist on paying my part, he climbs from the seat and heads to the counter. Knowing it's useless to again insist I pay for our meals; I pull some of my tip money out of my pocket and place some bills on the table for Vivian.

Brody and I wait by the back door for TD, who pauses at the table to drop off a tip and finds the one I left already. He shakes his head and returns his wallet to his shorts before walking to where we stand.

"Ready?" he asks when he joins us.

"Yep," Brody states instantly, pushing through the swinging door and walking down the short hall that leads to the staircase at the back.

I throw a wave to Vivian and the busboy before following them through the doorway. The two boys talk about Brody's limited work schedule as we maneuver the hallway and they open the lower door at the base of the stairs. TD pauses, waving me on to lead the way up the steps, his warm hand positioned on my back for the briefest of moments.

At the top of the steps, I unlock the door and step inside our small, but happy, apartment. Cool air hits me in the face, a welcomed and refreshing change from the warmth and humidity outside.

"I'm gonna grab a shower, 'kay, Mom?" Brody says, dropping the basketball onto the couch and already heading for the bathroom.

"Of course," I reply, toeing off my shoes and setting them on the rug by the living room window.

"Later, Coach. Thanks for the game. And dinner."

"You're welcome, Brody. See you at practice tomorrow," TD says, holding out his fist for a bump.

I'm silent as my son slips into his bedroom and grabs a fresh pair of shorts before entering the bathroom and shutting the door. I don't mind that TD hangs around for a bit, but my body definitely needs to unwind from the long, strenuous day on my feet. Since my son is currently occupying the only shower in the apartment, I'll settle for more water and putting my feet up for a bit.

"Come here."

I turn around and find TD pulling one of the kitchen chairs out from the table. "Umm, if it's all the same to you, I think I'd rather sit in the living room. It's more comfortable."

He points to the chair. "Just for a few minutes. Promise."

My eyebrows shoot for my hairline as I slowly make my way to where he stands. The chair is spun around, the back rest closer to the table than the seat, and when I reach out to turn it around, he stops me. "Have a seat, facing the table."

I look at the chair again, no doubt the confusion written all over my face. "Why?"

"Trust me, El." His voice is soft and calm, and I know without a shadow of a doubt, I do trust him completely.

I straddle the chair as instructed, feeling a little weirded out by the awkward position. This is how all the boys used to sit in chairs back when we were in school, and I've never found it particularly comfortable.

"Lean forward." When I do as instructed, I feel his hands on my shoulders once more. All question and thought flies right out of my head as he starts to massage my achy muscles again.

I have no idea how long I sit here, TD rubbing my shoulders, neck, and back, but it's heaven. That's the only way to describe it. I try to breathe normally, but it's difficult. Mostly because it feels too damn good to be massaged like this, but also simply because it's TD's hands on me. Sure, he's touched me before, but never like this. Never has he dug his fingers into my flesh, working out the knots and bringing me so much relief. And the crazy part is I like it.

A lot.

Too much so.

I can feel my nipples pebbled against my bra, a wave of wetness dampening my panties. I imagine his hands sliding down my back, cupping my rear. I think about them gliding around my waist, his big fingers angling to where I ache for his touch the most. I picture his mouth on my neck and my ears as he continues to touch me everywhere.

"You're tensing," he whispers, gently gliding his hands over my lower back and sides.

"Ticklish," I reply, even though that's not the reason. Yes, I'm ticklish, but that's the furthest from the issue right now.

The truth is I'm turned on.

Badly.

Trapped between wanting his hands on me for as long as I can get them and needing him to stop because I'm afraid the invisible line in the sand might be crossed.

A door opens in the hallway, breaking the spell I fell under. TD's hands pause before dropping from my back, and he clears his throat quickly. "Better?" he asks, taking a step back. I can feel the sudden distance between us instantly.

I nod, refusing to turn around. "Thank you."

"Go take a long hot shower and put your feet up," he says, already moving toward the exit.

"I will."

"Good." I hear the door open and his heavy footsteps pause. "Good night, Ellie."

"Night, TD," I whisper, risking a quick glance over my shoulder to where he stands. "Thank you for dinner."

He nods, the tension lines streaking around his eyes ebbing just slightly. "You're welcome."

And then he's gone, disappearing through the door and exiting the building as if his ass were on fire.

Sighing, I stand up and right the chair before walking over to the door and throwing the lock. I don't need to secure the other one at the base of the steps. I know TD already did it on his way out.

I can't believe I let myself get all worked up like that.

Over my friend.

Especially when he clearly didn't feel the same. It was obvious he was uncomfortable and ready to leave. I don't know what I did to cause such discomfort, but I need to remember to keep this pesky little crush buried as deep as I can. Nothing good can come of me wishing for him to finally see me as someone other than Ellie, his friend.

TD is my friend and *only* my friend.

We'll never be anything more.

CHAPTER four

TD

My cock is throbbing.

So fucking hard, it's painful to walk.

Of course, being in athletic shorts and basic boxers isn't helping conceal anything, which is why I had to get the hell out of her apartment. My cock was standing proud, trying to claw its way through my shorts to get to her, and the longer I had my hands on her, the harder it got to remember we're just friends.

Pun intended.

When I started rubbing her shoulders at the diner, I wasn't thinking clearly. I could tell she was hurting, no doubt from hours' worth of carrying those heavy trays full of food and being on her feet. So, I gave her a little back rub.

I wasn't prepared for the noises.

The noises that went straight to my balls.

Sounds that reminded me of sex.

I still have no idea what possessed me to continue the torture on my balls when we got to her apartment, other than I could tell she needed help relieving some of the stress and discomfort she was harboring. Of course, now I'm the one carrying that discomfort, but it was a small price to pay to feel some of those knots let loose between her shoulder blades.

It's about a half mile to my place, and the warm, night air is welcome. Being outside has always helped me clear my head, which is why I've always enjoyed anything outdoors. I grew up hunting, fishing, and playing sports, and when I got into high school, added working out and running to the list of things I liked. However, right now, I'd give about anything to have my truck nearby so I didn't have to walk. Especially with my nuts heavy and throbbing in my shorts.

I switch my line of thoughts away from Ellie and the reaction my body had to her and focus on the team. Our first game is this Friday, and I'm pretty pumped. We've got a great group of athletes, including Brody. He's become an integral piece of the team, providing leadership and mentorship to his fellow teammates. I truly believe a big reason he's turned out to be the amazing young man he's become is because of his mother. She instilled core values into his childhood from the very beginning, like compassion, hard work, and respect. I'm not blowing smoke up her ass when I tell her she's done an exceptional job raising him.

She has.

When I finally approach my block, I'm happy to report my cock has finally calmed down a bit. At least he's not standing at attention anymore, despite the fact I'm definitely going to need a little release. If I don't, my balls will swell up like grapefruits and I'll have to seek medical attention.

"TD!"

I'm unable to fight the groan, but fortunately, it's not very loud. Not that Shay would catch the annoyance in my sound and posture, but I try not to be a complete rude asshole to her.

I keep myself moving forward, barely slowing my steps. My goal is to get home as quickly as possible, not chitchat with my oldest friend's ex-wife. "Hey," I holler, offering a wave as I move along the sidewalk.

"Nice night, huh? I heard you had dinner with Ellie Daniels."

That makes me pause. One of the things I dislike most about our small town is the gossip mill. It's usually churning with something immediately. "Yeah," I reply, turning to face her as she practically sprints my way from her porch. She's wearing a tight white tank top that's barely able to contain her enhanced assets, as well as skimpy little workout shorts.

Shay flips her long, blond hair over her shoulder, allowing her fingers to linger there. This woman is a piece of work. Fake in both personality and body parts and thinks she's God's gift to men. Too bad for her, I'll never find her attractive. Not when I know what kind of vile, self-centered person she is on the inside. She made my best friend's life hell and is continuing to do so well after their divorce.

"Wanna come in for a drink? You look like you've had a long day," she practically coos. Most of the time, her act gets her the attention she's after from men, but not from me.

Never from me.

I'm not rude, because at the end of the day, she's still linked to Logan, even if only on paper with the business, so I'm not about to cause him more problems, but that doesn't mean I'm friendly either. "No thanks. On my way home."

She tsks and pops her hip out, trying to draw attention to the sliver of bare skin between her tank and the waist of her shorts. Too bad for her, her advances are about as refreshing as a ketchup-flavored popsicle. "You've been working hard all day," she whines, approaching, and I can see the glint in her eyes.

She's about to pounce, ready to invite me inside with promises of whatever in the hell I want. That's one of her biggest tools: sex. Always has been, always will be. She screwed the assistant manager of the hardware store back when she and Logan were separating, just to have someone on her side when it came to business. Bud ended up losing his job—and his wife—because of the misstep.

One thing about Shay is she's not afraid to go after what she wants. Or *who*. That person is usually married or has an elevated status to help her get whatever she's after. She's triggered more divorces than any singular person should be allowed to cause, and the fact she's only on the first one herself is surprising as hell.

"Later, Shay," I reply, continuing on my way, determined to make it home as quickly as possible.

She continues talking, but I keep walking.

Of course, the good thing about my brief interaction with the woman from hell is the fact I'm not sporting wood anymore. Nothing makes my dick and balls shrivel up faster than that woman. Her voice is like nails on a chalkboard to me, and her fake triple D's a huge turn-off.

Yeah, there may have been a time back when we were in high school—long before she stuck her claws in my best friend—when I thought she was hot. Hell, everyone did. She was beautiful, smart, and was driven to become the next big model. She was going places most people only dreamed about in our small town. Sure, she was quick to spread her legs, which a few of my then-friends took full advantage of, but I never did. She may have been gorgeous, but there was still something I felt like she was hiding from the world.

Turns out it was devil horns.

I prefer my women real. Soft skin and natural curves. The way my fingers dig into that skin as I hold her against me. Hair that slips my grip as I tighten my fist around those long strands. Plump lips ripe for kissing.

Why do I always picture one woman when I get to this point of the fantasy?

I reach my block, smiling as I glance to where my best friend's house sits. I can see into his backyard and notice his kitchen light is on. I shake my head, finding it funny—and not in a humorous way— that Shay bought a house with her divorce settlement only a few houses down from the ex-husband she's determined to torture for the rest of his life.

At least her place is in the opposite direction than mine.

When I reach my back door, I pull my key out of my pocket and slip it into the knob. The air-conditioning hits me in the face, a welcome reprieve from the warm August night outside. I secure the house and move straight to the bedroom. After a short run, that ended when I found Brody and Matt playing basketball at the park, I spent another hour shooting hoops with Ellie's boy when Matt had to leave for dinner before walking him back to the diner for a meal. Now, I'm desperate for a shower and a little...release.

Stripping out of my clothes, I turn on the shower and step inside the moment the water is hot. My cock is hard again in anticipation, but I choose to ignore it for a few minutes. Instead, I focus on washing my hair and my body, careful of the appendage protruding from my groin, begging for attention.

With a sigh, I close my eyes and will my erection into submission. Even after all these years, I feel guilty getting aroused when I think about my friend. Ellie thinks of me as a good guy, an upstanding friend. Little does she know I jack off to images of her and have since I was in high school.

But that doesn't stop me from taking my cock in my hand, knowing the only way to get it to go away is release. My balls instantly tighten as my cock thickens. I can feel precum oozing from the tip, the familiar tingles racing up my spine. This'll be embarrassingly quick, but I have no time to dwell on it.

I start to stroke, the pleasure racing through my veins at lightning speed. I gasp for air, letting the water lubricate my hand as I lean against the wall. My strokes pick up pace, my body gearing for the looming release, and all it takes is for me to imagine that sweet little moan she made while I was massaging her shoulders. That one noise, combined with the feel of her body beneath my fingers as I rubbed her down, has me blowing my load all over the shower tiles. I come hard, my legs wobbling as I press my back against the wall and suck in greedy breaths of air.

"Jesus, this is sad," I mutter at myself.

Grabbing the soap, I rewash my body before getting out of the shower. I grab a towel and run it over my body before wrapping it around my waist. Approaching the mirror, I place my hands on the vanity and lean forward. This is exactly how my life will go, isn't it? I'm thirty-five years old and rarely date. I'm a decent-looking guy, and I know there are women who would jump at the opportunity to go out with me for my uniform alone. I've been told it's a chick magnet, and while I guess I get the appeal, I'm just not interested in women like that.

How sad am I?

Single, mid-thirties guy not interested in women who want to bang me just because of the badge and uniform.

Instead, I'm pining after a woman who has me safely tucked in the friend zone, but sadly, I realize I'd rather be there than have nothing at all. I've always wanted Ellie Daniels, and I don't see that ebbing anytime soon.

So I'll continue to hide my attraction to her so I don't risk losing her.

Because a life without Ellie isn't a life at all.

"He told me he'd come back with the cash," Jeb, the old man who owns the small gas station on the edge of town, says. "He left me his ID as collateral." He holds up a State of Wisconsin driver's license, and as soon as I see the name, I have to fight a smile.

"I'm pretty sure you were scammed again, Jeb," I tell him, setting the license down on the counter and grabbing my notebook.

"You think?"

I nod, pulling my pen from my breast pocket. "Unfortunately. See the name? Sylvester Stallone is an actor, but the photo is Jason Statham, another actor."

The old man grabs the license and scans over the photo. "Really? His friend even called him Sly when they were in here."

"I'm positive. Sylvester Stallone doesn't live in Wisconsin, I'm sure. I'm going to assume this license number and the address are fake too, but I'll run them just to be certain." I give the man my full attention. "You know, you really should do pay-at-the-pump."

Before I even have the suggestion out, he's waving his hand. "Boy, that technology is past me. I'd have to update the pumps, and these babies have been working just fine. Had them installed myself back in the mid-seventies, and they still get the job done."

"But if someone had to use a credit card to turn on the pump, you'd have less gas-and-dash and are less likely someone will produce a fake ID with the promise of coming back with cash," I tell him, even though I know it's no use. Jeb Wilson is one of the most trusting fellas I've ever met. If a local doesn't have cash for gas, he'll pin a note on his bulletin board with an IOU. For those out of town, unfortunately, he'll take their driver's license as collateral, along with the promise they'll come right back with cash after visiting and ATM—something else he refuses to put in. Most of the time, his good faith bites him in the ass, like now.

"How much gas did they take?" I ask, making my notes.

"Uhh, a little over twenty gallons in a pick-em up truck and another couple in that fancy dune buggy they was pulling," he informs me, toying with the long, gray beard he's sported since I was a boy.

"Dune buggy? Or, like, a four-wheeler or side by side?"

"Yeah."

I crack a smile. "Which was it?"

He shrugs. "If they come back, I'll be sure to let you know."

"You do that, but I'm assuming, since it's been three days, they're probably not coming back," I inform him, realizing he's probably out close to a hundred bucks in fuel.

"Sly might need his ID," Jeb states, his blue eyes shining under the dim gas station lighting.

A wide grin spreads across my lips. "He might."

"All right, boy, better get back out there and catch the criminals. Wanna coffee to go?"

I glance at the pot sitting along the back wall and the fact it looks like it hasn't been cleaned since Nixon was in office. "No thanks, Jeb. It's eighty-three out there. No coffee for me."

The old man barely looks up from his newspaper. "How about a water then?" He turns and grabs one from the old cooler he keeps behind the counter. "It's the least I can do, since you came all the way out here to help me."

"That's my job," I tell him, reaching for the bottle. "Thank you for this. I appreciate it."

"You're welcome, boy. Just be careful out there. I heard Emogene Franklin was almost run over by one of those dune buggy things."

My eyebrows pull together in question. "She was?"

"Yep. She was getting ready to cross the street at the Methodist church, when one of those flying machines came barreling at her at Mach 10. Almost killed her."

I shake my head, wondering when this happened. We don't allow ATVs or side-by-sides on the streets in town. There's one path they're allowed to take, which covers Jeb's gas station, the diner, and Marcus's mechanic shop not too far away. "Is she okay?"

"Huh?" he asks, looking up from his paper once more. "Oh, yeah. She's fine. Swung her purse at him when he went by."

A snort slips out as I picture sweet little Emogene Franklin swinging that big bag she calls a purse at someone. "I can stop by and take her statement, see if I can find out who it was."

"Oh, they're long gone, boy. Happened probably ten, twelve years ago?" It comes out a question as he contemplates how long ago it was when this incident happened.

"I see," I reply, taking my bottle of water. "Well, I better get back out there. Thanks again for the water."

"Of course, boy. Be safe. Those flying buggies are buzzin' around something fierce right now. August brings 'em out in gangs."

I nod before pushing through the door and returning to my squad car. I let dispatch know what's happening with Jeb and decide to take a trip through Bluff Preserves. They have park rangers who patrol it regularly, but sometimes I want visitors to see my car too. Maybe I'll get lucky and spot Sylvester Stallone there and be able to convince him to pay for his damn gas at the station.

Probably not. Most likely, Sly is long gone, like I suggested to Jeb. I wish the old man would take the advice I've given, as well as about every other resident of Pine Village, and install new pumps. I know it's a big expense, but if a customer had to give a credit card to receive gas, he wouldn't be out hundreds of dollars every month when someone drives off or promises to come back and pay but doesn't.

I try not to let those kinds of calls get to me, but it pisses me off when out-of-towners take advantage of our residents. No, not all visitors are trouble, but there are plenty who are. And apparently, they could all use a reminder not to drive their ATVs and side-by-sides on undesignated routes.

I mean, poor Emogene was almost run over by one of their flying buggies.

Snickering and shaking my head, I drive toward the busy tourist park at the edge of our small town. Maybe after a pass through the area and chatting with a handful of visitors, I can stop by the diner for lunch and chat with my favorite server. Being greeted as I walk through the door with that familiar smile is the best part of my day.

There's nothing better than an Ellie smile.

It's what I live for.

CHAPTER *five*

Ellie

My nerves are through the roof as I find my seat in the bleachers. There's a buzz in the stands as everyone prepares for the first football game of the season. I greet fellow football parents and fans before looking out onto the field for my boy. A slight grin spreads across my lips when I find him, running to catch a pass from the quarterback. He easily snatches it from the air and runs to the next yard line before the whistle blows.

Brody tosses the ball back to the quarterback before jogging over to where TD stands. They talk a few moments, TD showing him something with his hands, before slapping him on the shoulder pads and sending him back to the line.

"Brody's looking good this year," Mr. Ramirez says a few rows behind me.

"He is," I confirm, glancing back and offering a polite smile to the man who runs the bank.

"I brought you popcorn," Hallie states, dropping onto the metal bleacher beside me.

"Thank you," I reply, taking the warm, buttery treat from my friend and popping a kernel into my mouth.

"You ready for this?" she asks between her own bites.

"As ready as I'll ever be. I'm super excited to watch them play, but it's also bittersweet. This is his last year."

She nods in understanding. "TD said they're looking good this year."

Now it's my turn to nod. "That's what I'm told."

"These seats taken?" Blair asks as she approaches where we sit.

"Of course not," I tell another of my closest friends. While Hallie stayed around Pine Village, Blair moved to Indiana when we were seniors in high school following her parents' divorce. She returned last year to help her father out at his medical practice, falling in love with Gabe along the way. She's here to stay now, living with Hallie's older brother and sharing the medical practice with him.

Gabe follows, sliding onto the bleacher behind us and says hello.

"Brother," Hallie states over her shoulder, narrowing her eyes at him as she shovels popcorn in her mouth.

"Sister," he replies, offering her a wide grin.

My eyes volley back and forth between the two before glancing up at Blair, who is sitting beside Gabe. "What's up with them?"

Blair rolls her eyes. "Gabe went over to help move some furniture at her condo the other day," she says, looking toward the walkway and smiling.

"Okay, I don't get it," I reply, my eyes seeking out Hallie for further clarification.

"He wasn't alone," she grumbles, shoving a whole handful of popcorn into her mouth so she can't close her lips.

"Hey, guys," Logan greets as he approaches, and that's when I realize why Hallie is so annoyed at her brother. She hates Logan. I'm not really sure why, other than the fact he can push her buttons like nobody can, but I do admit, it's amusing to watch.

"Ellie," Logan says with a nod before sliding onto the end of the bleacher, right behind Hallie. "Satan," he adds, causing her to do this weird growl, choking sound.

She chews quickly, getting all her snack down before turning to glare at the man behind her. "*What* are you doing here?"

"It's a football game," he replies casually, taking a sip from his bottle of water. "I like football."

"He used to play," I add unnecessarily. Everyone knows Logan Johnson used to play football. He went to college for it, playing at the University of Wisconsin as their starting quarterback, until his senior year when a knee injury ended all chances of him ever playing professionally.

Hallie narrows her eyes at me. "Yes, I know he used to play," she argues.

Shrugging, I reply somehow with a straight face, "Okay, just making sure."

"He went through my panty drawer."

That catches the attention of everyone around us, as all eyes zero in on Hallie.

"He what?" I ask, unable to fight my laughter this time around.

"My panty drawer! The jerk moved my dresser and went through my things," Hallie seethes.

Logan sighs. "Your *panties* were the least of my worries, cupcake. I pulled out the top drawer to try to get a better grip on her dresser, and the drawer fell out. The damn thing's older than I am, and the slide inside the drawer was busted."

"And my panties...went everywhere! He was holding them in his hand."

"I was picking them up. I could have just left them all on the floor, but I was trying to be a nice guy."

She snorts in disgust. "A *nice guy*," she argues, making air quotes. "A nice guy doesn't comment on another person's panties!"

Blair taps me on the back with her knee, as we all give the bickering couple our complete attention. Of course, they're not a couple in the traditional sense, merely acting like an old, bickering married couple every time they're together.

"All I said was you had a lot of granny panties," Logan says innocently, but we can all see the mirth in his eyes.

Hallie gives him her back, turning to face the field in front of her. "I hope you choke on a hot dog, Logan Johnson."

We all bust up laughing, hating to find such joy in their apparent hatred for each other. Of course, none of us really think they hate each other. It's more like foreplay. One of these days, those two will just erupt and the result will be explosive.

Hopefully on an orgasmic level and without any carnage.

"I am hungry for a hot dog. You want one, Gabe? Blair? Ellie?"

"No, I'm good," I reply, trying to hide my smile as he gets up.

"You want one, Hallie Hallie Bo Ballie?"

"I hope a football hits you in the head and gives you amnesia," she states bluntly, keeping her attention in front of her.

"Technically, I don't think a football could do that. Not enough force. It's unlikely to have enough power in a basic throw to cause any serious damage besides a mild concussion."

Hallie slowly turns around and narrows her eyes at Gabe. "Could you not be a doctor for, like, five seconds?" she asks bitterly.

He just gives her a wide grin. "Of course."

With a huff, she keeps her gaze forward as the players line up on the twenty-yard line with their hands over their hearts. We all stand as the high school band plays the national anthem, moving quickly into position for the school song. Once they begin the familiar beat, the crowd starts to cheer, the cheerleaders begin their routine, and the players slide their helmets onto their heads. Then, they run through the tunnel created by the cheerleaders and break through the banner donning the school name.

My heart is hammering as I watch my boy fire up his team, leading them in a chant. I'm so dang proud of him, of the player and teammate he's become since joining his freshman year. It's hard to believe this is the final season I get to watch him play the game he loves. When TD joins them, he says a few things to get them even more fired up, and they all break apart in unison.

"Last first game of the season," Hallie whispers, as if somehow reading my mind.

I swallow over the lump in my throat. "Yeah."

We take the field, preparing for kickoff, and I watch as Brody goes deep to receive. TD hollers something to him, and Brody nods in understanding. The whistle blows and the ball is in the air, sailing toward my son. He catches it easily and takes off running.

"Go, Brody!" Hallie hollers.

We're all still on our feet, eyes glued to my kid as he dodges one defender and then another. An opponent gets their hands on him, but he spins enough to break the contact and send the player to the ground. Brody stumbles a little but regains his footing and runs another ten yards before finally being brought down at the fifty.

"Great run," Gabe hollers.

The crowd takes a seat and watches the game. Our running back makes a few good plays, getting us near their thirty-yard line. When I see TD say something to Brody and slap him on the butt, he takes off into the game with determination.

"It's going to be a pass for Brode," I say softly, almost to myself.

Holding my breath, I watch as they line up. Dorian looks out at Brody and nods, and that's all the confirmation I need. The ball is snapped, and the players move. Dorian turns to Brody, who's running downfield, before firing it into the air. The ball spirals beautifully over the heads of the defenders and is snatched from the air by my son. He runs the remaining few yards for the touchdown without so much as being touched by the opposing team.

"Touchdown Panthers!" the announcer bellows over the loudspeakers.

I'm jumping up and down, cheering my heart out for my son and his teammates. High fives are given to my friends, as well as a few fans sitting near us. I watch as his teammates congratulate him on scoring points as they all jog off the field toward the sidelines. TD is right there, holding out his hand for a high five in celebration. Then, he slaps him on the shoulder pads twice and taps the top of his helmet. All I can do is smile, grateful for the relationships he's formed with his teammates and coaches.

Especially TD.

As if sensing where my thoughts are, the head coach turns to the stands and our eyes meet. He gives me a wide smile that makes my heart leap in my chest. I can't help but grin back, holding up my hand and giving him a thumbs-up. He winks before returning his attention back to the game in front of him.

We end up winning our season opener twenty-seven to seven, and even though Brody didn't score again, he had some great catches. It was thrilling to watch him, both on the field and on the sidelines, where he cheered on his teammates and celebrated every little victory. At the end of the game, TD leads them to the end zone, while the bleachers start to clear out.

"Great game," Gabe says when we all stand up and stretch from the extended period of time of sitting on the hard, metal bleachers.

"Gonna be a fun season," Logan replies.

"Next week is away, right?" Blair asks, looking my way.

"Yes. We're headed to Big Bay," I answer, referring to another small community about forty miles up the road.

"I should bring my fishing pole. I haven't fished in the bay in years," Logan replies. Like the lakes around us, fishing is a huge industry around Big Bay.

"Or you could just move there," Hallie grumbles not-so-quietly.

Logan gives her a big, cheesy grin. "You'd miss me too much, cupcake."

"I'd miss you like an STD."

"Okay," Gabe says loudly, stepping between the two bickerers. "Let's not talk about STDs, all right? Ellie, tell Brody good game for us. We're going to go to Miss Molly's for an ice cream sundae and head home."

My mouth waters at the thought of all the homemade ice cream goodness. "Sounds good."

"Wanna come?" Blair asks as we slowly make our way down the bleachers.

"Oh, no thank you. Brody and I have a tradition of homemade milkshakes and fries after the game."

Blair smiles, while Gabe takes her hand. "Let's go so we can beat the crowd to Molly's. I'll be mad if she's out of her mocha marshmallow ice cream before I get some."

They both wave, leaving me alone with Logan and Hallie. "I'm out of here. Hot date," Logan announces, but the look in his eyes tells me it's a big fat lie.

"Doubtful," Hallie mutters.

"Jealous?" he asks, leaning in and bumping her shoulder with his own.

"Of you dating? Hell no. I'm just surprised someone actually wants to spend time with you. Are you as annoying on dates as you are every other second of the day?" she counters.

Logan just laughs and turns to walk away. "See you guys later."

"Bye," I holler, as Hallie mumbles a soft, "Whatever."

"I can't decide if you two will someday kill each other or rip each other's clothes off and go at it like bunnies."

She makes a horrified face. "Gross! If Logan Johnson were the last person on this planet, my clothes would still be on."

"If you say so," I reply, not believing her for a second. "I'm going to head over to the locker room. Wanna come with me?"

"No, I have a few lesson plans I want to work on tonight before bed," she states. Hallie is one of the preschool teachers in town, spending her day with four- and five-year-olds. "Tell him good game for me too."

"I will. Talk to you soon," I say as my friend walks toward the school parking lot.

Looking out at the field, I notice the players are gone, which means they're in the locker room. I pass a few other moms who offer polite greetings, but for the most part, I keep my head down. I've always felt like the other moms look down on me. Not that I care. Much. The comments I've caught wind of only bother me if they affect Brody. In no way do I want to have my teenage pregnancy and single mom status upset him. I know this town. I grew up here. I've heard the under-the-breath remarks about him having no father or speculating *who* that person really is. I've dealt with my past and refuse to look back.

Forward is the only way to go.

Nothing good can come of looking in the rearview mirror, especially when a person refuses to acknowledge his part in the story.

As I lean against the brick wall of the school and wait for Brody to emerge from the locker room, my gaze is drawn to the man heading my way. There's determination in every step he takes and a gorgeous smile on his face as he looks up and meets my eyes.

"Hey," he says when he reaches my side, mimicking my position and leaning against the wall.

Playfully, I elbow him in the side. "Great game, Coach."

"Thank you," he replies with a big grin. "We had a hell of a game."

"Mom!"

I turn toward the locker room and find Brody still dressed in his pads and jersey, headed our way. "What's wrong?" I ask, despite the huge grin on his face.

"Nothing," he replies joyfully. "Did you see my touchdown?" he asks, stopping directly in front of me.

A bubble of laughter spills from my lips. "Of course I saw it. It was amazing!" I tell him, wrapping my arms around his back, despite being soaked with sweat and a bit smelly, and squeeze. "I'm so proud of you."

"I have something for you," he says when I release my hug. He holds up a football. "This was the game ball. The team voted for me to be the recipient of it tonight, and well, I couldn't have done this without you."

My eyes fill and I have to blink to keep them at bay. "Brody," I start, but am cut off when he places it in my arms.

"You've been my biggest fan. You and me against the world, right? Well, tonight, I scored that touchdown for you, so it's only fitting you get the game ball. Since it's my last season, I know you've been extra emotional and are trying not to cry right now, so I figured I'd do it now instead of at home. There, you'd cry like a baby. At least here, you'll try not to cry in front of all the people." He flashes me a cheeky grin.

Clearing my throat, I finally whisper, "I don't know what to say."

"Maybe how amazing I am, so I can have an extra hour out tonight with my friends?" he asks, his eyes hopeful.

Laughter slides easily from my lips as I shake my head. "I knew you had ulterior motives."

He chuckles loudly. "No, that part just came to me. I wouldn't mind a little extra time, though. The guys invited me to Miss Molly's for ice cream and then probably to the city park to hang out and shoot hoops."

"You just played an entire football game, and you want to go play basketball?"

He shrugs. "Yeah. I know we usually hang out after I get home and do our thing, but—"

"Go. You deserve this time with your teammates and friends. Ten thirty is fine. You have weights and game film walk-through in the morning," I remind.

He glances over at TD. "I know. Coach would make me run extra laps if I was late because I stayed out past curfew."

"Damn right he would," TD chimes in.

Brody leans closer to me and whispers, "See? Hard-ass."

"Go get cleaned up. Your friends are already coming out," I tell him, gently pushing his arm toward the locker room.

"Wait, Coach, can you take a picture for us?" Brody asks, and once more, I have to fight tears. How did I get so dang lucky? I won the lotto when I was given this child.

"Of course," TD agrees, pulling his cell phone out of his pocket.

Brody comes up beside me, throws his sweaty arm over my shoulders, and draws me close. I wrap one arm around his lower back and hold the football with the other. I smile happily as TD takes our photo.

"Thanks, Coach. I'm gonna run in and get cleaned up. Mom, I'll be home by ten thirty. Promise."

"Do you need the car?" I ask, wondering how much gas is in the old girl.

"Naw, I'm riding with Matt." Then, he leans in and kisses my cheek. "Love you."

"Love you too," I tell him before he turns and jogs over to the locker room and disappears behind the door.

"You all right?"

I shake my head, knowing if I speak, I'll cry.

"I know I've said this before, but you're raising an exceptional young man, El."

"Thank you," I whisper, cradling the football a little tighter against my chest. When my emotions are a bit more under control, I ask, "Are you going with them for ice cream?"

"No, I'll let them do their thing. They don't want me hanging around."

"I beg to differ. They all love you."

"As their coach. I'm not one of the guys."

Before I can reconsider, I find myself asking, "Do you want to come over? I've got ice cream in the freezer."

TD flashes me a wide grin. "Pistachio?"

"No. Nuts don't belong in ice cream, Thomas." I stick out my tongue in disgust.

"They most certainly do," he counters. "Even though you don't have the good stuff, I suppose I could stop by for a bowl."

Nodding, I take a step back. "I'll see you soon."

"I'll be there."

Turning, I practically speed-walk toward my car, my heart hammering in my chest with every step I take. TD is coming over. Why that makes me nervous, I'm not sure. He's been to my apartment a million times over the years. We've shared meals and snacks, watched movies, and talked. He's held me while I cried and laughed with me when I told silly Brody stories.

But for some reason, this feels different.

I don't know why.

Maybe it's because the last time he was over, he gave me a back massage and bolted quickly. Of course, he has no clue how he affected me. I had to touch myself in the shower after he left just to be able to relax enough to sleep, and I won't get into the number of times that's happened as a result of thinking about my friend.

Tonight will be different.

We'll share some friendly ice cream, and no one will touch anyone else. Hands will be kept to themselves, because that's what friends do.

They keep their hands to themselves and don't picture the other naked.

Okay, lies.

I totally do that.

A lot.

CHAPTER
six

TD

This is a bad idea.

Even though I've told myself that a dozen times in the last thirty minutes, I'm still outside her apartment and opening the door. My feet carry me up the stairs to the top, where I knock on the upper door. I don't know why I'm nervous. Maybe because the last time I was here, I had my hands all over her shoulders and back and got so fucking turned on, I had to go home and jack off just to find relief. And even then, I slept like shit that night and had to do it all over again the next morning.

Before I can turn around and leave, the door opens and Ellie's standing in front of me with a warm smile on her face. That familiar accelerated heartbeat thing happens in my chest, like it does most times I see her smile. I don't know what it is about it, but everything just seems right in the world when she grins.

"Hey," she greets, stepping back to allow me to enter.

"Hi. Thanks for inviting me." I tower over her tiny frame as I pass by and have a seat in the kitchen. It seems less intimate than the living room, which is what I need. If we move into the living room,

I'm gonna struggle keeping my hands to myself, and that's the last thing I need. No way do I want to make her uncomfortable because I'm lusting after her, my hands itching to touch her soft skin.

"Pick your poison. Cherry Jubilee or Cookies and Cream," she says, moving to the refrigerator freezer and glancing inside.

"Cookies and Cream, for sure, since you don't have the good stuff," I tease.

She narrows her eyes at me over her shoulder as she retrieves the frozen treat from the freezer and sets it on the counter. I'm up, knowing how much she grumbles when she can't scoop the hard ice cream out of the container. She takes the metal scoop out of the drawer and hands it over without protest.

"How many scoops do you want?" I ask, digging into the carton.

"Get yours first. You're the guest."

I just stare at her before plopping the first scoop into the bowl. Then, I add a second and a third. Once it's filled, I grab a spoon and hand it over. "That's not mine," she insists incredulously, staring at the heaping mound of ice cream in front of her.

"It is," I tell her, scooping the same into the second bowl.

"I can't eat all of this, TD," she grumbles, staring down at the sweet treat as if it's multiplying before her very eyes.

"I have faith in you," I state, slapping the lid back on the carton and putting it in the freezer.

We finally take a seat across from each other at the table. "You're going to eat what I don't."

"Done," I tell her before diving into my bowl.

"So tell me what's new with you," she instructs, taking much smaller bites than me.

"Loree and her crew are coming home for a visit in two weeks."

Her eyes light up. "Really? How exciting. When do they arrive?"

"Friday before Labor Day. They'll stay at Logan's cabin through Monday and fly back home. It'll be a short visit, but I'm glad they're comin'. I know she likes to go to Florida and visit Mom and Dad as often as possible, so I'm happy they're able to squeeze in a trip here."

"How are your parents?" she asks, concern filling her gentle green eyes.

"They're good. They leave soon for their Alaska vacation they've been saving for, which I'm sure is why Loree and her family are coming here instead of going to Florida."

"That's so cool they can take that trip. It feels like they've been saving for years," Ellie says, a dreamy look on her face.

"They have, and me too. I'm happy they're going. Between the airfare, six-day cruise, and then the week at an inclusive resort in Kenai, this trip is pretty salty, but it's been on their bucket list for a long time. I'm happy they're finally doing it."

Honestly, they've saved for years to be able to afford this experience. The two-week trip is over fifteen thousand dollars, but they consider it a once in a lifetime opportunity, and my sister and I agree. Dad will get to fish and Mom will enjoy a breathtaking view while catching up on her reading and knitting. I hope to be able to take vacations like this when I'm retired someday, even if it costs a small fortune to do it.

You only live once.

"I'm gonna help Logan make sure the cabin is ready to go next weekend. He says there were a few boards on the porch that needs replacing, as well as some critters that have been getting into the attic. He wants to make sure there's nothing living up there since the last time he did some repairs."

She pulls a face, wrinkling up her nose. "Critters?"

I shrug, scooping up another mouthful of ice cream. "Squirrels mostly. I think he had a few birds once."

She shudders. "Yuck."

"Happens, especially in the middle of the woods like that, surrounded by wildlife and water. Plus, the cabin isn't used nearly as often as it used to be, so with less human foot traffic, it's more likely that critters make themselves at home from time to time."

Ellie just stares at me with a blank look on her face. "I don't think I could ever go camping. I'm not a fan of bugs, let alone *critters*."

"It's not so bad, El. I think you'd enjoy it. Just make sure you have bug spray," I state, recalling how much my friend hates bugs, especially flying insects.

"I'll just stay here," she mutters.

We're both quiet for a while, enjoying our treat and lost in thought. I can't help but steal a few glances at her. She's always been the most beautiful woman I've ever known, and not just on the outside. Her heart is pure gold, and she'd do anything for anyone in need. I'm certain a big part of that is because of what happened to her as a teenager. She will forever be grateful to those who helped her during her time of need, especially after Brody was born soon after graduating high school.

"If you could go anywhere for vacation, where would you go?" she asks, breaking the silence.

I shift in my seat and give her my full attention. "That's a hard one, really. I'm a pretty simple man, so I prefer mountains and cabins, fishing and hunting, as opposed to beaches and fancy resorts. I might pick the Alaskan thing, like my parents are doing, but a simple cabin in Tennessee might be pretty awesome too. I always thought I'd like to go east to Maine for a trip or even to the Badlands in South Dakota. Would I turn down a trip to Hawaii or some fancy island? Probably not, but it wouldn't be my first choice."

She considers my comments and slowly nods in understanding.

"Where would you go if you could go anywhere in the world?" I find myself asking.

She shifts and looks uncomfortable suddenly. Her eyes are cast down to her dessert, her shoulders drawn in, and she appears to look smaller in her seat. "I don't know."

Realization hits me like a punch to the gut. As long as I've known Ellie, her entire focus has been on staying afloat and providing a stable life for her son. I rack my brain, trying to come up with a single instance where she took time away from work and went somewhere to relax and vacation with Brody, but I come up empty.

"Have you ever been on a vacation, El?" I find myself asking hesitantly. The last thing I want to do is make her feel more uncomfortable than I can tell she already is.

She lifts her slender shoulders and stirs her melting ice cream in the bowl. "When I was a kid, my parents would go to a church retreat every year, and I went with them. Though, not exactly my idea of a vacation," she says, a sad smile on her lips. "Once when I was seven or eight, we went to the Dells for an extended weekend. We rented a room in a big cabin resort place. I remember wanting to go to the nearby water park, but my parents said no. Instead, we swam in the lake behind the resort. It was fun, but I was so jealous of the kids talking about the water park." Suddenly, she looks up at me with wide, horrified eyes. "Do you think Brody is upset at me for not taking him to a water park? We've never been."

I'm moving before I realize I'm out of my chair. Dropping to my knees in front of her, I gently turn her to face me. "No, I don't think he's upset."

Suddenly, tears spring from her eyes and slide down her cheeks. "But...I've never taken him anywhere, TD. Not once. He's never had a vacation."

"He's had something better than vacations, El," I insist, taking her hands in my right palm and swiping at those damn tears with my left thumb. "He's had experiences. You made sure he has a season pass every year to the public pool. He's been able to attend camps out at Bluff Preserves as well as for any sport he's ever wanted. You've made trips to the county fair, year after year, making sure he always had a wristband to ride all the rides. You've done day trips to amusement parks and traveled around the area exploring, and you've spent more time with him one-on-one, creating more memories than most kids will ever get. Believe me when I tell you, Brody is not mad at you for not taking him on some big, expensive trip somewhere. He had everything he ever wanted here, with you."

The look in her eyes doesn't exactly tell me she believes me, but that's okay. I understand what she's saying. Most kids would want to go to Florida or California or somewhere far away, but knowing Brody as well as I do, I know he's happy as long as she's happy. He's incredibly smart. He's known they can't afford the fancy trips some of his friends have taken every year, but he never lets it bother him— at least not that I've seen—and he makes the most out of the smaller things he gets to do locally.

She sighs dramatically and gives me a sad smile. "I just wish...I just wish things had been a little different for us. Easier," she confesses.

"Me too," I reply honestly. Watching her work herself to the point of exhaustion has always been a hard pill for me to swallow, but knowing she puts Brody first in every decision she makes helps ease the hurt it causes me.

I want to give her everything.

I want to share the load.

Not take care of it all completely, because that's not what she wants or needs, but to *help* her.

And Brody.

Our eyes hold for several seconds, and so much happens in that short amount of time. I see her worries, her struggles, and her celebrations flash through those beautiful eyes of hers. I see composure, fortitude, and if I'm not mistaken, desire. It's there, reflecting in those stunning green pools, and growing with every passing second.

Her hands turn, her slender fingers sliding between mine as my free hand moves to cup her jaw. I've always known her skin to be soft and warm, but having it against my palm right this moment is a special kind of torture. All I want is to move my hand, to see if the rest of her body is as perfect, and it doesn't help when she angles her chin, as if seeking out my hand farther. The slight movement also brings her mouth just a bit closer. My eyes zero in on her lips, and the moment her tongue slips out, wetting them, I almost groan.

Because all I can think about doing right now...is kissing her.

Her pink lips fall open slightly, her warm breath tickling my chin. I lean forward, my mouth so fucking close to hers, it's killing me not to just take the kiss. When her eyes drift closed, I'm a goner. My brain tries to tell me not to do it, but my heart is screaming at me to *kiss her, kiss her!*

What's a guy who has been pining after one of his closest friends for years to do?

My fingers itch, my skin feels hot beneath my clothes, and my mouth is suddenly so dry, my throat is like a desert, but that doesn't stop my desire for Ellie. It consumes me, burning through my veins like an out-of-control wildfire.

I lean in just enough to touch her lips with my own. Her lips part, and my tongue delves inside, sliding across hers hesitantly, yet possessively. The first taste of her sends my senses into overdrive, and I realize my mistake immediately.

I never want to stop kissing her.

The softest mewl sound fills the room as she wraps her arms around my shoulders and presses her chest to mine. The tips of her fingers tease the nape of my neck, dancing along the top of my spine and tangling with the locks I've meant to get cut this week but haven't found the time. Feeling her delicate fingers sliding along my scalp makes me suddenly reconsider my decision for that haircut.

Her mouth is pure heaven. Sweet and ripe, like a delicious strawberry on a hot summer day. Her hesitancy is replaced quickly by desire, as she rocks her body against mine. My cock is so hard, it's trying to claw its way out of my jeans to get to her. I've fantasized about this moment, this kiss, for so long, it's hard to believe it's actually happening.

The only way to describe this is the best kiss I've ever had.

Just when I'm about to throw her over my shoulder and cart her off to the nearest bedroom, the shutting of a door nearby triggers something in the back of my brain. The sound of heavy feet on stairs is the next to register, and I realize quickly we're only a couple of seconds away from not being alone anymore.

I release my hold and pull back, opening my eyes and staring into her wide, shocked ones. I'm able to stand rapidly, my mind spinning—either from the fast movement or the kiss, I'm not sure which. Taking a step back, I turn to hide my groin as the kitchen door opens and Brody steps inside.

He doesn't seem surprised to see me here, but the moment his eyes find his mom, a flash of worry crosses his features. "Everything okay?"

"Yes!" Ellie bellows.

I almost smile.

Brody glance my way before returning his gaze to his mom. "You sure? You look a little...I don't know. Weird." He looks down to the melted ice cream bowls sitting on the table.

"We were eating dessert and talking. Your mom got a little emotional," I tell him, deciding to leave out the part about what happened after.

As if in understanding, Brody nods. "Ahh, I see," he states, relaxing his stance.

"Did you go to Miss Molly's?" I ask, realizing Ellie is still too shell-shocked to speak.

"Yeah, we did, but Matt had an early curfew tonight, since he leaves tomorrow after practice for his camping trip," he says with a casual shrug of his shoulders before walking over to the fridge and grabbing the gallon of water to pour himself a glass.

My sights turn back to Ellie, who's just sitting there, touching her lips. When she gazes up, her green eyes are still a bit glassy, but she's at least sitting a little more natural now. She clears her throat and smiles, even though I catch a hint of anxiousness.

"I'm glad you had fun," she finally says to her son.

His grin looks so much like his mom's. "All right, I'm headed to the shower. Early morning tomorrow," he says, bumping me with his shoulder as he passes.

"Watch it. Your coach'll make you run sprints," I tease. The last thing I want them to do is run the day after a game. Tomorrow will be for watching parts of the game film and reviewing plays that didn't work.

Brody laughs. "Night, Coach. Night, Mom," he says, placing a kiss on his mother's cheek before leaving the room and heading to the bathroom.

"Night, bud," she replies.

When the door to the bathroom clicks closed, I turn my full attention to the woman sitting in the chair. "Breathe, El."

She whimpers as she drops her face into her hands. "I can't believe I did that."

Gently, I grip her shoulders and help her stand. My hands wrap around her wrists and gingerly pull hers away from her face. "We. *We* did that, and it's okay."

She adamantly shakes her head. "We're friends, TD. Friends don't kiss."

My dick begs to differ.

"No, not usually, but it happened." Holding her gaze, I add, "I don't regret it."

Her throat bobs as she swallows hard. "It was a really nice kiss," she whispers, and her confession makes me want to pound my chest with pride.

"We probably shouldn't have done it but did. It's okay. We're still friends, El. I won't let anything like that come between us."

She relaxes just a bit and a faint smile plays on her lips. "Okay. But we can't do that again," she insists, a faint blush creeping up her neck.

Though I want to argue, tell her why stop when something feels so good, so right, I know she's correct. It shouldn't happen again, even if I really want it to. "Agreed. It won't happen again," I reassure her and watch as the tension seems to fall from her shoulders.

"Okay. Yeah. Good."

I lower my hands, realizing I was still holding her wrists, and step away. "I can help you clean up our mess," I tell her. What's left of the ice cream is melted and not very appetizing.

"No, I got it," she insists, turning to collect the bowls.

"I don't mind helping," I insist, but she stops me.

"No, really. I'm good. I think...yeah, I think I just need a few minutes alone. If that's okay with you," she says, making eye contact once more.

"Of course it's okay. You never have to worry about needing time to think or breathe, El. Never. I'll always give you anything you want," I state, realizing how true that statement is. I'd do anything for this woman, even walk away when everything inside me is telling me to stay.

She gives me a relieved smile and takes the bowls to the sink.

"I'll get out of your hair. Thank you, again, for dessert."

"You're welcome," she replies, rinsing the bowls.

Wanting to say more, but knowing this isn't the time, I open the door, prepared to walk out. "Lock up behind me," I remind, just like I always do.

She stops and faces me, a small grin on the very lips I kissed just a few minutes ago. "I will."

With one last glance at the woman in front of me, I exit the apartment, pulling the door tightly closed behind me. I pause, waiting until I hear the familiar sound of the lock engaging before descending the steps to the bottom door. Before pulling that one closed, I throw the lock to ensure no one can get in, and head out into the dark, warm evening, my mind still wrapped around the woman upstairs.

That kiss.

I've had a handful of decent kisses in my life, but none compare to that one. The crackle of electricity, the heat, the chemistry. It was all there in spades. The kind of kiss you get lost in and never want to be found. Even if that person you shared it with is one of your best friends.

I hope I haven't fucked this all up.

CHAPTER
seven

Ellie

It's been three days, and I'm still thinking about that kiss.

The kiss that shouldn't have happened, yet I'm secretly happy it did.

Because that kiss was everything.

I haven't seen TD since Friday night, not that I expected to. As the summer tourist season starts to wind down, his day job has been keeping him busy. Add in coaching, and I know he's stretched thin. However, I imagine he'll be by this evening when he drops Brody off after practice.

I still can't believe my son prefers to walk the few blocks to school instead of driving my car, but when the weather's decent, he chooses to hoof it with friends. He only drives when the weather turns colder, and even then, he may not drive every day. I've always wondered why, especially since most high schoolers will drive all day, every day the moment they get their license, but not Brody. He usually walks the block down the road to the grocery store he stocks shelves at or the few blocks to the park. Plus, even though he's never confirmed it, I think he enjoys having TD take him home after practice. TD's been his ride since he started playing freshman year, and I truly believe their friendship is a big reason for continuing that tradition. Brody looks up to TD so much, not only as a coach, but as a friend.

That's why I can't let that kiss Friday night change anything.

After I've folded my third load of laundry and put away the groceries, I decide I need a little fresh air. I don't get many days to myself, but I always schedule myself off on Mondays. I use that day to catch up on everything I wasn't able to get to throughout the previous week. Usually, that consists of lots of laundry, cleaning, and shopping. Sometimes, I even get to sneak in a bit of relaxing.

Like today.

Since I was fretting about the kiss last evening, I ended up doing a majority of the cleaning in an attempt to keep my mind from replaying the way his hands felt in my hair and his mouth dominated mine. It didn't work, of course, but I was still able to get the entire place dusted, vacuumed, mopped, and tidied up. Sure, the apartment isn't very big, but with two people busy living here, it can still get messy quickly.

Not to mention the stench of football equipment that seems to hang in the air like a fog of baked sweat and rotten feet.

However, now I'm somewhat caught up on the housework and anxious to go outside for a bit and enjoy the beautiful day. Grabbing one of the bagged chairs from the entry closet, I slip it over my shoulder and retrieve my tote. I slipped a bottle of water and a hardback book I've been wanting to read into it earlier, in hopes I'll be able to steal away a couple of hours of quiet.

And maybe a little sun.

Lord knows my complexion can use a little color in it.

Once my apartment is secure, I take off toward the park. When I reach the sidewalk in front of the building, I smile as the sunshine hits me in the face. I pass a few familiar faces and offer a friendly greeting, but continue on my way, past the bank and bakery before heading south. Pine Village Park is an entire block consisting of playground equipment, a basketball court, pavilion with picnic tables, a walking path, and a new pickleball court, with ample shade trees sprinkled in. There are a few wooden benches too, but I find them uncomfortable after a little while, which is why I now bring my own chair to sit on.

Since school is in session, the park is empty, with the exception of two ladies chatting as they walk along the path. I go to the big oak tree I like to sit under and set down my tote so I have both hands to pull the chair from the bag. I position the chair away from the street, so my view is a row of pine bushes used as a barrier between the playground area and the basketball court. It's just private enough and the breeze moves through the area well to help keep you cool.

I place the bottle of water in the holder on the chair, retrieve the book, and take a seat. A sigh of contentment slips out the moment I'm settled, my feet stretched out in front of me. The book is a historical romance I've heard great things about and has been featured on a streaming service recently.

The late morning transforms into early afternoon, and before I realize it, two hours have passed. I'm engrossed in the book, but my stomach is starting to remind me I haven't eaten anything since a piece of buttered toast and an orange for breakfast with Brody before he left for school. So, instead of continuing to read the chapter I'm on, I decide to pack it up and head home.

Just as I'm slipping my book into the tote bag, a shadow falls over me. "Not surprised to still find you here."

I glance up and find TD standing there, a small grin on his handsome face. "Hey. What are you doing here?" I ask, looking around to see if there's something nearby that warrants police presence.

He lifts his hand and reveals the plastic bag. "I saw you sitting here earlier today, and when I drove by just a bit ago and you were still here, I thought I'd stop and grab lunch."

"What if I've already eaten?" I ask, my stomach all but growling loudly.

TD smiles, and his entire face lights up. "Have you?" he asks, setting the bag on the ground in front of me and pulling out the first of two containers.

I take the lunch, the scent of chicken and ranch hitting me square in the nostrils. "Well, no, but I could have," I state, opening the lid and finding my favorite chicken BLT sandwich. Chopped crispy chicken, bacon, tomato, and lettuce, mixed with ranch dressing and stuffed in a fresh hoagie roll. Add in fresh fruit, and it's positively delicious.

TD snorts as he takes a seat on the ground in front of me and opens the second container, revealing the same lunch. "I've known you a lot of years, El. You always put everyone before yourself, which is why I assumed you haven't eaten. When you do finally get a little time to yourself, you usually get lost in it. Hence, the clock past one and you still haven't had lunch."

My eyes narrow a bit, annoyed with how well he knows me. "Don't say hence. You sound like Mrs. Eshelman from eighth grade English class."

He chuckles, and I hate how the sound goes straight to the apex of my legs. I should not get turned on listening to my friend laugh. "I forgot about her. Wasn't she a hundred and ten when she taught us?"

"She was in her fifties, silly," I comment, taking my first bite of my sandwich. The flavors explode on my tongue, and I have to rein in my groan.

"She cracked that ruler against the chalkboard like she'd been teaching since the fifties," he grumbles between bites.

"We should move over to the picnic area so you have a better place to sit," I suggest, closing the lid on my lunch container and preparing to stand.

"I'm fine, El. Sit. Eat."

"So bossy," I retort, remaining in my seat and reopening my container of food.

"You have no idea," he mutters, his focus on his own lunch.

A shiver sweeps through me at his words, as if they hold some sort of hidden meaning. I stare at my friend, casually sitting on the grass in front of me, and try to ignore how gorgeous he looks in his police uniform. The dark blue really makes his eyes look incredibly deep and rich, and I won't get into the way the pants hug his thighs and rear end. Even the black shoes seem to catch my attention.

Of course, all it does now is remind me of the kiss from Friday night. I've spent the last few days trying to forget it happened, but after only a few minutes in his presence, that kiss comes barreling back to the forefront of my mind, replaying every swipe of his lips and stroke of his tongue. I recall exactly how hot and bothered I was after he left, and exactly what I had to do to relieve the tingle between my legs his kiss evoked.

I feel my face start to get warm, and I pray he doesn't notice.

Clearing my throat, I finally ask, "Busy day?"

He shrugs and pops a grape into his mouth. "Not terrible. A few traffic stops early on, and Jeb had another gas-and-dash," he says shaking his head. "That man loses more money every month to gas-and-dash customers, I'm not sure how he can afford to stay in business."

"He told me not too long ago he'd never put in new pumps. If it ever got to that point, he'd sell or close it down," I reply before taking a bite of watermelon.

"Yep. I tell him every time I file a report, he's better off paying the money to put in the pumps. I know the cost is extensive in the beginning, but he does enough business with his location close to Bluff Preserves, he'd recoup the cost quickly."

"I get that, but Jeb grew up in a different time. He doesn't want anything to do with credit cards. When he comes to the diner, he always pays in cash."

TD sighs as he extends his legs out in front of him, his big feet sliding along the side of my chair. "I know that, really. I just hate when assholes take advantage of a good guy like him. I know plenty of times the gas-and-dash customers are accidental. When I get a hold of them after running their plates, you can tell it wasn't intentional. Those patrons are instantly embarrassed and apologize profusely, and most of the time, they do put a check in the mail to cover their gas. But there are still several who make it so you can't track them down to get payment or don't send it in. Jeb refuses to prosecute those assholes, and that never sits right with me."

"But it's his decision, right?"

He nods before taking another big bite of the sandwich. "These are really good. I can see why they're your favorite."

I offer him a small grin. "Would you believe it if I told you it was an accident we discovered this sandwich?"

"This is one delicious accident," he replies, his eyes burning into mine and causing my heartbeat to spike.

I look away quickly, returning my focus on what's left of my food. "We were playing around with a salad one afternoon, and when it didn't turn out the way Susie wanted because she said it had too much ranch dressing, she threw all the ingredients into a bowl and set it aside. It looked too good to waste, so I grabbed a fork and prepared to eat it, but the chicken was stripped too big. I cut it all into small pieces and ended up chopping the other ingredients the same way. Susie watched as I stirred it together once more, and suddenly, she was grabbing a hoagie roll and stuffing it. The result was so good, I suggested Fran add it to the specials board one day a week to see what the customers thought. When it took off and people were asking for it on days it wasn't a special, Fran put it on the regular menu. The rest is history," I state with a proud smile, recalling how excited Fran was to tell me she was adding it to the daily offering. It's not just my favorite sandwich, but a popular choice for the regulars.

TD is grinning from ear to ear. "It makes me happy to see you smile, knowing how much you love your job."

I shrug, shying away from the compliment turned my way. "I'm just a waitress."

He points a big, meaty finger at me and says, "Stop it. You're way more than just a waitress. You're an incredible, loyal, and dedicated employee and friend, the manager, and the customers love you. The regulars who know you always want to sit in your section every time they go. Everyone sings your praises, El, everyone, so don't for one second think you're just anything. You're so much more than that."

There's a fierceness in his eyes that steals my breath and makes it hard to think. I've always been fine with my career choice, even though I've secretly wondered if Brody was okay with having a mom who is a server. He's never complained about the fact I work at the diner, while some of his friend's moms have college degrees and nine-to-five careers.

"Stop it, El."

"What?" I ask, looking up.

"Get out of your head."

Sheepishly, I give him a slight grin. "Hard to do sometimes," I confess.

"I get that, but there's no need. You've got it more together than half this town, so stop second-guessing yourself every step of the way."

I try to really hear his words, and while I do, it's still hard to accept them sometimes. My parents washed their pristine Christian hands of me when I found out I was pregnant and refused to give up the baby, and I've been on my own a long time. My dad was a minister, and they couldn't fathom why I was ruining my life by having a child out of wedlock. Despite praying for me, they ultimately decided my pregnancy was too much for their faith to handle and chose to cast me aside. Within months, my dad relocated to another church, and I haven't spoken to them since. I've only ever had myself to rely on, along with a handful of close friends who I consider family.

That's why I have to forget that kiss Friday night happened.

I can't—no, I *won't*—risk TD because I let my hormones get the best of me.

Of course, those hormones have been lying dormant for a really long time. I haven't dated much recently. Okay, fine. I haven't dated at all. There was one guy when Brody was eight, but that fizzled and burned out after only a handful of dates. In fact, I quickly realized he was only after one thing, and once he got it, he moved on to someone else.

Since, I've devoted every free minute of my time and every ounce of energy to my son, not that I didn't do that before I met Mike, but after he all but ghosted me after getting what he wanted, I realized dating just wasn't for me.

Men are just too much work.

Clearing my throat and pushing thoughts of Mike from my head, I ask, "Are you ready for Friday's game?"

He nods, finishing off his lunch and shoving the container back in the bag. "Yeah, we're ready. Westwood's O-line is tough, so we're working on ways to get the ball outside as fast as possible. We know they'll be looking for the pass to Brody, so we're pushing plays with the tight ends too. Gonna be a fun one."

"I can't wait," I tell him after swallowing a small bite of cantaloupe. "It's still hard to believe he's a senior. It feels like yesterday I was getting him ready for kindergarten. Now, he's on the verge of adulthood and about to step out into the world on his own." I try to keep the emotions I've been wrangling at bay, but it's hard. I didn't expect to feel this level of sadness overcome me.

"Has Brode given any indication on what he wants to do after graduation?" TD asks.

With a sigh, I close the lid on my lunch container and reach for the bag. TD takes it, adding my trash to his. "No, he hasn't. Anytime I ask about it, he just shrugs and says he has time to figure it out. But honestly? I think he has an idea, and he doesn't want to say."

"What makes you say that?" TD's eyes are intense and focused, as if he's suddenly concerned along with me.

"Well, he gets this look in his eyes every time I bring it up. Like a flash of eagerness, only to watch him hide it as quickly as possible. The first couple of times, I assumed I misread him, but now I don't think I have. What if he's wanting to go away somewhere and is afraid to tell me? I've always reassured him he can come to me with anything, but I'm going to be honest, if he tells me he wants to study abroad in Paris or Japan, I'm not sure I can handle that." Then another idea hits me with the force of a thousand bricks to the chest. "Oh, God. What if he wants to go into the military? Not that the military isn't an honorable choice with so many career opportunities, but..."

"Breathe, El," he whispers, leaning forward and placing his big, warm palm on my bare knee. I try to ignore the jolt of electricity that simple, comforting touch possesses, but it's difficult.

I do as instructed, first with one calming breath, followed by a second. "You're right. If he were to choose the military, I would be so proud of him. It would just be equally as hard, you know?"

He gives me a small smile. "Yes, El, I do know. Your boy holds a very special place in my heart, and the thought of him going away like that tears me up inside too, but whatever he chooses, you've given him everything he needs to take that step toward his future. You've given him roots and wings."

I shake my head, processing his statement. I know Brody means a lot to my closer friends, especially since they've been right beside me every step of the way through raising him, but to actually hear TD say it does something to me. I know Brody loves TD, which is why us maintaining our friendship is so important to me.

Because it's not just about me.

It's about Brody too.

"Thank you for bringing me lunch. And for the talk," I say, knowing he's going to have to return to work soon.

"You're welcome," he replies, getting up and confirming my suspicion. He ties a knot with the handles of the bag, preparing to throw it in the nearest trash can. "Don't worry about Brody, El. I'm serious. He's a great kid and no matter where he goes in this world, he's going to do amazing things."

Tears fill my eyes and a lump forms in my throat, so I just nod in reply.

He bends down and places a chaste kiss on my forehead. My lips tingle with anticipation, but thankfully, he doesn't kiss me there. Not that I don't want him to. In fact, that's the problem. I do.

"Enjoy your afternoon, El."

"I will," I quickly insist, reaching for the book I've been lost in. "Don't work too hard, Thomas."

His eyes narrow before he slides sunglasses onto his face. "You'll pay for that," he states with a hint of humor in his voice before he turns to walk back to his squad car, tossing our trash in the bin as he goes.

A shiver sweeps through me.

Why do I secretly hope his threat is sexual?

CHAPTER
eight

TD

"Panthers on three! One, two, three…"

"Panthers!"

The team walks together toward the locker room at the end of our Saturday practice. Last night's game was a win, but it wasn't easy. In fact, for a while, I thought the Westwood Warriors were going to be victorious. They were definitely prepared for Brody, as well as our running game, but we made them work for every stop they made. Late in the fourth quarter, we were able to get around their strong offense and run in a score that put us on top. The defense was able to hold their late-game push for points, giving us the win in the end.

Hard fought game on both sides.

Now, the players are headed to the locker room at the end of our Saturday walk-through. However, my eyes search out one particular player, who seems a little off today, despite having a good game last night. I watch Brody head for the locker room, walking beside his friends. The others are still hyped up from the win last night, but I can tell there's something weighing on Brody's mind, and I plan to get to the bottom of it.

The assistant coaches take off, and once my office is locked up, I head for the parking lot. As players come out, I make sure to say something encouraging about last night's game, giving them compliments and accolades for the positives I saw. When the last group steps out, Brody is hanging toward the back. He's smiling as he listens to Matt talk, but there's still something different about him.

"Later, Coach," Matt hollers, heading this way to go to his car.

"Later, Matt. Good game last night," I reply, holding up my fist for a bump as he passes.

When I say goodbye to the other players, I turn my attention to Brody, who keeps walking. "Brody, wanna lift?"

He stops, and for a moment, I think he's going to turn me down. The kid definitely has a battle going on in his head right now, and while I won't push him, I'd love to help if I can. "Sure," he says, his lips curling up a bit in appreciation.

He throws his gym bag into the bed of the truck, climbs inside the cab, and the moment I turn over the engine, I crank up the air-conditioning. "You had a great game last night," I say, hoping to get him talking.

"We all played hard," he replies. That's one thing I've always noticed and appreciated about Brody. Anytime I compliment him, he turns it on to his teammates. "Matt's TD that last quarter was epic."

Smiling, I reply, "Sure was."

"I was worried for a bit. I didn't think we'd ever cross that goal line," he says, keeping his eyes on the parking lot in front of me.

"I knew you guys would do it. The determination was there. Just had to find the right play to make it happen," I state like the proud coach I am.

He doesn't say anything else as I pull out onto the road and head toward their apartment. "Everything all right with you?" I ask casually, trying not to be too assertive.

"Fine," he replies, almost too quickly.

"Okay," I say, keeping my hand nonchalantly on the wheel. "If you need to talk though, I'm here."

Silence fills my truck, and I decide now might not be the right time to push him. He's clearly working through a few things in his head and needs a little space to get through it. He knows I'm here for him when he's ready, and that's all I can do. Though, I may shoot Ellie a message later, just to give her a heads-up that I suspect something's on his mind.

I pull through the back alleyway and park in the lot behind the diner. Ellie's car is there, but I know she's working this morning. I stop in one of the first parking spots available and keep the engine running. Brody just sits there, staring straight ahead. My heart starts to beat a little faster as worry sets in. He's definitely battling something in his head, and it kills me I can't just fix whatever it is.

After a few minutes of silence, he says, "Can I ask you something, Coach?"

"You can ask me anything, Brody," I assure him softly.

He turns my way and asks, "Have you ever been camping?"

Okay. That wasn't what I was expecting.

"Uhh, sure. Several times. Why?"

He doesn't reply right away, just holds my gaze. "Matt and his dad go together every year, just the two of them. They went last weekend, and while I love hearing him talk about it, it makes me a little sad too." He swallows hard. "I've never been camping."

A lump forms in my throat, making it hard to breathe. "Do you want to go camping?"

He shrugs casually. "Yeah, I think so. He's always bragging about all the fun stuff he does with his dad, like fishing, cooking over a campfire, and sleeping in a tent. It sounds awesome, but..."

"But what?" I hedge, trying to gently give him a nudge.

"But I don't have a dad to do that kinda stuff with," he rushes to say.

This is the first time I've ever heard him talk about this, the first time he's ever mentioned not having a dad, and it tears at my heart. "You want to go camping, Brody?"

He nods insistently, his eyes a little glassy from emotion. "Will you take me camping? I know you're not my dad, but..." his voice trails off, and I hear what he doesn't say.

I may not be his dad, but I'm probably the closest thing he has to one.

My heart beats wildly yet calms at the same time. It's a wild reaction, and one I don't want to dive into right now.

Brody's green eyes reflect a whole mess of emotions. Worry, anticipation, and even embarrassment shine back at me, and I know there's only one answer I can give. Only one I *would* give. "Hell, yes, I'll take you camping."

He seems slightly stunned for a moment before he asks, "Really?"

"Of course. When?"

"Now?" he asks eagerly, making me laugh.

As if realizing it might not be the best time, he quickly backpedals. "We can go whenever."

But my mind has already sprung into action. "Actually, this might be a great time to go. I'm supposed to get Logan's cabin ready for my sister's arrival next week, so if you don't mind a little work while we're enjoying our camping, we can leave this afternoon."

His eyes light up huge. "Really? I mean, I was pretty sure this weekend was out of the question, but I don't mind helping you. That'll be cool, actually," he says, grinning from ear to ear. Then, just as quickly, that smile falls away. "Oh, wait. I have to work tomorrow at the grocery store."

"What time?" I ask.

"Two to six."

"Not a problem, Brody," I tell him, knowing he appreciates every hour he works at the local grocery store, stocking shelves. He's always been a big helper to his mom, working what he can between school and practices. "I'll make sure you're back in time to work."

"Thanks," he replies with a wide smile, suddenly looking so much younger than his seventeen years. There's an innocence in that grin, laced with a whole lot of happiness.

"You're welcome. Go on up and pack a bag. You'll need a few different changes of clothes."

"And a tent," Brody says, reaching for the door release.

"We can't just stay in the cabin?" I ask with a snicker.

"No way, Coach. We need the full camping experience. We're roughing it for the next twenty-four hours," he insists.

"All right, your call. I've got a tent, blankets, and air mattresses. The cabin already has the campfire equipment there, so we don't have to worry about that. We can stop by the grocery store and grab some food on our way out of town. Deal?"

"Deal!" he proclaims eagerly. "Wait. What about my mom?"

"Do you want to invite her?" Something flutters in my chest at the thought of sharing a tent and air mattress with Ellie.

He shakes his head. "You know how she is with bugs."

I chuckle at his comment, because, yes, I know exactly how Ellie feels about bugs. She's not a fan. "Good point."

"Do you think she'll let me go?"

Smiling, I tell him, "You let me worry about your mom. Go up and get packed, and then go down to the diner to see her. You know she'll want to visit with you before you go. Once I've talked to her, I'll run home and get all the supplies in my truck and be back to pick you up."

He nods impatiently. "Sounds good. Thanks, Coach. I mean TD."

"You're welcome, Brody. I'll be back shortly," I tell him. We get out of the truck together, and while he runs in the back door to go upstairs, I maneuver around the building to use the front entrance. Fortunately, it's still early enough to avoid the lunch rush, so once I step inside, it's easy to find Ellie. She's pouring water refills at a booth, smiling at something they say. That weird lurch happens in my chest, just as it does every time my friend smiles.

"Hey, what are you doing here?"

I blink, realizing she has turned her attention to me. "Hi. I wanted to speak with you for a moment, if you've got time."

Worry flashes in her eyes. "Is everything okay? Brody?"

"He's fine, El. Just wanted to run something by you."

"Oh. Okay," she replies, glancing toward the counter. "Viv, I'm going to step in back for a minute. Can you watch for the Pattersons' food to come out?"

"You got it," the other server says as she pours a cup of coffee for Victor Houston at the counter.

I follow behind as she steps through the swinging door. I know if you continue down the hall, you'll hit the back of the building where their stairwell is, but we don't go that far. She walks into a small office just off to the right.

"What's up?" she asks, her chestnut brown hair pulled in a high ponytail on top of her head and her green eyes shining like the most beautiful emeralds.

"Would it be okay with you if I took Brody camping tonight?"

Apparently, I catch her off guard because she doesn't reply right away and her gorgeous face registers confusion. "Camping?" she finally asks after several long seconds.

"Yeah. He wants to go, and I'll be out at Logan's cabin getting it ready for my sister, so it's the perfect opportunity," I tell her, deciding to leave out the part about Matt and his father always going together and Brody feeling left out. If she asks, I'll give more details, but for now, that's between Brody and me.

"Oh. Uh, I guess. He's never been camping, I don't think."

"No, he mentioned that too, and it's the perfect opportunity. He can help Logan and me at the cabin, and then we'll camp out afterward."

She seems genuinely surprised once more. "Like...under the stars? Why? You have a cabin."

"Real men tent camp, El," I tease, watching her make a face.

"My back would never recover."

Mine either, which is why I'll make sure to pack the air mattresses. "I'm going to grab some hot dogs, chips, eggs, and bacon, things like that we can cook easily over the fire. I'll have him back by one tomorrow so he can get ready for work."

She stares at me, her eyes filling with tears. "I don't know what to say."

"You're okay with it, right? I mean, I don't want to overstep."

Ellie moves, walking straight toward me with determination in her eyes. "You could never overstep, TD. Never. Thank you." Then, she wraps her arms around my waist and gently squeezes, hugging me the way she has for years.

My arms automatically go to her shoulders, holding her against me and breathing in the way her much smaller body feels against mine. Her hugs have always caused my blood to zing a little faster through my veins. Ever since we were in high school and I noticed how beautiful my friend really was. She had just started dating that asshole, Rusty Davidson, and she seemed really into him, so despite a bit of a schoolboy crush, I kept my distance. I thought perhaps the guy would be decent in the long run, but unfortunately, he proved me right in the end.

Man, I really fucking hate that guy.

When she pulls back, she gives me a tender smile. "Is there anything you need me to do before you guys go? Want me to pack lunches?"

I'm about to tell her no, but the truth is, sacked lunches might be just what the doctor ordered. When we get to the cabin, we're going to have to set up the tent and get everything organized. Plus, help Logan unload his truck and do a few of the miscellaneous jobs he's been putting off. A quick lunch of a cold cut sandwich and some coleslaw would do the trick.

"Actually, if you want to have the kitchen throw together a few cold sandwiches and a side, that'd be great. This way, we can get right to work when we get there and not have to worry about setting up the fire to cook lunch."

"I'm on it," she says eagerly with a pat on my chest. "Two?"

"Three, if you will. Logan's gonna meet us there."

She nods. "Coming right up." Ellie practically runs from the office and across the hall into the kitchen. I make my way up to the counter and have a seat where I can still see her moving around the large space. She stays on the refrigerated side of the kitchen, away from where George, today's cook, is working at the grill. After a few minutes, she comes up to where I sit and places two bags on the counter.

Pulling out my wallet, I retrieve a couple of twenties and set them beside the bags.

"Nope. Your money's no good here, Thomas Dexter."

A growl spills from my throat as I lean in and narrow my eyes. "You're not buying our lunches, Ellie Daniels."

She just gives me a wide grin. "It's a thank you. For taking Brody camping." She sobers as the smile falls from her face. "Something tells me this weekend is going to mean a lot to him, and because of that, it means a lot to me. So thank you."

Sighing, I slip my wallet back into my pocket and palm the twenties. "I'll buy pizza soon."

"Not necessary, but you know I'll never turn down pizza," she replies with a laugh.

Yeah, I know. It's her favorite.

"All right, I better get out of here and get the supplies. Brode will be down shortly to talk to you. He'll want to make sure you're okay with this."

"I'm okay with it," she assures me, rocking back on her heels as the bell dings above the door.

"We have good cell coverage out there, so call if you need us."

"I will," she promises.

Lifting the two bags, I can't help but ask, "What are you going to do tonight? A whole night to yourself."

She pauses, as if contemplating her evening. "Wow, I don't know. This doesn't happen too often. Maybe I'll call Blair and Hallie and see if they want to grab dinner or hang out. Or maybe I'll just take a bath, read a book, and go to bed early," she states with a laugh.

"Well, enjoy your time, El. You deserve a relaxing evening." Noticing the diner is starting to fill with customers, I step away from the counter and prepare to head for the exit. "You know, if you wanted to, you could come with us."

She wrinkles her cute little nose. "Camping? Outside? With bugs and wild animals? No thanks."

"You could stay in the cabin while the men are outside."

The sweetest grin plays on her lips. "Thanks for the offer, but I think I'll leave the camping to you guys."

Shrugging, I turn toward the door. "Suit yourself. Oh, and, El? Thanks for sharing your boy with me this weekend. He's a great kid."

Wetness fills her eyes once more as she nods. "Thank you for stepping in and helping me fill shoes."

That's all she says, but she doesn't have to say another word. I understand completely. She stepped up into the mother *and* father role when she decided to keep her baby in high school, and I was right there with her. Hallie, Logan, Ava, and a few others were there too, all willing to assist a friend in need.

Brody doesn't know his dad, because he's never been a part of his life. When Ellie found out she was pregnant, Rusty insisted it wasn't his baby and told the whole school she was cheating on him. Ellie never said a word to refute the lies, despite all of us encouraging her to do so. But she never did, stating she didn't want a man in her baby's life who didn't want to be there.

And Rusty Davidson never wanted to be there.

So we were.

I was there, and I'll never regret a single second of it.

Now, I get to take that boy camping, and I'm not sure I've been this excited about something in my life. Not just because of the time with him, but because he asked me. *Me.* And even though I'm not his father, I'm the closest man he has to one, and that's not something I take lightly. It's a big deal, and I'll do everything in my power to maintain that level of trust in him, because at the end of the day, he deserves the world.

Him and his mom.

CHAPTER
nine

Ellie

"I'm so glad you called," Hallie says, sliding into the booth across from me at the Mexican restaurant.

"Me too. I'm surprised you weren't busy, like Blair." When I called Blair this afternoon, she was on her way to one of the bigger neighboring hospitals to visit a couple of patients and was planning to go to dinner with Gabe once they were finished.

She waves off my comment before grabbing the second menu. "Are you kidding? I have no life. I spend my days with little kids and go home to the quiet."

"Still nothing with Curtis?" I ask curiously.

"Nope, and that ship has sailed. I'm over his broken promises. When he calls, I don't even answer."

Hallie and Curtis dated for a couple of years, but his focus seemed to transition from their relationship to work. He missed a bunch of events, but the straw that broke the camel's back was when he missed her birthday. She was so hurt she broke up with him afterward. I know he's made several attempts since, but she seems firm in her decision to end it with him.

"Are you seeing anyone else?" I find myself asking, wanting to ask about Logan. However, I know what her answer would be if I inquired about him specifically.

"Nope," she replies, popping the P. "And I'm not looking to yet anyway. As much as I want the husband and kids dream, Curtis left a bad taste in my mouth. I'm not in a big hurry," she insists as the server approaches our table.

"Hey, ladies, what can I getcha to drink?"

"Mango margarita. Big one," Hallie replies.

"I'll take a strawberry margarita, but make mine a small, please."

"Do you need another minute to look at the menu or are you ready to order?" she asks.

I already know I need to review the menu, so I say, "Give us a few more minutes, please."

The server nods. "I'll get those drinks for you right away."

Once she walks away, a basket of warm tortilla chips and fresh salsa arrives on our table and we both dive in. "A big one, huh?" I ask, trying to hide a smile.

"Long day. Had to go to the hardware store and deal with *Shay*," she mutters, referring to Logan's ex-wife.

"Was she able to help you?" I find myself asking, still finding it hard to believe Shay works at the hardware store.

"Not in the least, but she refused to let someone else help me and followed me around the store like a lost puppy dog. I mean, I don't want Logan's assistance at all, but I was praying he would come and take over."

Smiling, I ask, "Did he?"

"Nope," she states pointedly. "The asshole just stood behind the counter and smirked the whole time."

"What did you need?" I ask as the server brings our margaritas. Mine is a sensible size, even though I know I won't drink it all, but Hallie's looks like some sort of large fishbowl. "You're not driving, right?"

"Nah," she says before taking her first greedy slurp from the straw. "I walked. I was planning to drink one of these babies, so I knew better than to drive."

"Me too," I reply, taking a much smaller sip.

After we place our food orders, I turn my attention back to her. "So, what was it you needed to buy?"

"Guts for my toilet, and a new wooden rod for the coat closet. The landlord was coming over to fix it but wasn't going to make it to the hardware store before it closed, so he asked me to grab it. When I told Shay what I was looking for, she told me to just buy a new toilet, since mine was obviously old and gross, if it needed new guts, which she had no clue what that meant, by the way."

"I'm a little hopeless when it comes to home repair, but even I know what the toilet guts are," I reply with a snicker.

Shay Long was the Barbie doll of our class. She has long, beautiful blond hair, a perfect complexion, and bright blue eyes. Every guy wanted her, and every girl wanted to be her. Well, until you got to know her, that is. She wasn't exactly the friendliest person in our class, always looking down on the rest of us from her throne.

Our senior year, she did a little modeling and was awarded a contract out in New York. She was only out there a short time, refusing to tell anyone why she left the Big Apple and returned to our quiet, small town, but the rumors weren't kind. I've heard everything from she slept with someone married and got fired to her having an eating disorder and was sent to some sort of rehab. Whatever the reason, she ended up coming back to Pine Village and eventually marrying Logan. He was back after his own bright career playing football was derailed by an injury, and at that time, insisted she was different. He quickly changed his tune after putting a ring on it. The marriage only lasted about two years, but she's been a thorn in his side ever since.

"I had to just find it myself, because she kept wanting me to go pick a new stool. Then, when I told her I needed a wooden rod for the closet cut to four feet, she just looked at me with a blank face and asked if that was the same as a two-by-four."

A snort of laughter comes from my mouth, and I do my best to cover it. "Oh, God."

"Yep, and that jerk, Logan Johnson, just stood back and refused to step in. When I finally got what I needed, after almost thirty minutes of getting dumb questions from Blonde Barbie, mind you, I sent him a one-finger salute as I walked out the door."

Shaking my head, I take another sip of my margarita. It's a dang good thing I walked too, because I can already tell this tequila is going straight to my head. I hope my food arrives quickly.

"Enough about my run-in with Shay. Tell me all about the reason you're alone tonight," Hallie says, dipping a chip in salsa and taking a bite.

"Well, TD took Brody camping. Apparently, they are going to do a few updates to Logan's cabin, and then camp after. When Brody came downstairs, he was so excited. Like, just as excited as when he scored his first touchdown. I don't think I've ever seen him that happy to do something."

"That's awesome. I bet they're having a great time."

"When I talked to Brody before I left, they were just finishing up for the day and going to build a fire to cook hot dogs." Our food arrives, and after the server confirms we don't need anything else, I ask, "Have you ever been camping?"

Hallie dives into her burrito and nods. "A few times, but not recently. Remember that time we all went to Logan's grandpa's cabin and had that party right after graduation? Can you call twenty people piling into a two-bedroom cabin camping? I think a few people passed out outside," she says casually, trying to remember that night.

I actually do remember the party, but not because I attended. I was very pregnant, unable to continue walking up and down my apartment stairs unless absolutely necessary, and didn't attend any of the post-event celebrations. I heard all about the booze-filled party but had other obligations by that point in life. Hanging with my classmates to drink and toast our newest accomplishment was the last thing on my mind.

"Anyway, I went one other time a few years after that with Gabe. He was home for a long weekend from medical school, and we went with Dad. That was the last time, though."

I scoop up a bite of my chicken, rice, and queso cheese mixture, and say, "I've never been."

"No? It's pretty fun, if you're into the outdoors."

"Well, we both know I'm not a fan of bugs," I reply with a chuckle.

"You'd definitely need bug spray," Hallie insists. "But if you get a chance, I think you'd enjoy it. You can just sit around the fire and read or think. Sometimes that's the best part about it. Just being there, appreciating the quiet, solitude, and scenery around you. I bet TD would take you too."

"He offered," I say, stabbing a piece of meat with my fork.

"Oh yeah? I bet he's willing to share his sleeping bag with you too," she teases, the smile on her face evident in her voice, without even looking up and seeing her. "Don't act like you didn't hear me."

"I'm eating," I reply, even though that's only a partial truth. The fact remains, I don't want to think about sharing a sleeping bag with TD because that makes me think of the kiss before moving on to things that could happen within the confines of the sleeping bag, and that's the last thing I need to imagine right now.

"Mmhmm," she mutters, pointing her fork at me. "If you would look past your googly eyes, you'd see he's totally into you."

I look up, my stomach churning with uneasiness. "It's not like that, Hal."

Her eyes roll so dramatically, all I can see are the whites of her eyes. "Stop it. He's got it bad. I think he has for a really long time."

My heart starts to pound in my chest like a snare drum and my breathing seems a bit shallow. "We're friends."

"Friends who want to bang."

I can't help but snort a giggle. "Stop. We're just...there's a line. It can't be crossed," I insist once the giggle subsides.

"Says who?"

"Says me. I need him too much to mess it all up by getting romantically involved," I insist quietly, trying to keep the neighboring tables from hearing our conversation. "He's such a good friend, Hal. Like the best friend I've ever had, no offense. And Brody looks up to him so much, he relies on him for guidance. Look at this weekend. They're camping because my son has never been. TD stepped up when no other man in his life ever has. I can't risk ruining that for Brody. I won't."

My friend sighs and gives me a small grin filled with sadness. "I get that, Ellie, really, I do. But...okay, hear me out. What if...the reason there's such a close connection between TD and Brody and TD and you is because there's more there? Listen, I'm the last person who should be offering love advice, but from the outside looking in, I really believe there's something between you. Maybe I'm wrong, but I don't think so. None of us do."

My mind quickly jumps from thinking about how amazing our shared kiss was to the last part of her comment. "None of you? Who all thinks that?"

Hallie shrugs and lifts her fork. "Everyone."

Cheese and rice, everyone?!

I'm suddenly a little sweaty in the pits and the room feels like a sauna. "Like, *everyone*-everyone?"

She nods. "It's not like we all sit around and talk about you, but there have been comments over the years, Ellie. Everyone has seen the way he looks at you, dotes on your every move, and goes out of his way to spend time with both you and Brody. The man caught feelings, and I'm guessing he's had them a while. Why do you think he doesn't date?"

My mind is spinning. "There was that one woman. What was her name? The one from out of town who always smelled like fish."

She cracks up laughing. "Felicity Saunders. Yeah, they dated for like five minutes and that was three or four years ago. She only smelled like fish because of the seafood restaurant she worked at. Name one woman he's dated since."

I try to come up with a few names, but I can't. In fact, I can't come up with one. "I—"

"And how long has it been since *you* went out on a date?" she probes, turning the food and alcohol in my stomach into a mixture of concrete.

All I can do is stare at her, because it's too embarrassing to admit the number of years aloud. Yes. Years.

"I'm not trying to get you worked up or upset, Ellie. You're an incredibly smart, beautiful, badass, single mom, and anyone would be lucky to go out with you. I guess I'm just trying to tell you to keep your eyes open, okay? If you only feel friendship toward TD, that's okay. I'd never want you to risk what you two have. But, if there's a shot at something more, I really hope you take the time to truly consider it. Brody's a senior in high school, and soon will be off living his own life. You'll have a little more free time on your hands, and I'd love to see you finally put yourself first for a change and find someone of the opposite sex to do the same. Namely, orgasms, because by the way you ignored my question on dating, I'm guessing it's been a while on those. Find a guy who makes your toes curl and your temperature rise with just a kiss. The naked part falls into place afterward, but if he's not giving you at least two orgasms each and every time you're together, he's not worth it. Move on. There are plenty of dicks in the sea, as they say."

A loud laugh flies and I cover my mouth with my hand. "No one says that!" I declare, hiding my blush behind my hands. All I can think about is the way TD made my toes curl with his kiss, and my brain tries to conjure up images of the two of us naked in bed, his body hovering over mine.

Something tells me TD would be a two orgasm kinda guy.

"Well, they should. It's the truth."

I shake my head and flick some rice around on my plate with my fork. "I hear what you're saying," I tell her.

"Good." We resume eating our food, and after a minute of silence, she asks, "TD'd totally be a multiple orgasms giver, wouldn't he." It's not a question, but a statement.

My face burns with embarrassment. "I don't know," I insist, making her laugh.

"He would," she replies quietly. "It's the policeman in him. Quiet, determined, and full of stamina. I bet he just takes control too. In bed, I mean. Not like one of those extreme Dom/sub things, but I'm thinking he knows what he wants and takes it. Don't you think?"

My mouth hangs open. "Hallie!" I whisper-yell. "Stop it," I bark out over a giggle.

"What? I might be a preschool teacher, but it's not all rainbows and the ABCs in my head." She gives me that devious grin, a naughty glint in her eyes.

"Well, since you've thought of it so much, maybe *you* should be the one to date him." But the moment those words are out of my mouth, I wish I could take them back. The thought of Hallie and TD dating is enough to make my stomach queasy. Not because there's anything wrong with either of them—in fact, I love them both to death—but I just don't think I can sit there while he gives those breathtaking kisses to one of my closest friends. The fish lady was one thing, though I never actually saw them kiss, but Hallie would be another story.

"Hell no. He's not my type."

I take a hearty drink of my margarita. "Wait, he's not your type? You just said all those things—"

"Yeah, yeah. I said them, but not because I'm into him. TD is totally a friend, and I would never want to actually see him naked. Okay, wait, I wouldn't mind seeing it, but that's as far as it goes. Do you think he's tattooed everywhere?" she asks, leaning forward. "I've seen him with his shirt off, and man," she adds, fanning her face. "Hot. I bet he has hidden tattoos we haven't seen yet."

"I wouldn't know," I mumble, taking yet another drink to help cool myself off.

"Anyway, I'm serious. Not my type."

"What is your type?" I find myself asking. Hallie has always dated someone with a professional career, usually in a suit and tie, or at the very least a polo and khakis.

"Hell if I know anymore," she mutters, pushing away her empty plate.

Deciding to ask the question in the forefront of my mind, I say, "Logan Johnson?"

She makes a face. "Fuck. No. That man would make me crazy in two point five seconds. We'd never survive a date. We'd kill each other before the appetizer arrived."

Smiling, I want to tell her I strongly disagree but choose to keep my comment to myself. "I'm glad we did this."

Hallie gives me a grin. "Me too. We don't get to hang out very much. This whole responsible adult business is getting in the way of having fun, isn't it?"

"For sure," I reply with a chuckle.

"Let's do it again soon and try to get a night where Blair can come too."

"And Ava."

"Yes," Hallie says, pulling some cash from her purse and tossing it on the table. "My treat."

"You don't have to do that," I insist, grabbing my own wad of cash. One of the perks of being a server is I always have cash on me.

"Nope, I got it," she declares.

"Well, thank you," I state, adding a few dollars on the table. "At least let me get the tip."

"Fine."

We stand up and head for the door, alcohol buzzing around in my brain. I'm so glad I walked. We're able to go in the same direction for two blocks before having to separate. The diner is a block to the east and Hallie's condo is a few blocks to the south.

"Thank you again," I tell her, throwing my arms over her shoulders and squeezing.

"Thanks for calling. I had fun."

"Me too."

She steps back and starts to move in the direction of home. "Oh, and, Ellie? Don't be afraid to go after what you want. Especially if that's a tall, dark, and handsome policeman." She throws me a wink and walks off, leaving me standing on the sidewalk in silence.

Eventually, I turn toward the diner, my mind reeling.

Everyone has noticed the way he looks at me?

If only it were as simple as she suggested, but I know it wouldn't be. There's too much friendship, too many years of it between us to risk.

Right?

Why am I suddenly doubting myself for the first time?

And more importantly, why do I really want to know if he has more tattoos I haven't seen yet?

CHAPTER
Ten

TD

"This is the best day ever," Brody announces for probably the tenth time. He's currently on his fourth hot dog, shoveling the food into his mouth like he hasn't eaten in days. Of course, I do agree, there's something magical about dinner cooked over an open flame, even hot dogs.

"Glad you're having fun."

Night is falling and the light from the warm late-August sun is finally setting. It didn't take us too long to complete the few minor repairs Logan wanted for the cabin. The porch boards were replaced and will need to be stained, but not right away. The lighting in the kitchen and bathroom were updated to LED, and some new cabinets hung beside the stacked washer and dryer unit. Plus, we cleaned the cabin and made sure the linens and towels are ready to go.

Brody did his part too. He wanted to help every step of the way, absorbing every ounce of knowledge Logan shared as he made the updates. He also didn't balk when it came to the cleaning either. He jumped right in and dusted the entire cabin, while I vacuumed floors and Logan scrubbed down the bathroom and kitchen.

Now, we're sitting around the fire, our tent positioned not too far away. Brody's still insistent we have the whole camping experience, including spending the night in the tent. The air mattresses are blown up and my lightweight sleeping bags ready. He's even taken our outing a step further and said we're not able to use the cabin amenities at all, which is all fine and dandy until it comes time to use the bathroom. Then a nice toilet and toilet paper are gonna come in pretty handy.

"How is school going?"

He nods, swallowing the last bite of his hot dog. "Good. I've got all the standard senior classes this year, including the dreaded civics class. But Morgan Cooper is in that class with me, and she's offered to help me if needed."

Something flashed through his eyes the moment he said her name, and I can't help but wonder if he's got a little crush on the girl. "No shame in getting a little extra help if needed, especially from a pretty girl like Morgan," I say, hoping to draw some info out of him.

He doesn't reply right away, so I stay quiet, giving him time and space. One thing I know about Brody is if he wants to talk, he will. When he's ready.

He shifts in the lawn chair we pulled out of the small storage building behind the cabin and stares at the fire. After several minutes, he finally asks, "Hey, TD. Can I ask you something?"

"Always," I reply, trying to keep my posture casual as I wait him out.

Again, there's a pause, only this time, a much shorter one. "So, there's this girl," he begins nervously, and I know I hit the nail on the head with the Morgan Cooper crush.

"Yeah?"

He nods. "Yeah, I mean, she's really cool and smart and funny and plays tennis, and I kinda like her. I know it was a really long time ago that you were in high school, but I was just wondering, what would you do if you liked a girl?"

Ouch.

"Well, first off, it wasn't *that* long ago I was in high school."

"Almost twenty years," Brody insists, "And that's practically forever. Like ancient times when phones still had cords on them, and cars didn't have A/C in them."

A painful groan falls from my lips. "I'm thirty-five, Brode, not eighty-five. Cars had A/C in them when I was younger."

"But phones were all attached to the walls, right?"

Sighing, I concede, "I guess, but not all of them. There were cell phones, but they weren't as widely used as they are today."

"My point is things have changed. Maybe dating has too."

"I doubt it," I state. "A boy likes a girl, a girl likes a boy, and they go out on a date. If they hit it off, they become boyfriend and girlfriend. Same as it was when I was in school."

"Yeah, you're probably right. So? What would you do if you liked a girl in high school?"

"Ask her out," I reply, but I realize I'm not necessarily speaking from experience. Mostly, it's what I wish I would have done back then but didn't have a chance to before everything in life blew up in our faces.

"Did she say yes?" Brody asks, his eyes meeting mine from across the fire.

I open my mouth, but the words just won't come. I won't lie to him, so I stick with the truth. "Actually, I never got the chance to ask her. She started dating some asshole right when I finally built up the courage to take the chance, so I stepped back. I didn't want to cause problems for her."

"What happened?" he asks, leaning forward and giving me his complete attention.

I take a quick drink of water to wet my too-dry mouth and decide to go with the abbreviated version of the truth. "Well, they dated for a few months, and then he dumped her, leaving her high and dry when she needed him the most."

A flash of anger moves through Brody's green eyes. "What? That's cold. I can see why you called him an asshole. Did you swoop in and rescue her?"

"No," I tell him sadly, not even bothering to correct him on his use of profanity like I know his mom would have. "She had a lot on her plate by that point, and I decided it was best if we just remain friends."

He studies me, and for a minute, I wonder if he knows I'm talking about his mom. "What happened to her?"

That dryness in my throat is worse, and it feels like I may choke on my tongue. "She made an amazing life for herself, and that's all I ever wanted for her."

He nods, taking a drink from his Coke can. "What if the girl I like is a little out of my league?"

"No such thing," I tell him confidently. "You're one of the brightest, kindest, most hardworking kids I've ever known. If she can't see how amazing you are, then she isn't the one for you. You're not out of her league, she's out of yours."

We sit in silence once more, the sun having finally fallen completely behind the trees and the crickets starting to fill the night sky with the subtle sounds of chirping. I can tell he's thinking, probably about the girl he likes and wondering if it's the right time to ask her out. I hope he truly heard what I said. I wish I could tell him how I regretted not being a little quicker on the draw. Maybe if I had, she would have been dating me instead of that fucker who left her high and dry. Perhaps her entire life would have gone a little differently. Of course, she wouldn't have Brody if that would have happened, and I can't imagine life without him—hers or mine.

"Maybe I'll ask her out on Monday. I sit beside her in one of my classes, and she likes to go to the football games. Maybe she'll want to go for ice cream with me after the game."

"I think that's a great idea," I tell him.

He looks up and smiles. "Thanks, Coach. I mean TD."

"You're welcome, Brode. You can always come to me to talk."

He glances down before returning his gaze to mine. "You won't tell my mom, right? I don't want her to get her hopes up about Morgan. She's always encouraging me to ask out a girl, and I just don't want her to get all excited and then come to find out Morgan said no."

Well, it's good he finally confided in me who the girl he's interested in is, even if I had already figured it out. "I'll tell you what, B. I will keep your secrets as long as they won't hurt you, your mom, or someone else, okay? I want you to trust me, and I know that trust has to be earned. I won't say anything about girls or work or even school and football, as long it's not something bad. Does that make sense?"

He slowly nods. "Yeah, I get it. I understand what you're saying, and I appreciate you being willing to talk to me without running and telling my mom everything I said."

"I'd never do that unless it was absolutely necessary, B. Promise."

"Thanks, TD," he replies with a grateful grin. "Speaking of my mom," he starts, but doesn't say anything more.

My heart rate spikes as worry grips my chest. "What's wrong with your mom?"

"Nothing," he quickly insists, "but I've been doing some thinking."

"Okay, about what?"

"My mom. And you."

At first, I don't think I heard him correctly, but when he just continues to stare at me, I realize I heard him just fine. But, since this conversation could be about anything, I play it cool and ask, "What about your mom and me?"

He levels me with a look that tells me he's serious and blows my mind when he speaks. "I think you should date my mom."

After a few very long seconds, I open my mouth to reply, but nothing comes out. I shift in my seat, feeling the heat of his gaze as he stares back at me. Am I that transparent? I know I've fought this damn crush on Ellie for longer than any man should, but I thought I'd done a pretty damn good job of hiding it. Of course Logan sees it, but he's my oldest, closest friend and knows me as well as I know myself, so the fact he's caught on doesn't surprise me all that much. But Brody?

Well, shit!

"Listen to me before you say anything," Brody starts, moving on his seat so he's closer to the edge...and closer to me. "My mom is the best. She's smart, funny, sweet, can cook good food, which I know you like, and she likes football. She doesn't like bugs much and can't sing very well, but that's not something that should make or break this deal, right? She also works really hard and puts everyone but herself first all the time, but even then, she does everything with a smile and gives it her all. She's never once missed something I wanted her to attend and always has the good snacks in the cabinet, even though she'd rather I eat fruit or something healthy after school."

That last one makes me smile. "Brody—" I start but am cut off.

"And she's pretty, right? I know she's my mom, but I've heard people talk about how beautiful she is."

My throat tightens, making it hard to draw oxygen into my lungs. First off, I want to know who's saying this so I can beat their ass for looking at her, but I know that's not logical or sane in the least. "Yeah, Brode. Your mom is gorgeous."

"See? I knew it. And you like hanging out with her, otherwise you wouldn't come over so much. Plus, you're not dating anyone, so why not her?"

My head is spinning like I've drank too much tequila and haven't eaten any food. In fact, I might be a bit nauseous too. "Bud—"

"*And*...you said yourself you didn't ask that girl out in high school and regret it. Well, what if you regret not asking my mom out now?"

I'm stunned. So caught off guard, I have no idea what to say.

Do I confess the truth? Tell him his mom *was* the girl I crushed on in high school? If I tell him that, will he realize that crush hasn't died and is, in fact, alive and well?

With a sigh, I decide to step into this conversation delicately. "Your mom and I are good friends, Brody. I'm not sure dating is in the cards for us."

"I think you're wrong." The conviction in his voice gives me pause.

"Why do you say that?" I ask curiously.

"Because I see the way she looks at you, and she's just...I don't know...happier when you're around."

The air swooshes from my lungs as his words hammer into my brain, etching themselves in place like a tattoo.

"I have been thinking about this for a while now, and I have an idea."

The corner of my lip curls up. "Yeah? Well, lay it on me." Curiosity has gotten the best of me.

"I think you should take her to dinner, but not at the diner. If you guys go there, she'll end up in the kitchen, helping, and you know it. She talks about the steak house, but never goes because she doesn't want to spend the money. If you can afford it, take her there."

I want to smile but keep the grin off my face. "I can afford it," I reassure him.

"Okay, cool. I know everyone says cops and teachers don't make squat, considering all they do, so I wasn't sure," he adds.

"Definitely underpaid professions, but I can afford to take your mom out to a nice restaurant," I pledge.

"Great! When do you want to do it? Maybe Saturday? I checked her schedule before we left, and she works until two. That should give her time to get home and ready for the date, right? I know girls need a lot more time than guys do."

"They do, but—"

"And afterward, maybe you can take her to the movie in the park. I heard they're showing *The Wedding Singer*. You know Adam Sandler is her favorite, right?"

"Yes, I know that," I confirm. She loves his movies because they make her laugh, and she always says she'd much rather laugh and smile than cry when she's watching television or movies.

"So that's a great option, almost as if it was meant to be," Brody states. "Plus, Miss Molly's is open later on Saturdays, so you can probably grab some ice cream at the end of the movie. They'll probably even have plenty of your nasty favorite pistachio, because no one else orders it."

I bark out a laugh that echoes throughout the trees. "That's a low blow. I don't tease you for putting pineapple on pizza."

"Pineapple is amazing on pizza," he insists with a big grin. "So? What do you say? Wanna take my mom out Saturday night? She'll say yes if you ask her. I know it."

I was just blindsided by a seventeen-year-old.

And honestly, I'm not sure she will. I recall the fear in her eyes after I kissed her. Not because she wasn't enjoying the kiss, but simply for the fact she's afraid. Afraid of ruining the relationship we've built over the last many years, and I get it. Truly. Her friendship means more to me than just about anything in this world, and I never want to risk that.

But...

I can't stop thinking about that kiss.

About how my entire body was alive, energized, for the first time in...well, ever. No kiss before that one exists anymore. All I see, all I feel, all I want is her. I was fully prepared to tamp it down, beat my desire for one of my dearest friends into submission, but now? How do I do that when her son is sitting across from me, asking me to take her out?

Especially when all I want to do is just that.

"I guess I just want to finish by saying," he pauses, holding my gaze with determination and grit, "if anyone is going to date my mom, I really want it to be you." His words are almost a whisper by the time he reaches the end of his statement.

I'm completely speechless as I try to wrap my head around the direction this conversation has taken. Not for a second did I expect this, but now that he's said his piece, a bubble of excitement and maybe a little hope has appeared in my chest. I've thought about the day I ask Ellie out and she accepts a million times, but this is the first time since high school I've actually considered asking.

Leaning forward, I place my elbows on my knees and hold his gaze. "Well, let me start off by saying, I'm honored you'd think I would make a good fit to date your mom. She's everything you said she is, I don't disagree with that one bit."

"But you're going to let me down easy now, aren't you," he says, looking completely dejected.

"I should," I reply, a lump forming in my throat. "But I'm not."

He looks up so fast, he practically gives himself whiplash. "Really?"

I exhale deeply and decide to give him my truth. He deserves it after speaking his. "I like your mom, Brode. I always have. She's one of my closest friends, but...the girl I told you about in high school? The one I wanted to date, but someone got there first? That was your mom."

He grins from ear to ear. "I knew it."

"I've always wondered what would happen if we gave it a shot, but I know a big part of the reason she keeps me at arm's length is because of you. She knows how much my friendship means to you too, and she'd never want to jeopardize that."

"I respect that, but I still think you should ask. If it doesn't work out, then fine. I'm man enough not to let it come between our friendship too," Brody insists, looking and sounding much older than his young seventeen years. "As long as you were good to her. If you weren't then I'd have to kick your ass."

I hold a straight face, even if a part of me wants to crack a grin. He's completely serious, and I know he'd do whatever it took to defend Ellie, even throw a punch at me. "I understand, but please know I'd never do anything to hurt your mom. Ever."

He swallows hard, and if I'm not mistaken, tears fill his eyes. "I do know. That's why it has to be you."

I give him a nod. A promise. "All right, Brody. If you're okay with me asking your mom out, I'd be honored to, but not because you suggested it. I'll ask because I want to—have wanted to for a long time. Hearing you give me permission means a lot to me, and I know it will to her too, but just keep an open mind here, okay? We've been friends a long time, so she might not be ready to step over that line and go on a date with me. If that happens, I'm all right with it."

He nods quickly. "I will be too, but you should definitely try."

"Okay, I will."

He exhales in relief and leans back in his chair. "Good. Great. So, what do you think about Saturday night? Do you like my ideas or want more suggestions?"

This time, I do chuckle. "I think I'm good, B. Thanks for the tips, though. But I do have to admit, I don't know about next weekend, okay? My sister and her family are coming here for the weekend."

"Oh, that's right. I forgot. But maybe the weekend after that," he encourages.

We sit in silence for several minutes, both of us lost in our own thoughts. Mine flash to when we get home, to the moment I ask her to go to dinner with me. Sure, I could come up with a few ideas of my own for our date, but I do admit, Brody has put a lot of thought into this and his suggestions are on point.

My nervousness isn't about asking her, it's in not knowing what her answer will be. Will she be willing to give us a shot or is it too big of a risk for her to take? I know which way I hope she'll be leaning, but I'm not confident it'll happen that way.

"All right, I gotta use the bathroom," he says, jumping up and heading for the cabin.

"Wait, I thought we were roughing it tonight. No cabin privileges," I state with a cheeky grin.

"Yeah, well that was before I ate four hot dogs and drank the whole bottle of Coke. I'm not going to the bathroom outside," he insists, opening the door and stepping inside the cabin.

Well, good. Maybe he won't be so mad at me in the morning when I go inside for the cup of coffee I already set the timer on the pot to brew.

Smiling, I lean back in my chair and watch the fire flicker. This evening hasn't exactly gone the way I anticipated it.

It's been better.

CHAPTER eleven

Ellie

The apartment is quiet. *Too* quiet.

There have been dozens of times I've been alone, but for some reason, this night hits a little differently. I know he's safe and probably having the time of his life, just because he's with TD.

After they completed their work in the cabin, Brody called me to check in. TD was getting the fire going, and they had just finished pitching their tent and getting everything settled inside for the night. He was thrilled to be spending the night outside, and I'm certain a big part of the appeal is TD.

Now, I'm home from my dinner with Hallie and pacing the small living room floor. I don't know why I'm so anxious, but I am. Probably because of the conversation surrounding TD. Her mentioning everyone notices him watching me or thinking he has a crush on me is still swirling around in my head like a tornado of emotions.

I replay a few scenarios where TD seemed to be a little...attentive. He always comes over and says hello after football games, before he meets with his coaching staff to run through any issues that needed addressed from the game. He doesn't just drop Brody off at home following a practice or lifting. He always walks him up and says hello. And he makes sure I eat too. Case in point, he stopped by the park on Monday and brought me lunch.

But even with those few examples, I'm not sure I'm willing to risk our friendship to find out if it's more. What if it fizzles out or one of us has stronger feelings than the other? The last thing I'd ever want to do is hurt him, and I'm certain he feels the same way. We've been friends too long.

Plus, I'm not one to take a lot of risks in life.

Except for Brody. He was my biggest risk by not following through on my parents' demands, insisting I was ruining my life and probably that of a helpless baby.

My phone pings with a notification, so I put all thoughts of that last big fight with my parents out of my head and retrieve the device. I smile immediately when I see a text from TD.

> **TD:** Brody already broke his first rule of camping and went to use the bathroom in the cabin. Wonder if I can convince him to just crash in there too. I know my back would appreciate it.

> **Me:** See? Nothing about camping sounds like fun. No way would I want to go to the bathroom outside when there's a perfectly good toilet available inside.

> **TD:** Nothing sounds like fun? One word. Smores.

My mouth practically waters at the thought. Toasted marshmallow and melted chocolate between two pieces of graham crackers? Yeah, that might be the only thing listed in the plus column for me.

> **Me:** You play dirty.

TD: *insert laughing emoji*

Me: How's it going?

TD: Pretty good. Just relaxing by the fire for a bit before we hit the hay.

Images of TD sprawled out and sleeping, long, muscular legs taking up a big part of the air mattress fill my mind. What would it be like to be cuddled by his strong arms, drawn into his broad chest, and held tightly as I drift off to sleep?
No.
Don't go there, Ellie, or you'll never get that image out of your head.
Too late.

TD: I should have thought of this sooner, El. Brody seems to be having a great time and is completely at ease.

Me: It's not like you don't have a lot of other stuff going on. I glad he's having fun too.

TD: We both are.

Me: Good.

TD: How was your dinner with Hallie?

Me: It was good, but aren't you supposed to be roughing it right now? Cell phones are probably not allowed.

TD: Are you kidding? I'm with a teenage boy. Of course phones are allowed. Though, he hasn't been on his much. Just posted a few pics on that Snap-whatever-it's-called.

Me: I hate that app, but he's usually pretty respectable with it.

TD: He really hasn't been on his phone. He's soaking up the entire experience.

Me: Thank you, TD. It really warms my heart that he's able to do things like camping with you.

TD: I love that boy too, El.

A huge lump forms in my throat, making it hard to swallow. It's probably a good thing I'm texting, because there's no way I could talk right now. Hearing him say he loves my son is almost too much for this mom-heart to take.
Before I can reply, he fires back with another text.

TD: Alright, I should get off here. I just got in trouble. *insert laughing emoji*

Me: Enjoy! And take care of my boy.

TD: You don't have to worry about anything, El. I've got him.

Me: I know you do. Be safe.

TD: Always. See you in the afternoon.

Me: Can't wait.

And I realize immediately, I can't. I'm excited to hear all about their little trip, anticipating the moment they both return to share their stories. I know Brody has to work, but perhaps I can invite TD to come back for dinner, and we can eat, just the three of us.

As a family.

I shake my head, trying to dislodge that thought and send it to exile. We're not a family, and the last thing I need is to entertain that idea.

Placing my phone on the charger on my nightstand, I decide this is the perfect opportunity to finish reading my book. I retrieve the hardback book and move toward the bathroom. I'm not a bath person, but sometimes I do enjoy one every now and again when the opportunity strikes.

Filling up the tub with hot water, I add a lavender scented bath salt shoved way to the back of the small closet in the hallway. I'm certain it's been close to a decade since I purchased it, but these things don't expire, right?

Hopefully not.

I strip down and slide into the water, the fragrant salts and warmth soothing my muscles almost instantly. For a little while, I just lie back, my eyes closed, and relax. I try to keep my mind blank, but those images of TD keep replaying over and over again to the point I can't escape them, despite my insistence I try. He doesn't strike me as the cuddling type, but something tells me that man would surprise even me.

Not that I'd ever find out for sure.

I force myself to think about this upcoming week. I'm scheduled to work Tuesday through Thursday, giving myself Friday off then working again over the weekend. Brody's game is home, which I'm grateful for, but it's also the holiday weekend—the last big summer send-off, as the locals call it. Our small town will be filled with tourists, all trying to enjoy one last weekend at the lake, camping, riding, fishing, or boating. It's bound to be a crazy busy weekend, which means despite the toll it will take on my body, the tips should be good.

Grabbing the book, I flip the page to where I left off, and spend the next thirty minutes reading. I try to make sure the pages stay dry, but if I move much at all, there might be a splash or two of water meeting the paper. I refuse to stress about it though.

When my fingers and toes are pruny, I set the book on the toilet, release the drain, and carefully climb from the tub. Grabbing the towel on the shelf above the stool, I dry off before wrapping it around my body, picking up the book, and heading for my bedroom.

While standing in the middle of my small room, looking down at the pajamas I had already laid out this morning, I realize I'm all alone tonight. I could sleep naked if I wanted to. There's no one here to witness it. But then my brain is assaulted with thoughts of a fire. What if I had to escape quickly and wasn't wearing clothes? Or what if Brody came home early because he wasn't feeling well and found his mom without a stitch of clothing on?

Yeah, not happening.

Reaching for the comfortable pajama set, I slip on the top and shorts and flip off the overhead light, leaving the side table light on. Once I'm settled in bed, I grab my book, intending to finish it. There's only about fifty pages left, which should be easy to complete, especially having no interruptions. However, my brain has other ideas when it conjures up more images of TD sleeping naked.

Yeah, this might be a long, sleepless night.

"Honey, I'm home!" Brody yells as he crosses the threshold of the apartment, grinning from ear to ear.

"How was it?" I ask, reaching for his overnight bag.

"I got it, Mom," he replies, waving off my attempt to help. "It was amazing. We woke up early this morning and went fishing. I caught a decent-sized northern pike and three walleye, so TD taught me how to clean them. It was awesome, but you wouldn't like it. Lots of blood, and the fish are watching you the whole time."

I shiver in disgust as TD enters the kitchen, laughing. "Don't make her pass out, Brode. You know how your mom is with the sight of blood."

"True. TD and I will stick to the fish cleaning. Don't worry, Mom." He turns to the man behind him. "Thanks again, TD. I had the best time."

TD grins back at my son. "Me too, B. We'll go again soon. Promise."

"Cool." Brody throws his duffel bag over his shoulder. "I'm going to run and get ready for work."

"Leave your dirty laundry by the washer and I'll start a load shortly," I tell him.

"Thanks, Mom. You're the best," he replies, taking a few steps my way and throwing his long arms around my shoulders. He places a kiss on my forehead before releasing his hold on me, throwing his coach a wave, and heading off to his bedroom.

I give my full attention to the man in front of me. He looks…wow. His blue jeans are slightly dirty, as if he was rubbing the dirt off his hands on his legs, and his blue T-shirt hugs his muscular arms and torso to perfection. His chiseled jaw is full of stubble, which makes my thighs clench, and even though there's a hint of exhaustion, his dark brown eyes are bright with excitement. I can see why all the women fawn over him like they do; I'm just not used to myself being one of them.

"Did you have a good night?" he asks, the deep timbre of his voice vibrating through my veins like a tornado of pleasure.

Clearing my throat, I press those thoughts aside. "Yes, very good. I slept hard for a solid nine hours," I reply, still shocked by that fact.

He takes a step closer, the scent of outdoors mixing with his distinctive deodorant smell. Sandalwood with fresh air. I never expected something like deodorant to tickle my senses this way, but here I am, trying to refrain from leaning forward and taking a big ol' whiff near his armpits. "That's because you needed the rest, El. You work long, hard hours, on your feet the entire time."

"Not the entire time," I mumble, even though we both know I do.

"Mmhmm. Listen, Brody and I were talking, how about you both come over for dinner tonight. I'll cook up the fish we caught this morning, and we can tell you all about our excursion."

My heart does this weird flip-flop in my chest at the prospect of going to TD's house. I'm not there nearly as much as he's here, but it's a great little place with a big backyard and a breakfast nook. I always thought that'd be the perfect spot for a bit of family time before the day gets underway.

"What can I bring?"

"Just you," he replies, his voice low and gravelly. Then, he clears his throat, and adds, "I'll whip up a few sides too, and I've got plenty of drinks."

"I don't mind," I start, but he's already shaking his head.

"You include me plenty in your meals with Brody, El, so let me do this."

The intensity in his brown eyes makes my throat dry and my heart skip a beat. "All right."

"Good. Why don't you come early? We can hang out and talk," he suggests.

The hairs on the back of my neck stand up. "Is something wrong?"

Shaking his head, TD sniggers. "No, El, nothing is wrong. I just enjoy your company."

"Oh." I take a deep, calming breath. "Okay, yeah. Sorry, you know how I am with worrying about anything and everything," I add with an awkward chuckle.

He reaches forward and takes the strand of hair hanging near my cheek and pushes it behind my ear. The light brush of his finger against my skin sends my heart beating like a drum at a rock concert. "Yeah, El, I know." There's a faint smile on his lips.

Have his lips always looked that...kissable?

Why does my skin tingle where his finger faintly touched?

"Uh...what time?" I ask, my brain still thinking about the way he moved my hair.

"How about four? Send the car with Brody, and he can drive over when he's off work."

"Okay," I state, noting I'll have to walk to TD's house if Brody has the car, which is completely fine, I don't mind walking. But if I'm going to make something to contribute to dinner, I'll have to be sure it's lightweight and easy to carry.

"I'll pick you up just before four."

I blink a few times, staring at him. "You don't have to do that," I insist.

"There's no reason for you to walk, El. I want to pick you up," he states pointedly.

"Oh. Okay. I just don't want you to have to make an extra trip."

He slowly smiles, showing his pearly white teeth through the dark stubble and lighting up his entire face. "It's no hardship, El. Promise." He takes a step back, putting the needed space between us so I don't end up doing something stupid, like recreating that kiss from last Friday night. He turns toward the door and opens it once more. "See you in a few hours."

"I'll be ready," I assure him, watching as he nods before exiting the apartment. His heavy boots echo down the stairs until the bottom door closes and I'm left in silence.

What is going on with me?

Honestly, I should probably avoid TD for a while. This weird crush thing that I've developed is consuming me, and that's the last thing I need. What I need is to stop blurring the lines between friendship and more. There's nothing there, and the sooner I realize that fact, the better off I'll be.

But he kissed me.

And a kiss that amazing doesn't deserve to be forgotten.

So, I'll force it to the back of my brain and only pull it out on special occasions.

Like when I'm alone at night and need to take the edge off.

I'd be mortified if anyone knew how much I really thought about my sexy male friend when I was looking for a little release. My hands inch below the waistline of my pajamas and his face would appear. It takes only a handful of seconds to push me over the edge, especially with the dirty images my mind comes up with.

Images that will never be talked about with anyone.

Ever.

So, while I know I should just decline his offer and stay here, Brody will be looking forward to it, and I refuse to disappoint him for something like this. I can get through a few hours of hanging out at his house and pretending I'm not thinking about that kiss, right? Eventually, those images and the feelings they conjure up will fade away, and I'll return to what I consider normal friend territory.

A place where no one thinks about the other one naked.

Give it a few days, and I'll be past it.

I'm certain.

Easy peasy.

TD

My phone starts to ring, causing me to step away from the salad I'm making ahead of time for tonight's dinner. A smile spreads across my face when I see my sister's name on the screen.

"'Lo?"

"How's my favorite little brother?"

"Bigger than you are, sister," I tease, knowing she hates it when I pick on her shorter stature.

Sighing dramatically in annoyance, the only way a sister can. "Anyway," she starts, drawing that single word out, "I'm calling to talk about next weekend. We'll be in early afternoon Friday and are renting a vehicle to drive to town. We should be there around four or so."

"Logan has the key. Can you stop by the hardware store when you get to town?"

"Yes, perfect. Then, we'll get settled at the cabin before heading to the high school for the game."

A smile stretches across my lips. "I'm happy you're able to see a game while you're in town. We've got a great team this year."

"Super proud of you, little brother. Do you know your work schedule for the rest of the weekend?"

Usually I spread out my hours so I only have to work a few hours over the weekend, but with this holiday, it'll be busier than normal. "I have football duties Saturday morning, and working for a few hours on Sunday morning, and then I'm on duty Monday. County will cover when I'm not on and call me if anything arises."

"All right, so what about Sunday? Your nephews would love for you to come out and take them fishing at some point."

"I can do that. How about after I patrol for a bit, I'll run home and change and come out to the cabin."

"They'll be so excited," she insists. "Okay, so let's talk about Saturday. We were invited over to my friend Eloise's place for a cookout. You're invited too. If we don't have any plans yet, I thought it'd be fun to go over there for a while and let the kids play."

My potential date with Ellie flashes through my mind. I've always liked my sister's friend and her family, but if I have an out for Saturday night, I'm going to take it. "I might have plans Saturday night," I say casually, hoping she doesn't dig her teeth into my comment and refuse to let go.

"Plans? Like what? A date?"

So much for not digging her teeth in...

"No comment. We can hang out a little bit Saturday before you head over there if you want, and then when I'm done patrolling Sunday, I'll meet you at the cabin."

"Fine, fine, but let's go back to your Saturday plans. Do I know her?"

"What if I'm hanging out with Logan Saturday night?" I ask, trying to steer her away from the topic of me dating.

"Then you would have said you were hanging with Logan," she points out, the hint of victory in her voice.

Shit.

"I'm not getting into this now," I tell her, looking to change the subject, but also realizing she'll most likely just continue it Friday in person.

"Fine," she grumbles. "But for the record, I was really hoping you'd say you were finally dating Ellie. I've always liked her for you."

I try to swallow, but there's a lump in the way. Before I can say a word, Loree continues.

"I know, I know, you're just friends, but deep down, I've been secretly wishing you two would get together. I adore her and Brody."

Me too.

But I keep that to myself.

"Anyway, good luck with whoever it is, and don't think for one second I won't spend the entire time trying to get it out of you," she adds goodheartedly, but I'm certain she'll do just that.

I snort at that comment. "No doubt you will."

"Anyway, what do you think about Sunday having our own cookout or something?"

"Yep, it's a great idea," I tell her.

"Perfect. You can invite Logan. It's the least I can do as a thank you for letting us use the cabin for our stay. Oh, and Ellie and Brody too, if you want."

"Sounds good," I tell her, refusing to comment further.

"All right, see you Friday night. Love you."

"Love you more," I tell her before signing off.

Shaking my head, I set my phone aside and finish putting together the salad. Once it's ready, I cover the bowl and place it in the fridge before checking the time once more. I've got about thirty minutes before I need to pick up Ellie, which leaves me just enough time to run through the shower.

A wave of nervousness sweeps through my veins.

I'm not anxious to be around her. I love having her near. I'm worried her answer to the question I'm going to ask won't be what I hope. But if anyone will be worth putting it all out there for, it's Ellie. Time to man up and ask her on a date.

I'm going to pray like hell she doesn't say no.

"Let's sit outside for a bit," I say to Ellie after she slips the dessert she made into the fridge. I knew she'd bring something, even after telling her not to. I do admit, her Twinkie dessert looks a hell of a lot better than the store-bought cookies I picked up earlier.

"All right," she replies, grabbing a bottle of water from the fridge and moving toward the back door.

She takes a seat in the double lounger in the corner, as I knew she would, and sighs contently. She convinced me to purchase that big thing years ago, back when I bought my house, and picks it anytime we sit back here. The deck is tucked in between the kitchen and master bedroom, giving it a touch of privacy. Originally, I thought about screening it in or turning it into a four-season room, but I just haven't gotten around to it.

I choose to sit at the round pub table. From my seat, I can have this conversation straight-on and watch the way she reacts to what I say. My heart starts to pound a little harder now as I prepare to ask one of my dearest friends out on a date.

"I love it back here," she says, relaxing into the plush cushion. "This big lounger was your best purchase ever."

I snort a laugh. "It only gets used when you're here," I tell her, a hint of a smile on my lips as I watch her stretch out.

"That's a travesty. You were supposed to use it. I bet if you tried it, you'd like it. Come on, Thomas. Just try it."

"That sounds just like peer pressure, El, and I won't fall for it. No means no," I quip, earning me the grin I was hoping for. When a few moments of silence pass, I finally start what I've been wanting to talk about. "So, there was something I wanted to run by you."

"Okay," she says with a touch of hesitancy in her voice, shifting in her seat to sit up a bit straighter.

"We've been friends for a long time," I start.

She nods in confirmation. "We have."

"I'd like to think that over the years, we've grown pretty close, and you're one of the people I trust the most and rely on when I need someone to talk to, to make me laugh, or tell me when I have my head in my ass. To be honest, you've become more than just a friend to me. You're the person I want to spend all my free time with, which I know isn't always a lot. The person I want to call just to see how your day went. And the one I want to take out on Saturday night, not as a friend, but as a date."

Ellie stares back at me, those big green eyes full of confusion and shock, and after several very long, painful seconds, she still doesn't speak. My heart practically stops beating as fear grips my chest. She's going to turn me down. I can see it in her eyes.

So I need to make sure that doesn't happen.

Slowly, I get up out of my chair and approach where she sits.

"May I?" I ask, pointing to the vacant spot beside her.

She continues to watch me with hesitant, confused eyes, but after a couple of moments, she nods.

Once I'm seated beside her, I turn and meet her gaze once more. "I've been thinking about this for a while now, and I keep coming up with a thousand reasons why this is a bad idea, as I'm sure those same reasons are flying through your head right now. But every one of those reasons is trumped by the reasons I should ask you. I think you're the most beautiful woman I've ever seen, and my heart does this weird beat thing anytime you're near. I want to spend more time with you and hold your hand. Maybe even steal a kiss every now and again, because that kiss last Friday night was hands down the best kiss I've ever had.

"I know this is scary, El. Really, really scary. I'm not just nervous but terrified I'm going to fuck up one of my longest, greatest friendships I have in my life, but I don't want to regret not asking again, so here I am, asking." I take another deep breath. "Will you go out with me this Saturday night?"

Again, she doesn't say a word for what feels like eternity. Then, she gives her head a slight shake and asks, "Again? What do you mean again?"

I rack my brain to recall what part of my word-vomit she's referring to when it hits me. "Oh, that," I start, running my hand through my hair and giving her a sheepish grin. "I, uh, sort of had a little crush on you back in high school. I had just convinced myself to take a chance and ask, but then you started seeing someone."

Her eyebrows pull together and her nose wrinkles up in confusion. "Seeing someone? The only person I dated was—oh." A red blush creeps up her neck and stains her fair cheeks.

"Yeah, I was a day late."

"I'm sorry," she whispers.

"Don't be," I quickly insist. "It turned out exactly as it was supposed to, El. If I had asked first, you wouldn't have Brody."

She contemplates my comment for a few moments before nodding. "Yeah, I guess you're right."

"I know you struggled a lot as a single mom, but what you did took guts and I admire you. All your friends do. You were presented with a difficult decision, and you faced it head-on. We're all proud as hell."

She shakes her head and sighs. "I messed up so much over the last eighteen years, but that decision wasn't one of them."

"Fuck no, it wasn't. You raised a kick-ass kid, El."

She watches me for a few long seconds, and I can tell there's a battle raging on in her head. I don't want to push her, but I could probably help sway the decision a bit.

"I know you're worried about our friendship. I promise you, it will still be there, completely intact. Whether you tell me no right now or we give it a try and it doesn't work, I will always be your friend, El. No hard feelings. I can't imagine life without you, and what we have means the world to me." I take a deep breath and add, "But

I can't help but feel like, maybe, something is missing, and I want to see if there's more there than just this amazing friendship we have. I'd like the opportunity to take you on a real date."

"I don't know what to say," she whispers.

"Well, you can say yes," I quip with a chuckle, "but only if you want to."

"I want to," she replies adamantly before blushing once more, as if she surprised herself with her immediate response. "I mean, I do want to. Yes, I'm scared of losing you as a friend."

"Won't happen," I reassure her, reaching for her hand and lacing our fingers together. "You're stuck with me for life, El."

A small smile spreads across her lips. "Umm, I should probably talk to Brody about this first," she states, shifting a little in her seat, which I know is something she does when she's nervous.

"Actually," I say, turning a little more so we're facing each other. "Brody is aware I'm asking you out."

"You asked him?" Shock is written all over her pretty face.

"Well, yes?"

Her eyes narrow a bit. "Why was that a question?"

I run my hand through my hair once more and then down the back of my neck. The last thing I want to do is embarrass her, but I think she deserves to know about the conversation I had with her son. "Brody was the one who encouraged me to ask you out."

That pink hue to her cheeks turns her a dark crimson color. "What? Oh my gosh," she mutters, dropping her face into her hands. "That's so embarrassing."

"Why?" I ask, reaching for her wrists and gently pulling them away from her face.

"Because!" she bellows. "My son is trying to set me up!"

"Well, if it makes you feel any better, I'm pretty sure I'm the only one he asked, *and* I'd like to add, him suggesting I take you out wasn't the reason I did it. It was the nudge I needed to finally take the plunge, but I have been battling with myself for a long time. A really, *really* long time."

She exhales deeply. "Still mortifying."

I shrug my shoulders. "It's more embarrassing it took me so long. But if you don't want to, I'd completely understand, all right? No pressure."

Ellie snorts. "No pressure? My son tried to set me up with one of my best friends."

"Yeah, but that friend is me, so I don't see the problem," I tease, even though I'm not teasing at all. The thought of Brody trying to hook her up with anyone else causes my skin to feel tight and itchy. After a good minute of silence, I ask, "So what do you say, El? Wanna go out with me Saturday night?"

She looks over, and I know her answer. It's written all over her face, etched in the depths of her soulful green eyes. "I'm probably really bad at dating, TD. It's been...awhile."

"Me too, El. That's the beauty of this situation. It won't be awkward, because we already know more about each other than most married couples."

Thinking about my comment, she gives me a nod. "That's true." Swallowing hard, she asks a very soft, "Will this be weird?"

"No," I insist. "If it feels weird or uncomfortable at any point, we call it off. There's no pressure here, no expectations."

"I should say no," she finally states, almost absently. "I need your friendship, TD."

"And I need yours. This won't jeopardize it, I promise."

Holding up her hand, she asks, "Pinky promise?"

Smiling, I reach out and wrap my much-bigger pinky around hers. "Pinky promise."

Her lips curl upward at the childish gesture we all used to do back in grade school. "All right, then let's give it a try."

"Yeah?" I ask, unable to keep the smile from my face.

"Yeah. I'm terrified though," she confesses, even though it wasn't much of a confession to me.

"I know you are. I promise not to take your trust for granted."

She exhales before falling back and closing her eyes. "I can't believe I just agreed to go on a date with you."

Deciding to join her, I lean my back against the plush cushion and stretch my legs out in front of me. "You're right, this thing is pretty comfy."

"I'm always right," she sasses, bumping my shoulder with her own. It's the first time we don't keep inches of space between our bodies. Not that we're pressed against each other, but we're aligned to where her arm could easily brush against my own if one of us moves just a touch.

After a few minutes of enjoying the quiet, I say, "I'm glad you said yes, El."

She glances over before resting her head against my shoulder. "Me too, but you should be warned, I might suck at this. I think I can count on one hand how many dates I've had in the last decade."

A possessive growl threatens to erupt from my gut. "You won't suck at it. You can't, because you're you and I like everything about you."

Even though I can't see her face, I feel her cheek move when she smiles. "I like everything about you too, Thomas. Except for that nasty ice cream you like."

A bark of laughter flies from my mouth. "I take it back. I like *almost* everything about you. Stop calling me by my given name, *Ellie*."

"Never, Thomas Dexter."

I sigh contently and lean the side of my head against hers. "You're lucky I like you."

Smiling, she replies, "I like you too."

And that's how we sit until it's time to get the fish ready to bake.

I can't believe it. Ellie—*my Ellie*—agreed to go on a date with me. Actually, I never thought I'd have the balls to take the chance. Not because I haven't wanted to for as long as I can remember, but because I felt her own answer would be a rejection. That's why I'm determined to ensure our friendship remains one-hundred-percent intact if a relationship shouldn't work out.

But something tells me it'll not only work out but be worth it in the end.

She thinks she might be bad at this?

Im-fucking-possible.

I'm going to give her the best fucking date of her life.

CHAPTER Thirteen

Ellie

Me: Mayday, mayday! I need help!!

Blair: What's wrong?

Hallie: Are you ok?

I'm pacing my bedroom, while Brody is taking a shower and preparing for bed. That's exactly what I should be doing, honestly, but my brain won't slow down, swirling with the questions on whether or not I did the right thing earlier tonight by accepting TD's date request.

> **Me:** I'm fine, physically. I might have a date Saturday night, and I'm kinda freaking out a bit.

Blair: A date? Yay!!

Hallie: With who?

Blair: Why are you freaking out?

Me: Please don't freak out...

Because I'm kinda freaking out...

Me: TD asked me out.

Hallie: OH! MY! GAWDDDDDDD!!! I knew it!!

Blair: I'm so excited for you!!

Me: I might throw up.

Blair: No, honey, why?

Me: What if...everything goes wrong?

Blair: But what if everything goes right?

Hallie: Yep, what she said. I'm so excited this is finally happening.

Me: I'm still not sure this is the right move, but I'm willing to give it a shot. He promised we would always be friends if it didn't work out.

Hallie: It'll totally work out. You two are going to be so stinking cute together.

Me: I don't know about that.

Blair: I agree with Hallie. What are you going to wear? Where are you going?

Me: That's just it. I have nothing in my closet date worthy. Everything I have is made for comfort or Friday night football games.

Hallie: We've got you. Between my closet and Blair's, we're sure to find something that works.

I exhale and close my eyes for a brief moment. Thank goodness for good friends. I know Hallie has a ton of clothes in her guest bedroom closet she doesn't wear anymore. When she dated Curtis, he was always shopping for her, and most of it she didn't find to her taste. Only to his. And Blair lived in Chicago for years, so she's sure to have a top or something that'll work.

Me: No dresses. I want to feel comfortable, especially since I have to work until two that day.

Hallie: Got it. We'll come up with great options for you. We'll be there at four. Does that give you time to shower and shave all your lady bits?

My lady bits are suddenly paying close attention to the conversation.

Blair: Don't overthink it, Ellie.

Me: Too late.

Hallie: Stop. Just breathe, El. There's no need to stress about this. It's TD.

Me: Or that's all the more reason to overstress.

Hallie: *insert eye-roll emoji*

Blair: We'll be to your apartment at four. We can help with hair and makeup too.

I take a deep breath and slowly let it out.

Me: Thanks, guys.

Blair: Of course!

Hallie: That's what friends are for. But seriously, buy a good razor. You don't want rashy razor burn on the beave.

Me: OMGosh! Stop it!

Hallie: Well, just something to think about. My mom always taught me to keep the girly bits well groomed. You never know when you'll have the opportunity to show them off. *insert eggplant emoji*

Blair: *insert laughing emoji* *insert crying emoji*

Me: I'm blocking your number.

Hallie: Don't! I'm the best advice-giver on the planet!!

Me: That's debatable.

Blair: Don't freak her out any more than she is. You don't have to show your beave on the first date, Ellie.

Hallie: Ha! Says the woman who slept with my brother the first night she was snowed in at his house!

Blair: Your brother is a smoke-show, Hal. Total fire. Like, gorgeously hot, and his *insert eggplant emoji* is HUGE!

Hallie: No no no!!! Block her, Ellie!

I'm laughing so hard, I have tears in my eyes, and I realize how much I needed this. I needed my girlfriends, even if it was just via text messaging.

Me: Alright, I'm going to bed.

Blair: Night, babes. Gabe and I will stop over for lunch this week and see you.

Me: Sounds good.

Hallie: Ugh, I want bacon-wrapped meatloaf now.

Me: I'll save you a slice.

Hallie: With mashed potatoes and candied carrots?

Me: Well, the mashed potatoes are a given, but I'll see what he's doing for the vegetable.

Hallie: Put in a good word for the carrots.

Me: Will do. Thanks, friends.

Blair: We got you, girl.

Hallie: Yep! No worries.

Easier said than done, but I don't tell them that.

I place my phone on the charger and move to the kitchen to make sure the door is locked. As I'm returning to my bedroom, Brody steps out of the bathroom in sleep shorts, a billow of hot steam following in his wake.

"Hey," he says, offering me a cheesy grin.

"Got all your homework done?"

"Yep, all good. I want to do a little studying for my chem test, but I won't stay up too late."

"Sounds good, bud." Before I can walk away or chicken out, I add, "Listen, I wanted to run something by you."

He stands up a little straighter. "Okay."

"So, I'm going on a date Saturday night."

My son almost cracks a smile. I can see the way his green eyes light up with excitement and his lips threaten to curl into a grin. "Yeah? That sounds like fun. Anyone I know?"

I had already made the decision to not mention the fact I know about his conversation with TD. For one, I wouldn't want to embarrass him, but another major reason is I want him to continue to trust TD, and if he felt like things he said would be shared with me, then that trust wouldn't exist.

"Actually, yes." Clearing my throat, I quickly state, "TD."

This time, he does smile. Big. "Yeah? That's great."

"You don't think it's weird or anything? I mean, I've been friends with him for a lot of years, but he's your football coach."

His eyebrows draw together in confusion. "Why would that matter? He's a great guy, right? He's funny and has a steady job, and all the women drool over him when he stops by the grocery store. Plus, he's great with kids, right?"

I nod in agreement, a smile stretching across my lips. "He is all those things, but I worry about how it may affect my friendship with him. And yours too," I tell him honestly.

"Why?"

"Well, for one, it might look bad, considering he's your coach."

He blows out a breath. "I'm not worried about that. It's not like he's a teacher or anything. Mr. Hamilton dated Vi's mom last year for months. Everyone might have teased her about getting a better English grade because of it, but it was all in good fun."

"You don't think everyone will tease you if they find out your mom is dating your football coach?" I ask.

"Oh, they definitely will," he replies with a laugh, "But I can handle it." His face sobers and he holds my gaze. "I just want you to be happy, Mom, and if Coach—TD—does that, then I don't care about anything anyone might say."

My throat is thick with emotion, and I find myself wrapping my arms around his chest and hugging him. I don't know when my little boy grew up into a fine young man, but I'm so damn proud of him and honored to be his mom. "It might not go anywhere. It's just one date."

He squeezes me back a bit too tightly. "I think you're selling yourself short, Mom. You're awesome, and TD knows it. He's lucky to go on a date with you," he tells me sincerely, causing my eyes to mist.

Reaching up, I cup his cheek in my palm and give him a small grin. "You're the best thing to ever happen to me, Brody Daniels. I love you so much."

"Love you too, Mom." He clears his throat and glances over my head for a quick moment before returning his gaze to mine. "While we're on the subject of dating, can I talk to you about something?"

My heart skips a beat in my chest. "Of course you can."

He looks a bit sheepish and grins. "There's a girl."

My heart.

Even though Brody's a senior, he's one of the youngest in his class. He just turned seventeen during this summer, and as far as I know has never had a girlfriend. At least not one he's talked to me about. That's pretty telling, if you ask me.

"Yeah? Do I know her?"

Brody rolls his eyes. "It's Pine Village. Of course you know her. It's Morgan Cooper."

I want to throw my fists in the air in victory. I adore Morgan. She's the sweetest girl ever and has been friends with my son since they were in elementary school. The fact he's interested in her makes me very excited for him. "Morgan is great."

His smile is full of...elation. "She is. We've been talking a bit lately, and I think I'm going to ask her out."

"I think that's a good idea."

"TD thought so too," he replies, and my heart stutters in my chest.

A flash of jealousy hits me, but only for a second. Yes, Brody apparently went to TD to talk about Morgan before me, but do you know what? I'm happy he felt comfortable enough to talk to him about a girl he likes. Since he lacks the male father figure in his life, and he finds it in TD, that's more than okay with me.

He couldn't get a better man to look up to.

"I was thinking about asking her out, maybe for ice cream after the football game Friday. Do you think that's okay?"

"I think it's perfect. You can take the car if you want," I suggest. "This way you'll have transportation to and from the ice cream shop, and if she's comfortable enough, you can give her a ride too."

He nods. "But then you'd have to walk, and I don't want that."

Oh, my sweet, sweet boy.

"I'll be fine. I've walked these sidewalks plenty of times."

"Well, you *could* ask TD for a ride home," he suggests, a big grin on his face.

Now it's my turn to roll my eyes. "I could, yes. That's not something we need to worry about now."

"But it's definitely an option. He'll probably be in a good mood too. You know, after we beat West Central's hind end," he boasts, making me snicker.

"Don't get too cocky," I insist, shaking my head.

"Not cocky, Mom. Confident. We're gonna run circles around the Rebels." He bends down and places a kiss on my cheek. "I better get in there and review my chemistry worksheets."

"Don't stay up too late," I remind him, turning and stepping into my bedroom.

"I won't. Night, Mom. Love you."

"Love you too, bud. See you in the morning."

I watch as he enters his room and closes the door. I can faintly hear him moving around his space. The flooring between my apartment and the diner below is well insulated, but the walls up here aren't that great. When I lie in bed, I can hear his bed creak from movement or his faint footfalls on the old floors.

I know someday soon, those little noises will be gone. Even though I'm not certain what his next step is after graduation, I do know he won't live here with me forever. So, for now, I'll soak up every creak of the floor, every muffled conversation he has with friends on the phone, every laugh I hear when he's watching TV. One of these days—one day soon, too—those noises will be replaced with silence.

And that might be the scariest part of motherhood.

Letting them go.

"Ellie!"

I turn and find TD's sister, Loree, waving and heading this way. "Hi, Loree. So good to see you again," I reply as she wraps her arms around my shoulders and gives me a hug.

"What a beautiful night for a football game, huh?" she asks with a smile, turning to take in the sights and sounds of the crowd filing into the bleachers.

"Sure is, though, it'll get cooler once the sun finishes going down."

"We brought sweatshirts," she states, taking a seat beside me. "It's definitely cooler here already than in Arizona. It was in the lower nineties before we boarded the plane," she adds, taking a bite of her popcorn. "You remember my husband, Kenton, right? And my boys, Hagen and Rogan. They're so excited to see Uncle TD in action."

"Well, it should be a good game. Both teams are two and oh going into this matchup."

"Ohhh, a true test of wills," she replies as Logan approaches.

"Hey, guys."

"Hi, Logan," Loree greets, as Logan goes to sit down beside Kenton. They immediately fall into a conversation, while the boys sit on the bench below us and point out onto the field.

"There's Uncle TD!" the younger one, Rogan, announces.

Both boys stand up and start waving the moment TD turns to walk back to the sidelines. He glances up and sees his nephews waving and quickly returns the gesture, a smile spread across his handsome face.

He's so good with kids, and he clearly adores his nephews.

Loree waves at her brother as well before turning her attention to me. "Oh, before I forget to say something, we're having some people out at the cabin on Sunday for a cookout, and we'd love it if you and Brody came."

"What time? I have to work until two," I state, after mentally running through my weekend schedule.

"Probably mid-afternoon for fishing or whatever, but we'll eat later, around five."

I nod, knowing Brody would love to go. He doesn't mind spending time with the younger boys, especially if he has another opportunity to go fishing. "I can make that work. What can I bring?"

"Just you and Brody."

"How about a dessert?" I offer.

Loree laughs as Hallie joins us on the bleachers. "What's this I hear about a dessert? I'm all about the sweets." Hallie says, making Logan snort. When she turns and glares at him, he just continues talking to Kenton and watching the field as the players warm up, completely ignoring Hallie.

"What was that about?" Loree whispers as she leans toward me.

"They have a love/hate relationship," I respond.

"No love. It's hate/hate," Hallie insists, reaching over and taking some of my popcorn out of the bag.

"If you say so," I mutter, making Loree laugh.

Blair and Gabe arrive, as well as Ava and Marcus. I don't see them often, so it's nice to catch up with how Ava's fifth grade class is doing, as well as hearing about Marcus's busy schedule at the mechanic shop all before kickoff. However, now that the game is ready to start, we all stand up and prepare for battle.

The whistle blows and the ball is in the air. We receive and take off toward the goal line, but the Rebels ensure we don't return it nearly as far as we want. Brody jogs onto the field with the starting offense, and my heart starts to beat a little harder. They huddle together to receive the play call before taking their positions. Brody is way outside, and I can tell by the way he flexes his hands, the ball is headed his way.

Holding my breath, I watch as the ball is snapped. Dorian scrambles back as the linebackers blitz, but he's able to get the ball in the air before being sacked. Brody is running downfield, glancing over his shoulder to find the ball. He extends his arms up at the same time I feel a hand clench my wrist. I don't even turn to look at Loree. I know it's her hand. My eyes are glued to my son as he grabs the ball out of the air just as a defender reaches forward and tips the ball. Both players go down hard, the football falling from Brody's hands and landing on the grass beside him.

"Shit," I hear Logan mutter as I wait for my son to get up.

The defender bounces up first and extends his hand to Brody, who takes it. They're both standing a moment later and jogging off toward their respective huddles, and it's in this moment I realize we're in for a tough fight. West Central is another two and oh team, which means tonight's game will be a hard-fought win for either team.

TD turns and meets my gaze. So much passes in that brief moment. He's letting me know my son is all right. He's telling me tonight's game is going to be rough. And he's assuring me he'll do whatever he can to protect all his players. That look goes a long way to calm my erratic heartbeat, but it doesn't help settle the churning in my gut.

I hand my popcorn over to Hallie, because I'm suddenly not hungry.

Our team breaks out of their huddle for their second play, and even though Brody's still in, I know it's not a pass to him. Our center hikes the ball and hands off to the running back, Matt. He darts straight, but the defensive line is blocking any forward motion, so he spins to the left and sprints around the line. He's about to get outside but is brought down after only a yard or two gain.

We clap for our boys, trying to show them support. Brody jogs out and heads straight to TD, who places a hand on his shoulder and talks to him. I watch as my son nods in understanding and waits on the sidelines for his next opportunity to go in. However, on the next play, one of our players doesn't get back up. He's reaching for his ankle, and you can tell he's in pain. The trainer and TD both jog onto the field, and after several heart-pounding minutes, help the player off. He's hobbling, but able to put a little pressure on his injured ankle.

"Oh man, I hope that's just a sprain or something," Loree says.

"Me too. Justin's our halfback, and a key player for the offense."

After making very few gains, we end up punting the ball to the Rebels as our defense prepares to take the field. Brody keeps his attention on the game, cheering on his teammates and trying to keep them motivated. But after only three plays, the Rebels score a touchdown, celebrating in the end zone and leading the game for the first time.

"Shoot!" Rogan hollers as their kicker sends the field goal high into the air and straight through the uprights.

"Come on, Panthers! You got this!" Hagen yells to our team as the kickoff return team gathers around TD.

Brody is still pacing the sidelines, anxious to get back in the game. When the ball is in the air, we return it for about fifteen yards and the offense takes the field once more. TD hollers something to Brody, who nods before turning and running onto the field. For the next four plays, I watch as my son struggles to gain yardage for his team. The Rebels cornerback is all over him, ensuring any catch he makes doesn't end up in the end zone, and that's if the pass isn't broken up before Brody catches it.

I watch as my boy becomes more and more frustrated with each play of the game, hoping he's able to catch a break and make a big play. But the Rebels did their homework and were prepared for Brody's speed and agility to snatch those hard-to-grab balls from the air.

By the time halftime comes, we're down twenty-four to seven, and our team looks dejected as they head for the locker room.

Tonight's going to be a long night.

CHAPTER
fourteen

TD

That was a tough loss.

They're all hard, but when you're two and oh going into the game against an equally matched opponent, it can be a bitter pill to swallow.

After a few adjustments at halftime, our third and fourth quarters were much better, scoring three more touchdowns to their one. However, in the end, we just couldn't top the Rebels. They had studied our offense hard and made sure to cover Brody well, essentially taking him out of the game. Every catch he made was for yards, but they were able to stop his runs every time to keep him out of the end zone.

After meeting with my team and telling them to keep their heads up, I make my way through the crowd to where Ellie and my sister will be waiting. I get there in just enough time to see Brody hugging his mom, a sad and slightly worried look on her beautiful face. He took some big hits tonight, that's for sure, and while he'll definitely be a little sore tomorrow, he didn't sustain any major injuries.

"Uncle TD!" Rogan hollers, running my way and leaping just before he reaches me.

I grab him easily and give him a hug. "Hey, buddy, good to see you. How was the airplane?"

"Cool! We went through a storm and the plane shook," he boasts with an excited toothless grin.

"Yeah? Did your mom freak out?"

"Oh yeah," he confirms, holding out his fist for a bump.

"I didn't freak out," Loree grumbles, heading my way for a hug.

"I believe Rogan," I insist, setting my nephew down and pulling my sister tightly against my chest.

"He's six," she mutters as her air wooshes from her lungs. "Can't breathe."

Relaxing my arms just a bit, I quip, "Doesn't matter his age. I can picture you gripping the armrest and trying not to pee your pants up there."

Her eyes narrow. "One time. I did that one time, and I was eight," she argues, hitting me in the arm.

Laughing, I place a kiss on her cheek before releasing my grip and holding up my knuckles for Hagen to bump. He's nine now, and might be too cool for uncle hugs, but I can't help but notice the boy barely pays me any attention. Once he taps his knuckles to mine, he turns back to Brody and hangs on his every word in complete rapture.

That's when I notice Ellie has moved over to stand by the wall. She's letting the young boys talk to Brody, who is answering all their questions and talking football with them. I walk over and lean against the wall beside her. "You good, El?"

She sighs and doesn't take her eyes off her boy. "Yeah, I'm good. Tough game."

I nod. "It was. Brody played very well. The opponent was prepared for him."

"He took some hard hits," she says softly.

"It's part of the game." I know that'll never make a mother feel better about watching her son get tackled repeatedly, but it's true. Football is the toughest, yet greatest sport ever, and the hitting is both a favorite aspect and a curse. The key is to train well and be prepared for it.

"Uncle TD, are you coming for ice cream with us?" Rogan hollers.

"Are you buyin'?" I ask the six-year-old.

He laughs. "I don't got no job. You're buying."

"Deal," I tell him, pushing off the wall. "You coming?"

She looks over at Brody, who now has his attention on Morgan. "Actually, I'm going to skip tonight. I think Brody is taking Morgan for ice cream, and I don't want him to think I'm there just to spy on them."

"He wouldn't," I insist.

"Maybe not, but I do have an early morning tomorrow. I have to open at six." She glances at me out of the corner of her eye, the hint of a smile toying on her lips. "Plus, I have a date tomorrow."

My chest starts to pound and my cock getting a little too eager in my pants. "Yes, you do. Can I still pick you up at six?"

"You can," she confirms. "Brody is spending the night with Matt tomorrow."

"So you don't have a curfew?" I tease, keeping my voice down so my sister and anyone else nearby can't hear.

"Technically, no, but I do have to work again Sunday at six in the morning."

"I know. I won't keep you out too late," I say.

"Are you going to tell me where we're going?"

I shake my head and take a step away. Her subtle perfume is doing things to me, making me want to reach out and pull her into my arms or kiss the hell out of her, audience be damned. "It's a surprise, but I think you'll like it."

She makes a face. "How am I supposed to know what to wear?"

"Just be you, El. Be comfortable," I state as my nephews run over and grab my hands.

"Come on, Uncle TD. Brody said the chocolate chip cookie dough ice cream will be gone if we don't get there soon! I can't miss the cookie dough," Rogan insists, pulling on my hand.

"Yeah, and then we'll have to get gross pistachio ice cream," Hagen adds, sticking out his tongue.

"Pistachio is the best," I insist, but it falls on deaf ears.

Rogan starts gagging and acting like he's throwing up, while Hagen lists every flavor of ice cream that's better than pistachio, which includes black licorice apparently.

I start to walk over to where my sister and husband stand, but glance back over at Ellie. Her eyes are glued to my ass, making me smile as big as the Mississippi River. When she looks up and realizes I'm watching her, her beautiful face turns ten shades of red as she covers her mouth with her hand. Winking, I return my attention in front of me with a little extra spring in my step.

Ellie was staring at my ass.

I'll take that as a good sign she might be as attracted to me as I am her.

And tomorrow night, I'm taking her on a date. It's not my usual first date activities but geared more toward Ellie and her comfort level. I don't think I've ever been as excited for a first date as I am for ours. I'm hoping tomorrow is the first of many dates.

The start of something great.

I raise my hand to knock on the door, only to have it open before my knuckles connect with wood. Ellie is standing there, wearing a pair of jeans that hug her curves and an off-the-shoulder, three-quarter sleeved sweater in a rich green that practically matches her eyes. Her hair is curled and left down, something she doesn't do nearly enough because of her job, and her makeup is subtle and flawless. She's the most beautiful woman I've ever seen and takes my breath away.

"Wow," I find myself saying, my eyes slowly returning to her face after their leisurely stroll up and down her gorgeous figure. "You look amazing."

Ellie blushes. "Oh, uh, thank you," she replies nervously, fidgeting with her hands. "You look pretty great yourself."

I'm wearing a pair of comfortable bootcut jeans and a black polo shirt that cost more than just about anything else in my wardrobe. It's nothing fancy by any means, but a bit more dressed up than I'm used to. "Thanks. Are you ready?" I ask, holding out my hand.

She nods and locks the door before placing her hand in my own. Once she makes sure the door is secure, we descend the stairs and head for my truck. "Any hints yet about where we're going?"

"Mum's the word, El," I reply with a wink.

She chuckles and shakes her head. "All right then, keep your secrets."

I open the passenger door for her, just the way my dad taught me when I was a young boy, and the moment she slides inside my truck cab, everything just seems to click. Sure, she's been there before, but this is different. My heart feels happier once I've seen her there, as if I've been waiting for her to take her spot beside me all this time. As cheesy as that sounds, having her there just feels right.

Once I shut the door, I head around to the driver's seat and suck in a deep breath of cool air. The nights are getting longer now, the temperatures slowly starting to drop. Before we know it, snow will be flying and the cold winter in full swing. I take a quick second to calm myself and open the door, climbing behind the wheel.

"It's starting to get cooler out," I state, starting my truck and backing out of the parking spot behind the diner.

"I know. I'm not ready for heavy coats and thermal underwear for football games," she says, and while thermal underwear isn't exactly sexy, I can't help but want to see her in them anyway.

Smiling, I pull onto the main artery running through our small town and drive toward the last place she'd expect to be taken on a date. "You'll have your blanket with little footballs on it out in no time."

She chuckles. "It gets so cold," she replies, taking in the scenery as we drive.

"I don't feel a thing."

"Do you remember that coach from up north who wore shorts every Friday night, despite the temperature?"

I laugh. "Coach Nelson. Great man and coach and, apparently, doesn't mind the freezing temperatures."

"He's nuts," she proclaims animatedly before returning her gaze outside. "Wait, where are we going?"

Pulling onto my street, I head toward my house and turn into my driveway. Once the truck is in park, I release my seat belt and turn to face her. "Well, I was thinking all week about where we could go for the perfect date night, but nothing felt right. I know you worked all day today and are tired, so I thought we could have a nice, quiet, relaxing night here. Plus, I know how your mind works and if we would have gone somewhere, you'd fret about everyone seeing us and asking questions, so I thought for this date, our first one, we could just keep it simple. And private."

I start to get a little nervous when she doesn't say anything, just stares at me with those big, green eyes.

"If you want to go to the steak house, I'll gladly take you," I blurt out nervously. "I just thought you'd prefer a little privacy, so I planned a whole...thing. Shit, I'm fucking this up."

"No!" she insists, reaching over and grabbing my hand. Her fingers send tingles of awareness up my arm and through my body. "This is...this is perfect, TD, really." She glances over at my house. "I was a little nervous to go out in public, not because I don't want to be seen with you, but because it's no one's business. And there's always whispering and questions, and I just...that's what I hate about small towns."

I give her a smile. "I know, El. That's why I thought we'd just hang out here tonight. Kameron made us dinner, and it's inside in the warmer, and there's an Adam Sandler movie cued up and ready to go. I know it's not a fancy restaurant and movie theatre, but this just seemed more...us."

"You're right. It is."

I let out a long breath. "Okay. Are you ready?"

She nods eagerly, releasing her seat belt and opening the door.

I'm out of the truck and at the passenger side before she can climb down, so I take her hand and assist her. Not because she can't do it on her own or because my dad insisted I always be a gentleman, but simply because I want to hold her hand, even for a few seconds.

Anxiously, we walk up the steps together, and as soon as the door is unlocked, I step aside for her to enter. Kameron was just here, so I know the kitchen is set and ready. With her hand still nestled in my own, we follow the scent of delicious food.

"Oh, wow," Ellie says when we step into the kitchen.

"It's good to have a chef friend who owns a restaurant," I quip, referring to one of our friends who went to culinary school, returned to our hometown, and purchased an old building downtown to transform into a steak house.

"My mouth is already watering. This smells amazing," she replies as I pull the chair out for her. "Thank you."

"I gave him free rein on our plates, so I'm not sure what we're having," I tell her once she's seated. "Well, I take that back. I told him no broccoli or gross cheese."

Ellie giggles, which makes me smile. I love the sound of her happiness. "Did you say gross cheese? He probably had no clue what you meant."

"Actually, he figured it out right away," I tell her, retrieving the bottle of wine Kameron left to complement our dinner.

"Why would anyone put blue cheese on anything? It's so nasty."

"I do agree with you. Wine?" I ask, popping the cork.

"Sure."

I pour two glasses, even though I'm not a big wine drinker, and join her at the table. Ellie lifts the lids off the plates and the aromas hit with the force of a punch. Filet mignon, skewered smoked shrimp, a weird breaded hash brown thing, and asparagus. My mouth waters just looking at it.

"Oh my word, this looks amazing," Ellie says, grabbing her fork and knife. She uses it to cut the piece of steak, but it moves through the meat so easily, I bet a knife isn't even necessary.

I make a mental note to send Kameron a text of gratitude later this evening.

Slicing into my steak, I take a small bite and moan. "Holy shit," I mumble, slowly chewing as the flavor explodes on my tongue.

"Right? That man is a genius," she adds, cutting her asparagus into bite-size pieces and removing the shrimp from the wooden skewer.

"Tell me about your day," I suggest, sticking my fork in the breaded hash brown creation and taking a small bite. It's like a creamy hash brown casserole with ranch seasoning, rolled into a ball, breaded, and baked.

"Crazy busy," she announces between bites. "I love holiday weekends, but they're definitely hectic."

"Tips are probably great though, right?"

"Yep. That's why, selfishly, I always schedule myself to work those weekends," she states with a chuckle.

"That's not selfish. You could use the tips, and I'm willing to bet some of the staff would rather have it off to enjoy the holiday weekend anyway, right?"

She nods. "Actually, yes. Some of the younger evening servers request it off for whatever reason, so there are plenty of hours left for those who want to work it."

We chat about her work, mine, and Brody, and before I know it, our plates are clean and we're both stuffed. "I'm going to have to give Kam one hell of a tip. That was delicious," I state, tossing my napkin on the table.

"It really was. I can't believe I've never had that before," she says, scooting back from the table and starting to collect dishes.

"Leave them," I insist, standing up and moving toward her. "They'll wait until tomorrow. Grab your glass."

She picks up her stemmed glass. "It wouldn't take that long to wash them now," she informs me. "Fifteen minutes, and everything would be done and clean."

Reaching for her hand, I slide my fingers around hers, reveling in the feel of her soft skin against my rougher hand. "Yes, but this is a date, and there will be no dishwashing this evening. I will happily take care of them in the morning, El. Now, come on. We have the next phase of our date night to get to."

"You're smiling," she says, keeping her hand tucked inside mine and walking with me toward the fridge.

"Do you mind if I switch to beer?" I ask, pausing at the fridge.

"Of course I don't mind. I'm surprised you drank that wine, honestly. You're not much of a wine drinker."

I shrug and pull a bottle of my favorite beer from the refrigerator. I'll have just one tonight, making sure I'm good to drive her home at the end of our evening. "I thought I'd try it. Kameron said it would go well with the meal, so I gave it a shot."

"And did it?" she asks, stepping through the back entrance when I open the door.

"It wasn't bad at all. He didn't turn me into a wine enthusiast, but I did enjoy it with dinner," I say.

When we're filing onto my back porch, I find myself holding my breath in anticipation of her reaction to the change. Logan and I put a lot of late-night work into finishing this space, something I've wanted to do for a while but needed the right push.

"Oh my goodness, what did you do?" she asks, still holding my hand as she slowly turns to take it all in.

"I just finished it, El. You know I've thought about doing this for a while now. I guess I just needed the right inspiration," I tell her, bringing her hand to my mouth and kissing her on the knuckles.

A light blush stains her perfect skin as she smiles up at me. "It's amazing. I really like it."

Getting less sleep a few nights this week was worth seeing this look on her face, watching the delight reflect in her green eyes. I realize I'd do it all again with no sleep at all if it makes her smile like that all over again.

What does that mean?

I'm pretty sure I already know, but now isn't the time to get into the nitty gritty of my feelings. Now, I get to execute the rest of our evening together, and a wave of exhilaration courses through my veins.

"Good. Now, let's get to the second half of our date."

CHAPTER fifteen

Ellie

I can*not* believe he did this.

His back porch is completely transformed into a cute little space, great for entertaining. But not just hosting a group, it's cozy and intimate, and so very perfect for date night. There are twinkle lights hanging from the ceiling like a million bright stars in the sky. The double lounger I talked him into purchasing is sitting prominently in the space, facing a big television on the wall, which I'm pretty sure is the one from his living room, now that I think about it. There are flowers and battery-operated candles positioned on the tables and on the floor. But the element that's the biggest surprise is the fact the porch is now enclosed, screened in to keep the bugs out.

He couldn't have done that just for me, right?

Tears fill my eyes as I take in the space he's transformed into an outside oasis. "This is so beautiful. How did you do all of this in a few days?" It wasn't like this Sunday when Brody and I were here for dinner.

TD sets his beer down on the table. "Logan and I've been talking for a while now, and I told him Sunday night I wanted to make it happen. We had it enclosed by Thursday, and Hallie came over and helped me with a few of the other details, like the shades and those plants in the corners. Apparently, they don't take much water, which is good because, I'm sure I'll forget to water them," he says, running his left hand through his hair and down the back of his neck, like he does from time to time when he's nervous.

"They're called succulents, and they don't take very much water," I tell him. "I'll help you water them."

"Okay, good." He spins around and grabs the remote control off the table. "Have a seat."

I climb onto the lounger, careful not to spill my wine, and slide over to the left side. TD turns on the television and cues up his streaming service. When the movie fills the screen, I can't help but laugh.

"I know there's a movie in the park tonight, but again, I thought you'd be more comfortable here for our first date."

"This is my favorite," I tell him unnecessarily. He knows Adam Sandler is my go-to actor, and this movie always makes me laugh.

"I know," he states, grabbing his beer and having a seat beside me on the lounge chair.

A bubble of anticipation sweeps through my entire body as his arm rests against mine. We've sat close before, but this time, it holds a different sense of familiarity and excitement. We're on a date, which means touching is not only allowed, but encouraged. At least it is as long as both parties agree to it, and this party definitely agrees.

And is a little hopeful, really.

TD reaches for a blanket at the foot of the lounger and unfolds it, covering our legs. There are small pillows lying around us too, but once we get into position, he slips his arm behind my neck, and I realize quickly those pillows are useless. All I need is a strong arm holding me and a warm, hard body to snuggle against.

"Comfortable?" he asks.

"Oh yeah," I say, instantly wishing I would have replied with something else, like a simple yes. Instead, those two words were filled with interest and pleasure.

"Good. Me too," he says, turning up the volume as the opening scene to *50 First Dates* fills the screen.

Man, I love Adam Sandler.

It's not lost on me that TD is well aware of the fact and catered tonight's date around me. From the private dinner at his place to the movie choice, it's the most personal, thoughtful date I've ever been on. And that's not counting the fact he did a small remodel project on top of it.

He shifts a little at my side, and even though the fact I'm cuddled in his arm isn't lost on me, the fact I really like it isn't either. It gives my skin—and other parts of me—tingles of awareness. I've never noticed how soft his arm is or paid attention to the way his cologne tickles my senses and causes me to lean just a little closer into his body. It's definitely messing with me, being this close to one of my best friends, but not in a bad way. If anything, I can't help but wonder why we haven't done this sooner.

You know why, silly.

I'm still battling those emotions that tell me I shouldn't be on this date, but curiosity—and attraction—have won out. The fact remains, I like him. I'm definitely interested in my friend, have been for a while, and we seem to have a lot of chemistry, so I'm willing to push those discomforts and worries aside for the sake of giving this a try.

"You seem to be thinking awfully hard."

"Sorry," I reply, giving him a sheepish grin.

"What's the matter? Are you not okay with this?" he asks, starting to pull his arm out from behind me.

"No," I blurt out quickly, watching as hesitancy fills his eyes. "That's not it, really. I mean, I guess I was just overthinking this whole...us thing, but not in a bad way. I was just realizing how right it feels, even if it's still a little scary."

The smile that spreads across his lips is both energetic and youthful. It's also a little crooked, which I suddenly find wildly attractive too. "I get that, El. If at any point you feel uncomfortable, please tell me. We can't work through it if I don't know how you're feeling, deal?"

I nod, that kiss we shared flashing through my mind in vivid detail and making me wiggle.

TD watches me intently, studying me like a test. "This is one of those times you tell me how you're feeling," he murmurs, his voice suddenly deep and raw.

"Oh, well, I was just replaying that kiss from two weeks ago and wondering if it would be as great now as it was then."

His eyes darken to black onyx. "Yeah? You were thinking about our kiss? Maybe we should try it again and see."

I want to grin at how cheesy his line is, but the hum between my legs has my full attention right now. Well, that and the fact his mouth is moving closer to mine. My tongue slips out and wets my dry lips as my heart starts to hammer in my chest.

The first brush of his mouth across mine is like an electrocution. If it weren't for his larger body anchoring me to the chair, I might have actually levitated from the power. His right hand moves to cup my jaw as his tongue slides along the seam of my lips. My mouth automatically opens for him, and the result is explosive. This kiss rekindles embers from our last kiss, consumes me, and burns me alive.

I mewl, ready to swing my leg over his and climb onto his lap, to feel every hard muscle beneath my fingers. Never have I been so brazen, so bold, yet here I am, on the verge of throwing caution to the wind and taking what I want. I know in this exact moment, if he were to suggest moving this to his bedroom or ridding ourselves of every stitch of clothing we wear, I'd do it in a heartbeat.

Unfortunately, that doesn't happen.

TD rips his mouth from my own, breathing heavily and looking a little dazed when he opens his eyes. It's in this moment I realize I'm still holding my breath and let it out in a rush of air. I hold his gaze, trying to come up with something to say, but my brain isn't braining right now.

He clears his throat. "Uhh, wow."

"Mmm," I mutter, my lips feeling delectably swollen and well kissed.

"That wasn't part of my plan," he confesses softly, running his thumb over my bottom lip.

"You didn't want to kiss me?" I ask, a little confused.

"Oh, no, I definitely wanted to do that. I didn't want to overwhelm you tonight. My plan was to win you over with my charm and first date etiquette, not my stellar kissing abilities."

A giggle bubbles up from my gut, breaking through the sexual tension surrounding us and lightening the mood. "They are pretty stellar," I concede.

Giving me a wink, he adjusts his body so I'm tucked comfortably against his side once more and turns up the volume on the television. Adam is at the diner, getting ready to meet Drew Barrymore's character, and I'm here for it. It doesn't matter I've seen this movie a hundred times. It's still amazing and makes me smile, especially the antics of his best friend.

I lean my head against TD and slightly shift my body, pressing myself against his side. His warmth seeps into me, his strength comforting me, and for the first time I'm truly wondering why we haven't tried this before. It's still a little scary, but there's relief in dating my best friend too. No one knows me better, has seen me at my best and worst, and still wants to spend time with me despite it all.

There's a smile on my face as I allow myself to truly relax for the first time in I don't even know how long, because I know TD has me. I may not know where this road will lead, but I feel comfortable enough to get in the car with him. If it were anyone else, I'd still be standing on the side of the road, worrying and watching.

With a deep exhale, I let everything go and just be in the moment.

I'm here, with TD.

My friend.

Best. Date. Ever.

"Ellie."

I open my eyes and stare straight ahead at the words moving up the television screen. Then, I turn to my right and find TD gazing down at me with a hint of a grin on his face. Realization slaps me across the face like an unwanted zit on your first date.

I fell asleep.

On our date.

Hells bells, this would be a great time for the ground to open up and swallow me whole.

In fact, I'm praying for it.

"Don't do that," he mumbles, lifting his arms up and stretching them over his head. The action causes his shirt to ride up just a bit, revealing a sliver of tanned skin across his abdomen.

"Do what?" I ask absently, my eyes locked in on the flesh.

"Well, not that. You can gawk at me all you want," he quips, drawing my eyes back up to his face. Of course, I blush, the burn of embarrassment stinging my skin. "I meant don't get embarrassed for falling asleep. You were tired. You worked most of the day, getting up pretty early this morning."

"Yeah, but it's rude," I grumble, noticing for the first time my foot is kicked over his.

"No it's not. In fact, quite the opposite. I'd find it rude if you forced yourself to stay awake, despite being exhausted, just to try to make me happy. I think the fact you were comfortable enough to fall asleep—in my arms, mind you—was the best compliment I could have had."

I shake my head and chuckle awkwardly. "You're nuts, you know that?"

"Probably, but still. I didn't mind, El. In fact, I rather enjoyed holding you in my arms while you slept. That's why I didn't wake you until the end of the movie. I liked snuggling, and you know I'm not a snuggler."

Shaking my head, I can't fight the smile. "You are *so* a snuggler. A big one."

He groans and tosses the blanket off our laps. "Keep it down, will you? I have a reputation to uphold." When our gazes lock once more, he asks, "Ready to go home?"

"Yeah. Four thirty is going to come awfully early in the morning," I state, stretching a little before climbing off the lounge chair. "This was the best purchase ever, by the way."

"I finally see the appeal," he replies with a wink before getting up and turning off the TV.

I turn to grab my forgotten wineglass and his beer bottle, which is almost full.

"Leave that. I'll get it."

"I'm not going to let you pick everything up after you take me home. It'll take two minutes to do it before we leave," I insist, spinning around to see what else needs to be taken inside.

"El." When I look up and meet his gentle eyes, he whispers, "Leave it. Please."

I can tell this means something to him, so I don't fight. "At least let me take this inside and set it by the sink," I state, holding up my wineglass and his beer bottle.

He gives me a slow grin that somehow pulls some invisible string from his lips to my female region, because my lady parts take notice. "Thank you, Ellie Daniels."

I roll my eyes. "You're welcome, Thomas Dexter."

We move inside, and even though I hate the idea of leaving tonight's dishes for him to clean up later, I do as asked. Setting the wineglass by the sink, I empty the beer bottle and toss it in the trash. Then, I take his outstretched hand and allow him to lead me through his house to the front door. He opens the passenger door to his truck, something that's not lost on me. I've always told Brody the importance of chivalry and manners, but honestly, this is the first time I've witnessed this firsthand. No one seems to open doors for others anymore.

When he climbs into the driver's seat, he starts the truck and backs from the driveway. Once he's moving forward, he reaches over and takes my hand, linking our fingers together so fluidly, it's as if we've been holding hands our whole lives. As if we just…fit.

Together.

By the time we pull behind the diner and park, I'm starting to get a little nervous again. This night has been unlike any I've ever experienced, and I know it's because of who I was with. Any other first date might have felt uncomfortable and ended with an awkward goodbye at the door, but with TD, the entire evening felt thoughtful and catered to me.

He meets me around at my door and pulls it open, extending a hand to help me down. "Thank you. I had a really great night," I tell him as we make our way toward the back entrance to the diner.

"Me too," he replies, taking my keys and releasing the lock on the first door. We step inside and make our way up the stairs, flipping on the light as we go.

Finally, we reach the upper door, and TD unlocks that one too. I step inside the kitchen and set my purse down on the table. When I turn around, I find TD leaning against the doorjamb, watching me. I fidget with my hands, trying to keep my fingers busy for the sake of having something to do.

He pushes off the wall and approaches like a lion stalking a gazelle. When he's directly in front of me again, he cups the sides of my face in both hands and gazes into my eyes. "Is it all right if I kiss you good night?"

My heart skips a beat. "I'd be disappointed if you didn't," I tell him, running my tongue over my bottom lip.

His mouth descends, pressing firmly against mine. I grip his upper arms, loving the softness of his skin beneath my fingertips. He doesn't deepen the kiss the way he did at the start of the movie, but that doesn't mean it doesn't pack a punch. There's something incredibly intoxicating about kissing TD, and I hope this isn't the last one I experience. Something tells me they'll continue to get better and better as our relationship starts to grow.

He releases my lips but doesn't pull away. "I want you to know, tonight was everything I had hoped it would be."

"For me too," I whisper, our gazes locked.

"Good."

Then suddenly, he's stepping back and putting distance between us. I open my mouth to invite him to stay, but the words fall flat as he asks, "Can I call you?" The corner of his mouth curls upward in this incredibly sexy way.

Clearing my throat, I reply, "Of course."

He nods and reaches for the doorknob. "Lock up behind me. I'll make sure the bottom door is secured."

Just as he starts to move, I stop him. "TD?"

He glances back, his eyes locked on me. "Yeah?"

"Be careful going home."

He flashes me an easy smile. "I will. I have a girl to call soon."

I return the grin and nod. "Good night."

"Night, El."

Then, he's gone, the heavy sound of his boots on the stairs moving away from me. It's only when the door is closed downstairs do I finally exhale the breath I was holding. I spin in the middle of the room, holding my arms out like a child and letting my head fall back.

I can't believe I just went on a date with TD.

And the best part, it was amazing. Every moment was easy, and all I can hope is he enjoyed it as much as I did and that he'll call me soon, maybe even for a second date.

I hear his truck start up in the lot out back and it takes everything I have not to run to my bedroom to look down at him while he leaves. But the ringing of my cell phone has me retrieving my purse and pulling it out. I smile again when I see his name.

"Hello?"

"I told you I'd call."

A giggle slips from my mouth. "You did," I confirm.

"Is it too soon? Should I have waited the customary twenty-four hours post-date?"

"No. I think I prefer the twenty-four second post-date phone call," I tease, even though it's true.

"So, I was thinking," he starts, but doesn't continue.

"About?"

"A second date. Is now a good time to ask what you're doing tomorrow?"

Still smiling, I tell him, "I'm working until about two, and then Brody and I are going to the cabin for your sister's cookout."

"I'll pick you up at two thirty."

"It's a date."

"Yes, it is. See you tomorrow, El."

"Good night, Thomas Dexter."

"Night, Ellie Daniels. Sweet dreams."

And they are, because TD stars in them from beginning to end, with his charming smile, sexy body, and lips made for kissing.

Oh, yes.

These dreams are definitely sweet ones.

CHAPTER
sixteen

TD

"You're smiling. A lot."

I glance over at my sister, who's obviously picked up on the fact I'm a bit happier to be around Ellie, especially after our date last night. And the fact I was given a kiss when I picked her up this afternoon to bring her to the cabin. Brody had just left, using their car to go pick up Morgan, so I was able to hold her in my arms and kiss her lips without anyone seeing.

"I enjoy being here," I reply lamely, not wanting to get into the whole dating conversation again.

"How'd your date go last night?" she asks casually, clearly fishing for details.

My eyes betray me as they instantly seek Ellie out, and I realize it a moment too late.

Loree gasps and grabs my arm, bouncing up and down in excitement. "Holy shit, I knew it!" she bellows, drawing the attention of those in the near vicinity.

"Knock it off. We're not exactly public with it yet," I argue, turning to face the grill once more, flipping the burgers.

"You have no idea how happy this makes me," she states quietly, handing over the package of hot dogs to add to the grill. "I've always known you've had a thing for her."

"Yes, well, we're testing the waters and taking things very slow. Don't start planning a wedding," I tease.

She gives me a fake shocked look. "Would I do that?"

I snort in reply. We both know she would. "All I'm saying is please don't get ahead of anything that may or may not happen."

Loree does this weird little happy dance right in front of me.

"I said don't get ahead of anything!" I insist, trying to keep my voice down so Ellie doesn't overhear. I glance over my shoulder and find her at the water's edge with Brody and Morgan, who was invited to come along for today's cookout.

"What aren't we getting ahead of?" Logan asks, appearing out of nowhere.

Asshole.

"TD and Ellie," my traitorous sister proudly announces to my best friend.

"I've never seen a man so whipped so quickly before," Logan chimes in, about to earn himself a fat fucking lip.

"Really? Why do you say that?" Loree asks with a twinkle in her eyes.

"You mean he didn't tell you what he did for date night?" Logan bumps me out of the way and takes the spatula, flipping the burgers.

"No! Tell me!"

My friend goes into great detail, spilling all my secrets about the nice meal I had catered, enclosing my back porch, and setting up the area for a movie. He even tells her about all the extra decorations Hallie talked me into buying because it would really "bring the space together."

"I hate you both," I mutter, pushing him aside and reclaiming my position as grill master. "You're no longer my friend."

"You'll never get rid of me. I know all your secrets, including where you used to stash the *Playboys* you were hiding from your dad," Logan announces smugly, crossing his arms over his chest.

"I got them from you, asshole," I mutter, flipping the hot dogs for even grilling.

"Oh yeah," he replies with a laugh. "Best money I ever spent."

"That's just sad," Loree replies, reaching over and patting his arm. "No wonder you're single."

A bark of laughter flies from my mouth. "Burn."

"What's so funny?" Ellie asks, making the hairs on the back of my neck stand up with her nearness.

"Logan was just threatening to out TD on where he hides his *Playboys*," Loree states, grinning from ear to ear.

"*Used* to hide. Jesus, you're not helping," I mutter to my sister, turning my attention to Ellie. "I was just getting ready to disown my sister and drop Logan's burger in the dirt. Do you want cheese?" I ask, redirecting.

"Yes, please, but where did you hide them? Was it under your mattress like all fifteen-year-old boys?" she asks, and there's no missing the sparkle in her eyes. In fact, that joy reflecting back at me has my heart doubling its beats and causing my cock to threaten to stand at attention.

"Stop encouraging them," I tell her, turning to face the grill once more and placing slices of cheese on most of the burger patties. "And for the record, no, they weren't under my mattress. My mom found those when she was changing my sheets once. I kept the good ones in my closet behind my shoe rack."

When Ellie giggles, I wink and reach for the serving pan. "Food's done!" I holler, hopefully catching the attention of our small group.

Loree takes the tray from me and heads for the cabin, where she has the other food ready to go. The rest follow behind, their stomachs drawing them toward the delicious smelling food. My nephews run up beside Brody, who despite having the girl he likes by his side, still gives them his attention as they discuss fishing. My brother-in-law, Kenton, strikes up a conversation with Logan, and together, they move toward the cabin as well. That leaves Ellie and me outside for just a few short moments.

Making sure the grill is turned off, I give Ellie my full attention. "Having fun?"

"I am. Your sister and her family are good people."

"They are. Just don't tell her I said that. I'll never hear the end of it," I tease, causing her to chuckle the way I had hoped.

"Everything all right over here? It seemed a little intense earlier," she asks, clearly referring to my conversation with Loree.

"It's fine," I assure, "But Loree might have figured out who my date was with last night."

Ellie's eyes widen is surprise. "Really? How?"

I run my hand through my hair and down the back of my neck. "Uhh, apparently, I can't keep my eyes off you."

She blushes, just as I knew she would. "Oh. Well, I suppose that's a good reason, right? And it's not like Logan and Brody don't already know, so really your sister finding out was probably inevitable. You and I both know this small town knows how to gossip," she says with a grin.

Reaching for her hand, I slip my fingers around hers. "Very true. Speaking of Brody, he seems pretty happy to have Morgan here."

"Doesn't he? I just adore her. She's the sweetest girl. I'm secretly hoping they decide to date more seriously, though I'm also torn because I want him to enjoy his last bit of youthful freedom before adulthood crashes down on him."

I find myself bringing her hand to my lips and kissing her knuckles. "I know, but I don't think you have anything to worry about with him. He has a great head on his shoulders, thanks to you. I think adding a girlfriend will only enhance his great qualities."

She gazes up at me with conflicted eyes, and I already know where her mind has gone. "I just don't want him to find himself in a situation where he's forced to grow up sooner than he's supposed to." Her words are just over a whisper.

"Like you," I deduce. This time, when I bring her hand to my face, I maneuver her palm so it's resting against my cheek. I could bathe in the heat of her skin, in the softness of her touch.

She exhales slowly. "I messed up at his age."

"Maybe, but you didn't do it alone. In fact, the one who messed up was the asshole we won't name, who walked away from his responsibilities instead of being a fucking man and owning them." That familiar itch causes my skin to tingle every time I think about that piece of shit who knocked her up in high school and walked away with a college scholarship and not a care in the world.

"You know what, it's fine. Would it have helped to have him in Brody's life? Sure. But not if he didn't want to be, because ultimately, he would have walked away at another point in my son's life. So, fuck him."

The biggest smile spreads across my lips. "Say it again," I instruct, noticing the blush already creeping up her neck.

"That slipped out."

"No way, El. Say it again, because it's how you really feel. Yell it."

She giggles, covering her mouth with her other hand. "I can't yell it."

"Sure you can. Let it fly, baby."

Her laughter is the balm that heals my scarred, scared heart. "Don't make me," she counters through giggles.

"Do it," I encourage, chanting those two words three more times.

Ellie closes her eyes and says, "Fuck him."

"Louder, El."

"Fuck him!" she bellows, covering her mouth with her hand when she realizes just how loudly she yelled the profanity.

"Uhh, Mom?"

Ellie spins around and finds Brody and Morgan standing on the porch. Brody's face shows sheer shock at hearing his mom not only curse, but practically screaming it, while Morgan's trying not to laugh. "Oh my God!" Ellie whisper-yells, the mortification all over her face.

Brody just shrugs, holding his plate full of food, as he walks down the steps and heads for the chairs around the fire. "Don't worry about it. Sometimes, the situation calls for a good fuck-him, Mom."

"Brody!"

The seventeen-year-old chuckles as he passes by where we stand. "Sorry, Mom."

Ellie spins around and faces me. "See what you made me do? I just cursed in front of my son. Your nephews are right inside and probably heard it."

"That was sexy as fuck, El. I think you should curse more often. Besides, my sister curses. Believe me when I tell you, they've heard it all."

She shakes her head. "It's still not my place to say it in front of them."

Suddenly, I'm smiling again, something I find myself doing often when she's near. "When can we go out on our third date?"

Her eyebrows shoot upward as she gives me a look of humor mixed with confusion. "Third date? What happened to the second one?"

"Today was the second one," I insist. "I picked you up. I'll take you home. Maybe steal a kiss or two outside your door. That constitutes a date in my book."

"Ahh, yes, you did mention that last night," she says, sliding her hand down my arm. It's not meant to be suggestive, but that little touch goes straight to my dick, reminding me of exactly how badly I want her.

"I did. So, date three?" I ask, trying to pull my brain away from the naughty route it's trying to take.

"How about Saturday again? Since we have an away game Friday, it'll be late when we get back home. Plus, I have to work Saturday morning, but I'm off Sunday."

"Deal. Any thought of what you want to do?" I ask, ideas spinning in my head.

Ellie shrugs her shoulders. "I don't need anything big and fancy. I actually prefer a more intimate setting like last night."

I nod, just as the rest of the group comes out of the cabin. "I've got you. Besides, date three is my favorite date of all."

"Why?"

"Second base, El."

She barks out a laugh that draws her son's attention, but he quickly goes back to his food and Morgan. "Says who?" she teases.

"It's a rule."

"Oh? And who made these rules?"

"Logan. When we were sixteen."

She continues to laugh, which was my goal here. I'm not expecting to get to second base, or any base by a certain number of dates. I've always felt it will happen when we're both ready, even though I *really* hope we'll be ready soon. I'd never push her, never take more than what she's willing to offer, more than *anyone* is willing to offer.

"That makes sense," she responds, shaking her head. "Back then, he listened to a lot of Usher and Robin Thicke."

"Ha!" I proclaim, shaking my head. "He really did. He played that damn twerking song on repeat." Man, I enjoy walking beside this woman down memory lane. "Why don't you go make a plate, while I finish cleaning the grill. Then I'll join you."

"Sounds good," she replies, heading for the cabin. Just before she crosses the threshold, she glances over her shoulder and holds my gaze. Invisible sparks dance around us, and I know I'm completely gone. My crush I've harbored for way longer than appropriate is growing, crossing lines without one fuck to give. "Oh, and just so you know, I'm not against the third date rule."

Then, she slips inside the cabin, leaving me breathless and with a sudden raging hard-on in the middle of a family cookout.

Game.

Set.

Match.

Once I help Rogan bait another hook and watch him cast, I step back to take in the scene. Logan is helping Hagen and comparing fish stories about who caught the bigger fish, while Ellie and Morgan sit over by the fire and chat. I walk over to where Brody sits in a folding chair, his line out in the lake as he tries for the biggest catch of the day.

"How's it going?"

"Good. Getting lots of bites. Fish just ate my bait, though," he tells me as I drop down onto the ground beside him.

"It's a great day to wet a line," I say, kicking out my legs and leaning back on my hands. "Things seem to be going well with Morgan."

A goofy grin spreads across his face. "They are. She's over visiting with Mom for a while, but she says she'll come back over and fish in a bit."

"It's good that you have similar interests."

He nods. "We do. Like you and Mom."

Now it's my turn to smile. "True."

"So, I don't want all the gory details, but how did last night go?" he asks, somewhat hesitantly.

"It went well, actually. We're going out again Saturday night, as long as our schedules still allow it. I know she doesn't know everything you're up to this weekend, so if we can fit in a dinner, we will."

"I have to work Saturday afternoon for a few hours, but I want to ask Morgan to dinner. I thought about taking her to the Mexican restaurant and maybe some ice cream afterward."

"That'll be fun," I tell him.

"Speaking of, I was invited to a Wild hockey game next month with Matt and his dad. They took me a few years back to a game against the Blackhawks. Pretty cool Mr. Elliott gets tickets through his work," he states, referring to his best friend's dad.

"Yeah, there are some jobs that have a lot of perks, but usually those are the ones with different types of stresses."

Brody seems to consider that a few minutes. "I see what you're saying. He has to deal with math and numbers all day long. I bet that can be pretty stressful."

Knowing Matt's dad works for a big accounting firm in St. Paul, I'm sure he has plenty of shit he deals with. "I'm sure."

"Anyway, if I go out with Morgan, that means my mom will be free. Well, until curfew," he says, trying not to grin.

The corner of my mouth curls up. "Noted."

"Maybe Sunday we can hang out, the four of us. You, Mom, me, and Morgan."

"I think that's a great idea, Brode," I tell him.

"We could probably have Logan, Hallie, Gabe, and Blair come over."

"Logan and Hallie will probably kill each other, but I bet we can make that happen. I'll say something to your mom when we leave here about having it at my place. We don't have many decent summer days left before it gets cold."

"Good football weather," Brody reasons with a cheeky grin.

"Very true."

We watch the water ripple for a few long seconds, my nephews talking and reeling in their lines every time they think they have a bite. "I was wondering about something," Brody says, grabbing my attention once more.

"What's up?"

"How did you know you wanted to be a police officer?"

Well, that question wasn't expected. Clearing my throat, I speak my truth. "I figured it out in high school. I was drawn to the profession after one of my classmates had a bad accident one night and I came upon it when I was on my way home. The police officer for Pine Village at that time was a man named Frank Overlong, and he handled the situation with professionalism and empathy. It was the first time I really got to see him in action, working the scene and helping those involved. I ended up going and speaking with him one night at the diner and asked him a million questions. I knew before I left that night I'd be applying for the police academy."

He holds my gaze and asks, "It's tough, right? Being a cop?"

My throat is thick. "Yeah, Brode, it's tough. But it's incredibly rewarding too. Some of the stuff in our small town is minor compared to the big cities. They have more crime, drugs, murder, and a whole lot of stuff no one wants to think about. But there's also a lot of good there, just like there is in our town. I get to help my neighbors and the people I grew up with. Police work is hard. It's stressful. But it's one of the most rewarding jobs there is."

Brody stares out over the lake, lost in thought, so I let him be. Choosing your career path for the future is a big step, and something tells me he was asking for a very specific reason. I don't want to speculate, but my head is telling me he's interested in police work. First off, he'd make an excellent cop. He's caring, attentive, and smart, and if he were to pick this line of work to make a career of, I know he'd excel.

But I also know Ellie, and there's no denying the dangers that come with the profession. I guess all I can do is listen and give advice, if and when the time comes for it.

Until then, I have a third date to plan.

CHAPTER
seventeen

Ellie

TD: I'm on my way.

A wave of anticipation races through my veins as I give myself a quick once-over in the mirror. Deeming my outfit appropriate for date three, I flip off my bedroom light and head for the kitchen to wait for TD.

Brody left fifteen minutes ago to pick up Morgan for their date, and he seemed incredibly excited for the evening. Of course, he's also still riding the high of last night's big win over Salt Ridge. He had thirteen receptions and scored three touchdowns during their road victory, the most points he's scored in a single game to date. And to him, the icing on the cake was Morgan was in attendance to witness his incredible game. Yes, he was happy I saw it all too, but there's nothing like the girl you're seeing being in the stands and cheering you on.

He's growing up right before my eyes, and there's nothing I can do to slow down time.

A knock on the door grabs my attention. I quickly walk over and open it, revealing a mouth-watering TD, wearing well-fitting dark jeans, a dark blue Henley, and his boots. He's freshly shaved and his dark eyes sparkle with an eagerness I'm becoming accustomed to witnessing.

"You look beautiful," he says, his eyes trailing my body from head to toe.

"Thanks," I reply, turning to grab my purse to try to hide my blush. "Just for the record, I haven't bowled in about ten years. Remember when we took Brody when he was seven or eight? I think I bowled a one-fifteen, and that was with bumpers."

He snickers. "Oh, I remember. Brody bowled a better score than you did that day, but I have faith in you, El. You can do it."

My eyes narrow. "Or you just want to show me up on our date."

He laughs hard now. "Not in the least. If it makes you feel better, I will make sure to suck more than you."

"I would appreciate that," I state, bypassing the need to dwell on his statement. It's been a while since there was any *sucking*, but something tells me I wouldn't mind giving it a shot tonight.

We slip in his truck and take off for Hudson where the bowling alley is. It's the first time I've been out today, and I can't help but notice how quickly the temperature is dropping. Last night at the game, I had to dig out my stocking cap and gloves but was able to keep warm with just a hoodie and down vest. Tonight, I'm glad I have a jacket with me, because there's definitely a chill in the air.

"How was work?" he asks after reaching over and entwining our fingers.

"Not bad. You can tell the summer tourist season is winding down, but I kind of enjoy the slightly slower pace."

He nods. "Don't get too comfortable though. The colder seasons are right around the corner, and before you know it, snow will be blanketing everything, and the temperatures will be freezing."

"Ugh," I groan, shaking my head. "I hate winter. Why'd I stay up in northwest Wisconsin again?" I quip, not really looking for the reason. The truth was, I was too scared to leave. I was barely eighteen with a baby, living above the diner, paying pennies for rent compared to what the going rate was for rental properties around town, and working every chance I got to be able to afford diapers and formula.

"You love it here," he teases, bringing my hand to his mouth and kissing my knuckles.

He does that a lot, and I really like it.

"If you say so. How was your day?"

"It was good. A couple of traffic stops and an argument over at Dixon's Apartments over a parking spot."

"Really?" I ask, curiosity getting the best of me.

"Oh, yeah. Someone parked in a spot deemed 'theirs' by another tenant, and when they went outside, a confrontation ensued. The person who declared the spot theirs went inside her apartment and grabbed a carton of eggs and proceeded to throw them all over the car."

My mouth drops open. "Seriously?"

"As a heart attack. By the time I got there, the eggee was standing on the sidewalk in tears and the egger was smiling smugly on her front steps. Unfortunately for her, egging is vandalism and a pretty serious offense. She wasn't too happy with me when I put her in cuffs, especially after explaining that there were no designated parking spots in that lot and the eggee had a right to park anywhere, including that spot in front of the egger's apartment."

"What a mess."

He nods, tapping his thumb on the top of the steering wheel and looking sexier than ever as he drives. "Emotions get the best of people sometimes, and they make bad choices. Like today. Those eggs cost her more than three bucks now."

Within fifteen minutes, we're pulling into Hudson and driving toward the bowling alley. It's early enough we secure a parking spot near the front and are standing at the service counter only a few minutes later.

TD reserved us a lane for two hours, and our plan is to order dinner from the bar and restaurant attached. They'll come over, take our order, and then deliver the food once it's ready. It's actually a pretty great feature, as long as you follow their rules and keep the food and drinks in the designated spot by your lane.

"Ready?" TD asks, taking my hand and both pairs of ugly bowling shoes and leading me toward our lane.

The computer system is already set up, so once we are wearing our fancy shoes, we're off to find the perfect balls. Mine is a bright pink, sparkly one that weighs nothing—no doubt intended for a young girl—while TD chooses a solid black ball that probably weighs as much as me. Setting the balls in the return rack, we prepare for our first game.

"Ladies first," he says, waving his hand toward the lane.

Standing, I strut up to retrieve my ball, putting a little extra swing in my hips, which he clearly enjoys, if his eyes being glued to my ass is any indication. "Thank you, kind sir."

I take my position, hoping I don't make a complete fool of myself.

Is it too late to request bumpers?

I exhale and swing my arm, letting my ball fly down the lane at Mach speed. Thanks to it weighing an ounce over a feather, it gets there quickly, but unfortunately, only takes down two pins in the process. Turning around, I pin my date with a look. "You promised to suck more than me, right?"

TD crosses his heart over his chest and holds up two fingers. "Boy Scout's honor."

Chuckling, I grab my ball when it returns once more. "That'll probably be hard for you. You've always been a natural athlete. Bowling under a two-fifty is going to be difficult for you."

He's kicked back in one of the chairs, a smile on his lips as he watches me. "I can throw gutter balls like no other, El. Especially if it helps me seal the deal for another kiss later."

My throat is suddenly dry.

There have been stolen kisses throughout the week. He stayed for dinner a few times after bringing Brody home from practice, and there was even one quick, yet incredibly hot kiss after the game last night when he pulled me between two SUVs in the parking lot and laid one on me. But there has been no talk about second base since Sunday's cookout at the cabin. To be honest, that's all I've thought about. My body is humming for his touch.

True to his word, I win our first game, despite my dismal one hundred and thirty-one pin game, and to celebrate, I make him pose with me in front of the scoring screen, selfie-style. TD wraps his hands around my waist and draws me back against his body for the picture. As he does, his hard-on brushes against my backside, but he doesn't adjust our positions. He has to know I can feel it, considering it jumps and starts to get harder within seconds, but he never says a word. He just smiles for the photo as if he doesn't have a care in the world.

That hum in my veins turns into a full-force tsunami, causing me to blush and my skin to prickle with awareness.

Before we start a second game, I take a moment to regroup in the bathroom, while he orders a pizza and two waters. In the mirror, I spot a woman with minimal sexual experience, who looks wild and excited for what could come next. Her cheeks are flush, her eyes wide and shiny, her lips full and glossy. She's been thinking about her friend in a way she's tried to deny herself, but now can't stop that train of thoughts.

She wants him.

Bad.

But with limited experience—thanks to getting pregnant in high school after her first sexual boyfriend and a few very select dates in the years since—comes a lot of nervousness. What if I'm no good at this? What if TD expects at least some level of experience and what I have to offer falls flat on his expectations?

Closing my eyes, I try to push those worries out of my head.

We're not there yet. He hasn't made any indication he's looking to get naked right away, so why am I worrying about that now? That's a bridge I'll cross when the time arises.

Shaking my head, I take a deep breath and exit the restroom. Just as I'm arriving where he's waiting, I notice a group of teenagers approaching.

"Coach!" the boy leading the pack hollers. I recognize him instantly. Patrick is a year younger than Brody and plays on the football team. He's with a group of five others, two boys and three girls, all of which I identify.

"Hey, guys, how's it going?" TD asks, turning and giving me a smile as I step up into our designated lane.

"Pretty good," Patrick replies, noticing me for the first time. "Hi, Miss Daniels."

"Hello," I greet politely, even though my heart has jumped up into my throat. I knew there was a chance we'd be seen tonight, but I wasn't expecting it to be some of Brody's teammates and friends.

"We'll let you two get back to your game. We're down on the end. I bet PJ and Felix I would beat them. Losers have to do the milk mile challenge," Patrick says, a wicked grin on his face.

TD laughs. "That sounds terrible." Glancing over Patrick's shoulder, he asks, "You girls didn't agree to this challenge, did you?"

"Heck no!" Gia announces, while Claire offers a fast, "No way."

"I'm allergic," the third girl, Stephanie, adds.

"Probably for the best. Make sure you boys don't puke on my field," TD announces with a grin.

"Deal, Coach. See you later," PJ says.

"Be good," TD replies as the six teens walk down to the far end of the lanes.

"Do I even want to know what the milk mile challenge is?"

"Nope," TD states, "but I'm going to tell you anyway. The losers of their game will have to drink an entire gallon of chocolate milk between a mile's worth of laps. The person who pukes first...loses."

"Eww." I'm sure my face gives away how disgusting and revolting this challenge is.

"Exactly. And because it's chocolate milk it's thicker."

"My God, these kids come up with some crazy stuff."

"Yeah, but I'd rather see them do something like this, where the worst that'll happen is a little vomiting, than other challenges you hear about on social media."

"Very true," I quickly agree, recalling how deadly the laundry pod challenge that went around for a while turned out to be.

"Anyway, are you ready for game two?"

"Sure, but you know, maybe we should do our own bet?" I suggest.

"Yeah? What do you want if you win?" he asks as our pizza and drinks are delivered.

"If I win, I get to drive your truck home. Oh, and I get to pick our next date location."

"Fine," he replies, sliding a piece of pizza onto a plate and pushing it toward me.

When he doesn't tell me his terms of our bet, I finally ask, "What do you want?"

He looks up, his eyes darkening into molten pools as he licks his lips. "I want second base, El."

My thighs clench and my nipples pebble against my bra. My tongue is so thick, I can barely speak, but somehow, I get out that single word. "Deal."

"Thank you for another lovely night," I say, releasing my seat belt and turning to face TD.

"You're welcome." He sits perfectly still.

On the other side of the truck cab.

Since our second game, he hasn't mentioned the bet, or when he plans to collect his winnings. The thought of feeling his hands on me, sliding under my sweater, and cupping my breasts has had me hot and bothered since the first ball he threw. It was a strike, as were five more of them. He didn't just win the game. He cremated me.

Now, we're sitting in his truck—which he drove back to Pine Village, mind you, since he won the bet—and he's clear over on the other side. Except for basic hand-holding, with our hands resting on the console, he hasn't made one move to collect his winnings. Not that I expected him to try while driving down the road, but I did think there might be a little more touching.

"You're all the way over there," I whisper, the words sounding hesitant and unsure.

"I am."

"Why?"

"Because if I move any closer, I'm going to pull you onto my lap and kiss you until neither of us can breathe."

Yes, please!

"That doesn't sound so terrible," I mumble, my cheeks already heating from a blush.

"Is that what you want, El? Do you want me to kiss you?"

"Yes." My response is breathy and a plea.

He releases his own seat belt and pushes the console up. His hands reach for me at the same time I move in his direction, eliminating the space between us. When I'm on his lap, his mouth finds mine, hot and urgent. Our tongues dance as our lips crash together. My hands grab for his hair, while his rest on my hips. I want to beg, to rock my hips against his growing erection, to throw caution to the wind and just...feel.

I move my hands to his Henley and slide them beneath the material. His skin is hot and smooth beneath my fingertips and all I want to do is continue my exploration.

"Ellie?"

"Yes?" I whisper against his lips.

"I don't want to do anything you're not ready for." His words sound pained but insistent.

"I don't have any problem with you collecting on your winnings, TD. In fact, I really hope you do." To prove my point, I grab his hand and place it against my side beneath my own sweater.

He groans, flexing his fingers before gently gripping my flesh. I move my hand and allow him to explore, leaning forward and pressing my lips against his once more. This kiss is slower, but still packs quite the punch, as his hand begins to move up. His fingertips trace the cup of my bra before he cups my breast in his palm. His index finger glides over my pebbled nipple as his tongue plunges into my mouth. I can feel his cock, hard and ready, against the apex of my legs, and it seems to only intensify my desire as he lightly strokes my nipple.

A whimper falls from my mouth as I rock my hips, trying to get closer to the glorious friction. Sadly, I could actually get off like this, with just enough pressure between my legs, but he doesn't take it any farther. The kissing is hot, and his hands feel amazing against my body, but second base is as far as it goes.

After what feels like hours of making out like teenagers, he pulls back and whispers, "You better get inside. I heard something about a curfew, and I'd hate for you to miss it." TD strokes my swollen bottom lip with the pad of his thumb.

"You're probably right, it's getting late." I pull back and meet his hungry gaze. Then, I slide off his lap and climb back over to the passenger's seat, noting how steamed up the windows are.

Okay, well that's a little embarrassing.

TD climbs out of the truck and walks around to my door, helping me down. Once the door is closed, he guides me to the entrance to my apartment and pauses just outside. He pulls me into his arms and whispers, "Best. Bet. Ever."

A giggle slips from my mouth as he brushes his lips against my own. "I'd lose a bet like that again in a heartbeat."

He laughs and pulls back, putting distance between our heated bodies. "I'll text you."

"When you get home," I insist, wanting to make sure he arrives safely.

"Of course. Night, El," he murmurs before kissing me one last time. "Lock up behind you."

"Night, Thomas."

I have no idea how I walk into the building and climb the stairs. It feels like I'm floating, my feet not even touching the ground. I slip inside the apartment quietly, listening as his truck starts and pulls out of the lot.

Just as I close and lock the door, I spin around and lean my back against it. A grin takes over my face as I replay the hot and heavy make-out session that just transpired in TD's truck.

"You're late, young lady."

My eyes widen as I see Brody standing in the mostly dark kitchen, his arms crossed over his chest and a stern look on his face.

Busted by my seventeen-year-old.

Could this be any more mortifying?

CHAPTER eighteen

TD

Dating my best friend is awesome.

It's been almost four weeks since our hot and heavy make-out session in my truck, and even though we haven't taken it any farther, I'm having an amazing time with her. We steal moments together where we can, kiss as often as possible, and text or talk on the phone way later than we should. Every day these feelings I have for her grow deeper and become harder to fight.

This weekend is a big one for us. I've invited her to go camping with me, and surprisingly, she agreed. Of course, we'll be staying in Logan's cabin, which I'm certain is the reason why, but that's okay. The cabin is much more comfortable than the tent and sleeping bag anyway. Plus, the temperature has transformed from gorgeous fall weather into the beginning of bitter winter, but that's October in northwest Wisconsin for you.

First, I have to get through tonight's game.

Brownville is the top program in our conference and currently undefeated with two games left in the regular season. We sit at a five and two record, with our two losses being incredibly close, hard-fought games. Tonight is going to be a true test of will, power, and determination for my boys, but I believe they have it in them.

I head for the locker room to give my team a final pep talk before we take the field. When I get the door open, I can hear voices. Instantly, I recognize Brody, Matt, and Dorian giving them the speech I was about to give. Not the exact wording, but the gist is the same, so instead of rounding the corner and taking my place before the team, I remain where I stand and let the three outgoing seniors take care of it for me.

"Make your plays, hold your positions."

"Stay low, especially on D. This team is bigger and faster, so we have to stay low and put our shoulders into them. Backers need to be able to see behind their line, so keep them low."

"And wrap up. Their speed is their biggest asset, so when you zero in on your target, wrap up and hold on tight."

"Watch Coach for cues, D. We all know he'll get in his groove and start reading their movements. He's killer like that, so wait for his calls before you get into position."

Smiling, I listen to the three captains give pieces of talks I've made in the previous several weeks, all key ingredients to tonight's game. They picked out all the parts pertinent for this opponent, and I am damn proud of the leaders they've become.

"All right, Panthers. Let's go out and kick some Wildcat ass!" The players all cheer and get into a huddle. Even though I'm not in the room, I know their routine like the back of my hand. "Panthers on three. One, two, three...Panthers!"

When I walk around the corner, the players take a knee and wait for my speech. I look around the room at their eager, hungry eyes, and know this is our night. We can do this. I sense their determination seeping from them, feel their excitement like waves in the ocean. The locker room is electric, the team ready for battle.

"Sounds like your captains have done a fine job at firing you up, and everything they said is pretty much what I'd be telling you, so let's skip the bull. Protect your teammates, protect yourselves, play smart, and above everything else, have fun out there."

The team comes together for one more huddle before taking the field in Brownville. I steal a few glances before kickoff to the stands and find Ellie. She's bundled up in her down coat, hat, scarf, gloves, and a blanket over her legs. Chances are, she's wearing insulated boots under that pile of material too, and that prospect makes me smile. She's cute as hell when she's bundled up for a chilly football game.

It makes me anticipate tomorrow night's date at the cabin that much more.

The whistle blows, and I push all thoughts of Ellie out of my head, at least for a little while. For now, I have a game to coach.

And what a game it is. We're tied at twenty-one with thirty seconds left on the clock. Brownville has the ball but isn't within field goal position yet. Our defense has a chance here, if they can hold them. I hold my breath as the defensive play is called and we line up. The ball is hiked, and as expected, the quarterback falls back to throw. I look downfield, searching for his receivers, and realize exactly where the ball is going. But Brody is there. He's matching the receiver's stride, keeping pace, as he glances back to look for the ball. That's when the ball is thrown high into the air, sailing in a perfect spiral toward their receiver.

And toward Brody.

Just as the ball starts to drop, Brody lifts his hands and snatches it out of the air. The crowd behind me and the sidelines surrounding me erupts as Brody takes off running toward the end zone. He has a good seventy yards to get there and must also make his way through an entire field of defenders, but he's running and giving it his best effort.

By the grace of God, that boy somehow makes it downfield, with only the opposing quarterback standing in his way. My heart hammers so loud, I can hear it over the screaming surrounding me, as I watch Ellie's son dig deep for one last burst of energy and somehow make it past the final opposition between him and the end zone. With no time left on the clock, Brody scores a game-winning touchdown.

The team runs onto the field, but my feet are rooted to the grass where I stand. All I can do is watch their celebration, an overwhelming sense of pride for this player—but more than that, I'm overwhelmed with love for the boy. He's always been a part of my life, thanks to my friendship with his mom, but this—this feels different. It's paternal pride.

He may not be my son, but I'm as proud of him as if my blood ran through his veins.

Before they have too much time to celebrate, Brody is leading the team to the fifty-yard line to congratulate the other team on a good game. I line up at the end, extending my hand and shaking many of their key players' hands as I walk by. Many are crying, having just lost their first game of the season, with only one final game to go. I wish I had encouraging words for them, but I know whatever I say won't help their grief. So instead, I pat them on the shoulder and tell them great game. I do pull their head coach into a hug and tell him his team is outstanding and will go far in the post-season. He thanked and congratulated me on the win, before heading off to console his team.

When the Panthers gather on the field, the celebration continues, but as I approach, they all follow Brody's lead and take a knee, facing me. "I'm proud of each and every one of you. We knew going into this game, we were going to have to play our best football to date, and you did that. You fought hard. Every one of you stepped up tonight." One of the assistant coaches hands me the game ball. "Game ball tonight goes to Brody Daniels, who played hard on both sides of the ball, but secured that win tonight with a pick-six."

His teammates cheer for him as I toss the ball right into his hands. The grin he gives me just cements the affection I feel for him with another wave of overwhelming pride. I knew his sperm donor, but Brody is nothing like him. Brody may get his athleticism from the man who knocked up Ellie, but that's as far as it goes. This boy is all Ellie, and I can't help but feel a little sorry for his sperm donor because he's missing an incredible kid.

Dorian leads the team in one final huddle before they walk off the field to the visitor's locker room to change and gather their gear for the forty-minute bus ride home. I check the sidelines and grab my things, making sure the rest of the managers and coaching staff have our belongings and mess cleaned up. Then, I go searching for Ellie.

I find her, Logan, and Hallie waiting outside the locker room where our players are, and with determined steps, I eat up the distance between us. I'm so overcome with excitement, I pull her into my arms and lift her off her feet, spinning her around like I just won the Big Game, not a regular-season high school game.

Her mouth is pressed against my neck, and I try not to think about how amazing it feels to have her legs wrapped around my waist. "That was amazing," she whispers, squeezing me back tightly.

"It was," I agree, pulling back to meet her happy gaze. "I was just starting to run through scenarios for overtime. All I needed was D to not allow them any significant yardage. When I saw the QB drop, I knew it was headed for the end zone, and just prayed Brody or Jackson were able to keep up with the ball to break up the play."

"I can't believe he intercepted that ball and scored," she replies with tears in her eyes. "My throat hurts from screaming."

Chuckling, I maintain my hold on her and smile. "I was so overwhelmed. I just stood there and watched him celebrate with his teammates."

"I'm so proud of you. Both of you," she says right before pressing her mouth to mine. I quickly take control, coaxing her lips apart with my tongue and slipping it into her mouth.

"Uhh, I don't want to break up this...whatever this is, but unless you want to explain to your team about the birds and the bees—" Logan starts.

"Or be teased mercilessly on the bus ride home," Hallie breaks in with a giggle.

"Or that, yes, I'd suggest keeping it PG while in the presence of high schoolers and their families," my friend finishes, breaking through the sex-laced fog in my brain. I've never been one to let my little head do the thinking—at least not since I was a teenager—but he is clearly calling the shots at the moment.

Before I'm ready, I pull away from Ellie and gaze into her lust-filled green eyes. Even though I don't want to, I set her back down on her feet, which seem a little unsteady for a moment or two, so I let her lean into me a bit. Mostly because I love the feel of her pressed against me.

"Coach!" someone hollers, but I don't put even a millimeter of space between us yet.

"I should probably go make sure they cleared out the locker room," I say, loving the way she feels in my arms.

"Probably," she whispers.

"I'll drop Brode off at home when we get back."

"All right. You're welcome to come up if you want to," she replies, her voice husky and dripping with desire.

"I'd love to, but I have an early morning tomorrow. Plus, I have some work after film and walk-through with the team, and then I'm picking up my girlfriend and taking her camping."

"Wow, that sounds like fun," she murmurs.

"A whole night, just the two of us."

"Huh, that sounds promising. What are you going to do with this girlfriend when you get her in the cabin?"

My mind races with every dirty thought I've had in the last week. Hell, in the last almost two decades, and there have been a *lot* of dirty thoughts. "Whatever she wants me to do."

Now it's her eyes that darken as she shivers in anticipation. We haven't vocalized our desires for our night away, but I'm certain we're both on the same page. I feel it in her touch and in the way she kisses me.

"I have a list," she whispers. "A long one."

My cock kicks in my pants, anxious to be freed from his denim confines to get closer to her. "I can't wait to hear it."

Ellie finally drops her arms from around me and takes a step back. "Maybe I'll just show you."

This is the exact moment I have died and gone to heaven.

Tomorrow, she's finally mine.

"I can get the appeal of camping, if I was staying in a cabin," Ellie says, dropping onto the sofa beside me.

We've been here for a little over two hours, and I have yet to do any of the things I've been dreaming about. Namely, getting my hands on her. But I'm trying to take this night slow. After all, we have all night, and I want to make sure, without a shadow of doubt, we're on the same page.

Ellie glances at her phone and holds it out for me to see the screen. Brody is standing along the glass, a hockey player smiling on the ice behind him. "He says he was photobombed when Matt's dad went to take the picture. How cool is that?"

"Pretty epic. I bet he's already shared it all over his social medias," I say, kicking my feet up on the coffee table and holding out my arm.

Ellie types out a quick reply before setting her phone down on the table. She curls into my side, snuggling into my embrace. "I'm sure. He says he's having fun at the game and will be home by noon tomorrow."

Tonight was the big hockey game with Matt and his dad, which means I get Ellie to myself until midmorning, and I couldn't be happier. We arrived just after six, and the first thing I did was start a fire in the fireplace. We cooked dinner together, deciding against a traditional camping meal and opting for spaghetti and garlic bread. Comfort food, as Ellie called it. We also went for a short walk, checking out the property around the cabin and venturing down by the lake for a bit. It was dark, but no less romantic as we walked hand in hand, the sound of her laughter echoing off the trees.

Now, we're in front of the fire and she's in my arms.

Where she belongs.

"So we have about fourteen hours to kill, huh?" I ask, my finger casually caressing her arm, even though she's wearing a crewneck sweatshirt.

She turns her head and looks up at me. "Seems that way. What do you think we should do with all that time?" There's definitely a hint of flirting in her question, and it goes straight to my balls.

"Well, there's a Scrabble board in the closet."

"Oh, I love Scrabble," she says softly, burrowing deeper into my side, as if she can't get close enough. "But I had something else in mind."

"Checkers?" I quip, praying like hell that's not actually her suggestion. If it is, I'll gladly play a few board games with her, but my mind has us playing a different game. One with far less clothes.

Ellie moves, slipping from my embrace and climbing onto my lap. Before she's even in place, my cock is hard and ready. Straddling me, she places her hands against my chest. "That's a good thought, but still not what I was thinking."

My throat is thick and dry as I glide my hands around her hips and grip her ass. "No? Then, why don't you tell me."

A flash of nervousness flits through her green eyes, but it's quickly squashed away and replaced with determination. "I want you to take me to bed, TD."

My dick jumps in excitement, and despite the invitation, I hold my position. "Are you sure? I don't want to pressure you."

Leaning forward, she presses her chest to mine and rocks against my hard cock. "Oh, I'm very sure. I've been sure for a while now, but didn't want to come on too strong," she says, that familiar blush creeping up her neck.

The urge to roll my hips, to seek out that amazing friction our bodies create, is strong, but I hold still a little longer. "I'm pretty sure that's not possible, El. You know I want you, right? I've had a thing for you since high school, but that doesn't mean we have to take this any farther than you're ready to take it."

She rocks her hips again, and I'm unable to stop the groan. Pleasure races through my veins from the contact. Her fingers flex, her nails biting into my shirt and digging at my flesh. If it were possible for clothes to evaporate into thin air, now would be the time for it to happen. We're lined up perfectly, our bodies on fire with desire. I can see the light pink hue of her skin darkening as lust sweeps through her. Hell, I can see the hard peaks of her nipples pressing against the loose-fitting sweatshirt, causing my mouth to water for one little taste.

"TD?" She holds my gaze as she leans in and whispers, "I'm ready."

CHAPTER
nineteen

Ellie

I barely get the words out of my mouth, and I'm moving. That quickly, I went from straddling TD's lap to being flat on my back, his broad, hard body pressing me into the couch.

"Say it again, El," he whispers, nuzzling my neck with his nose.

Wrapping my legs around his waist, I murmur, "I'm ready, TD."

He starts to lower his mouth to mine but pauses just before we connect. "If at any point you want to stop, just say the word."

"If you don't quit stopping, I'm going to scream," I tell him bluntly, earning me a crooked grin.

"We don't want that now, do we?" he asks, moving his face into the crook of my neck once more. His lips slide along my skin, causing any response I may have had to vacate my brain. All I can think about—all I can feel—is how amazing his mouth is.

As his mouth moves to my jaw, I hitch my ankles over his hips. The movement causes my legs to fall open and a flood of sensations to strike my core. I've been ready for this moment for a while, patiently waiting for those intoxicating kisses to become something more, and now that it has, it's better than I could have possibly imagined.

And we still have our clothes on.

Any thought or worry about making out with one of my best friends doesn't even flit through my brain. He's been far more than just a friend for weeks now, and with each passing day, I start to feel myself fall deeper for the man I've always known was amazing yet was too scared to act on it. Well, not anymore. I'm taking what he's offering, what I want, for the first time in my life.

This just feels right.

My hands push up his long-sleeved T-shirt, exposing those hard muscles and taut skin beneath. His mouth finally claims mine as my fingertips explore his flesh. He's so warm, his skin surprisingly soft, as I caress. I even slide my hands up his chest and over his pecs, despite him caging me into the couch. My fingers dance over the spot where I know his tattoo is inked, and even though my mouth is occupied, my mouth waters to cover that spot with my tongue.

I can't seem to get enough of him.

When he rips his lips from mine, he asks, "What do you think about removing some of these clothes?"

"I think that's a brilliant idea," I state, my breathing labored and coming out in fast pants.

TD sits up to help me remove my sweatshirt, his eyes dropping to my breasts the moment he throws it on the floor. I can feel the familiar blush burning my skin, but I don't shy away and hide. Not from him.

Instead, I push his shirt up, hoping he takes my cue and removes the shirt completely. He reaches behind his head and pulls the shirt off in this incredibly sexy way that makes my mouth go dry and my core flood with wetness. If I were to try that, I'd be so tangled in the material, it'd never come off.

"Better?" he asks, lying back down and covering me with his body once more.

"This doesn't feel wrong," I whisper, only realizing it wasn't just in my head when he kisses my neck and glides his right hand down my bare side.

"Nope. Feels very fucking right, El."

I mewl as my own hands grip his back, exploring the muscles and valleys of his body like Magellan. My mouth finds his shoulder and lightly traces the ridges, my tongue wanting to get in on the action too. I can't help but wonder how it will feel to trace *other* muscles with the tip of my tongue. A shiver sweeps through my body at the thought.

"El?"

My lips don't want to leave his body. "Hmm?"

He pulls back and meets my gaze. "I want to taste you."

Yes, please!

TD sits up, and while keeping his eyes locked on mine, he reaches for my pants. Hoping tonight would go this way, I opted for a pair of warm leggings, perfect for hanging out around the fire. Also perfect for taking off, since there are no buttons or zippers to contend with.

Lifting my hips, he shimmies the leggings down, also removing my fuzzy socks. My toes are usually the first thing to get cold, but for some reason, my entire body is fevered. Actually, hold that. I know the reason, and his name is TD.

When I'm lying on the couch in nothing but the sexiest undergarments I own—a white satin panties and bra set with a bashful pink lace overlay—I start to get a little squirmy as his eyes devour me. That's the only way to describe it. They slowly caress my entire body from head to toe, as if committing every inch of me to memory.

"Fuck, El. You are the most beautiful woman I've ever laid eyes on," he states, his voice husky and gravelly as he drinks me in.

The urge to cover my abdomen is strong. Rarely do I let anyone see the toll childbirth took on my body. The stretchmarks are there, though slowly fading over the years. I never wear those crop top things clothing designers think all women want to wear, and my bathing suits are always one piece, and anyone else I've allowed get this close to me in the past never saw me with the lights on.

I take a deep, calming breath as he lowers his head. I expect him to go...*there*, but he doesn't. His lips softly caress the skin just below my belly button, right over the slightly puckered marks from carrying my son for nine months.

"You're so unbelievably sexy, El. Every inch of you," he whispers, as if he knows how self-conscious I am. Heck, of course he does. No one knows me better than this man.

Reaching down, I glide my fingers into his hair, just needing to touch him. His locks are soft and silky between my fingers, and as I bring the other hand up to get in on the hair-touching action, he shifts his position and lowers his mouth. The first brush of his lips across the apex of my legs almost causes me to jolt from the couch. TD spreads his big hand across my stomach as he glides his lips down the seam of my pussy.

A loud groan fills the cabin, and I don't even care it's mine. A wave of warmth floods my core, and he hasn't even taken off my panties yet. He doesn't either. Instead, he gently pushes the satin aside, exposing me to him. The ache between my legs is intense and growing stronger by the second, so when he lowers his mouth to my flesh, it's a mixture of pure bliss and torturous desire.

His tongue is hot and firm against my clit. Shock waves of euphoria sweep through my veins as I spread my legs wider on the couch. TD takes this as the only invitation he needs as he simply devours me. His tongue, his lips, his fingers, all three of them together are a deadly combination.

One single finger slowly pushes inside me as his lips wrap around my clit. I cry out again, rocking my hips and racing headfirst into the pleasure. His movements are gentle, yet precise. He knows exactly how to play my body, how to make me sing, and with each passing second, I start to drift higher toward the clouds.

TD moves his hand from my stomach, wrapping it around my thigh and spreading me open. His mouth starts to suck harder on my clit, his finger beginning to pick up the pace as it thrusts into me. I can feel my internal walls tightening around his finger, feel the way my body is electrically charged to the max. I'm going to come.

Hard.

I grip on to his hair, my hips rocking to the rhythm, seeking out more of the sweet pleasure he's providing. It's hard to breathe as his tongue slides up and down, his fingers stroking that magical sweet spot deep inside me. The moment his lips latch back on to my clit, I explode in an epic orgasm.

Crying out, waves of pleasure consume me, my body squeezing around his finger like a vise. I have no idea how long my release lasts, but it feels like it goes on forever. Seconds turn into minutes, which blurs into some unspecified amount of time, all while my body shakes with the ecstasy that consumes me.

When I'm finally able to open my eyes, I find him smiling up at me, his mouth still dangerously close to my body. "You good?" he asks, a hint of cockiness in his question.

"Very good," I tell him, still trying to slow my heartbeat.

He slides his finger out of my body and wipes his mouth with the back of his hand. "I'm happy to report, you tasted even better than anticipated. In fact, I'm pretty sure I'm going to have to have another taste very, *very* soon."

"Like how soon?" I find myself asking. "I was kinda hoping there was more on the agenda this evening."

Holding my gaze, TD stands up to remove his jeans. My eyes drop, following his every move with laser-focus precision. "Oh, there's definitely more."

Then, he drops his pants and kicks them out of the way, and all I can see is his erection through his boxer briefs. Big. Oh my God, so big. Like it'll never fit big, and that makes me a little worried. "Umm, TD?" I whisper, hating to even voice my concerns, especially since I took health class. I know it'll fit. But I also know I haven't had sex in a *really* long time, and as far as I know, the hymen went back to its sixteen-year-old state and I'm basically a virgin again.

As if sensing my apprehension, he drops to his knees beside the couch and reaches for my hand. "What's wrong? Do you want to stop?"

"No," I quickly reassure, licking my lips nervously. "Uhh, it's not that at all."

"Then what?" he asks, bringing my hand to his mouth and kissing it softly.

I really like it when he does that.

"Well, you seem to be rather...*large* everywhere," I tell him, dropping my eyes to where his erection stretches the material of his boxer briefs.

He doesn't crack a smile or laugh at me the way I expect him to. He brings my hand back up to his mouth and trails kisses across my knuckles. "I'll fit, El. And I'll take it very, very slow, but if you're not ready—"

"I didn't say that," I quickly reiterate. "It just might be a little tight."

This time, he does crack a crooked smile. "That's actually a good thing," he teases, making me giggle. Some of the tension starts to ease, just as it always does when he's near.

"Yes, but this might be overly tight. It's, uh, been a while for me."

He links our fingers together and rests his elbows on the couch beside me. "How long's a while?"

My face goes up in flames, and I divert my eyes. "Uhhh...a long while? Are you going to make me say it?"

"No," he replies quickly. "If you're not comfortable talking about this, that's okay. We can ease into that conversation, but just to be upfront with you, it's been about three years for me."

"Seriously? Have you seen yourself in the mirror?" My brain just can't compute women not lined up to date him. Not only is TD completely gorgeous, but he's a police officer, and I know the uniform is like catnip to a huge demographic of women.

He grins again. "I have seen myself in the mirror, yes, but I don't know, I just haven't been that interested in dating. I've been harboring a crush on one of my best friends for a while now, and everyone else just seems to pale in comparison."

"Oh." This is still a little wild to me. We've been friends for so long, and even though I'm past the whole dating my friend and messing it all up issue, it still leaves me a bit flabbergasted to know he was crushing on me as long as I on him.

"Yeah, so I'm just hoping I last longer than three minutes, El," he adds, pulling a worried look.

My mind races, and before I realize what's happening, I blurt out, "Nine years."

Shock registers on his face. "Did you say nine years?"

This would be the perfect time for the world to implode or some other equally devastating natural disaster that wipes out all living organisms.

I pull my hand from his and use it to cover my face. "Yes," I mumble.

Warm fingers wrap around my wrist and gently pull them out of the way. "This is going to make me sound like a complete asshole, but I'm a little relieved you don't have a black book three inches thick."

A giggle slips from my lips. "No black book, Thomas. Hell, I don't I even have a hookup's number in my phone."

TD growls and narrow's his eyes. "Let's keep it that way, shall we?" He leans forward and presses his lips to mine. "You know, I'm a little pissed off at the men in the area. There was this amazing, beautiful woman they could have had but were too fucking stupid to see it."

I shrug. "I'm a busy single mom. That doesn't exactly scream sexy."

He moves toward me once more, his eyes dancing with desire. "I think it's sexy as fuck, El. You're so damn sexy," he tells me, running his hand up my thigh and sliding it around to my rear.

"I think you're sexy too," I reply, my voice suddenly all breathy.

"What do you say? Wanna get naked with me?"

"Yes." My answer is instant and absolute.

He reaches for my panties, which are stretched and askew, and slides them down my legs. When they're gone, he moves to my bra and releases the front clasp. The warmth of the fire warms my bare chest, and my nipples pebble under his gaze. "Christ," he mutters, running his hand through his hair and down the back of his neck. "If I would have known you were this perfect beneath your clothes or swimsuit, I would have tried this years ago."

Smiling, I take a moment to enjoy my own view while he's distracted. But my view of his chest is ruined when he bends over, his warm mouth latching on to my right nipple. The smile falls from my face as zings of pleasure sweep through my veins.

TD licks and sucks the first nipple before moving on to the second. His big, warm palm cups the one he's not showering with attention from his talented mouth, rolling the nipple between his fingers.

Suddenly, he pauses. "You haven't gotten off in nine years?" he asks, looking at me.

I shake my head. "I didn't say I haven't gotten off in that amount of time."

His right eyebrow arches and a wicked grin spreads across his face. "I'm going to need to know more about that, El."

"No," I insist. "That's private."

"Yes, but also sexy as fuck. I can't stop thinking about you touching yourself. Did you use your fingers, like this?" he asks, slipping one hand between my legs and gliding his fingers through my wetness.

"Yes," I whisper through a gasp. "Like that."

"Did you push a finger inside your pussy, El? Like this?" he asks, slowly pushing a finger back inside my body.

A low groan rushes from my lips. "Yes, that too."

"One finger or two?" he asks, running a second finger around my entrance but not pressing it inside with the other.

"Two," I reply, but quickly add, "but my fingers are much smaller than yours."

"They are," he agrees.

My body is humming once more, the desire stirring to life within me. "You know, it wasn't always my fingers," I find myself saying without stopping to think.

TD pauses. "What else did you use, El? Toys?"

I nod shyly. "A little one. I only used it when I was alone in the apartment."

He groans painfully, closing his eyes for a few moments. "That is an image I'm never getting out of my head. I'm going to need to see you use it. Soon."

Blushing profusely once more, I give him a coy smile. "We'll see."

"Oh, we'll definitely see," he insists bluntly before standing up and slipping his fingers beneath the waistband of his boxer briefs. My breath catches in my throat as he pushes them down his hips and lets them drop onto the floor at his feet. His cock is magnificent. Long, hard, and making my mouth water for a taste.

TD grabs his erection in his fist and gives it a squeeze, causing moisture to seep from the tip. Reaching out, I hold his gaze as I swipe my fingertip across the wetness and bring it to my mouth. The moment my tongue slips out and licks it off, he groans and releases his hold on himself. He turns to his jeans and pulls a condom from the pocket.

"Awfully cocky, aren't we?" I tease, my eyes glued to him as he rips the package open and sheathes himself.

"Not cocky, El. I wanted one close in case you made me lose my mind, just the way you have. I wanted to be prepared." Then, he comes down on top of me, covering me from head to toe. He lightly kisses my lips, his tongue slipping out and tangling with my own for several very long seconds. When he releases my mouth, he kisses across my jaw and down my neck. My legs wrap around his waist, his heavy erection nudging at my entrance.

"Ready?"

Heck, yes.

"I'm ready."

CHAPTER Twenty

TD

I have to keep reminding myself to breathe.

The fact I'm about to slide into Ellie has my mind spinning and basic bodily functions like breathing seem to evade me. I lift my hand and cup her cheek as I shift my hips. That slight movement presses the tip of my cock into her tightness, and I instantly see stars. There's no way I'm going to last long, especially because I know I need to take this very slowly so I don't hurt her.

Ellie rocks her hips, drawing my dick inside her body a little farther, and I have to remind myself to fight against my body's natural desire to thrust. "More," she whispers, her lips so kissable, so ripe.

"I don't want to hurt you, El," I insist, even though I think my balls may explode soon.

She holds my gaze. "You won't. You'd never hurt me."

Shaking my head, I insist, "No. Never."

Her hand is soft against my stubbled jaw, and I can't help but lean into her touch. "I'm ready, TD. Please."

I will never deny this woman anything. Ever.

I release a shuddered breath and press forward, feeling her incredible tightness engulf my cock inch by inch. Slowly I pull back out and push back inside her pussy, each thrust, her grip on my dick loosening a touch and taking me inside a bit more. Finally, when I'm completely seated, I exhale through the euphoria crashing through my veins, begging me to move. "Jesus, El," I mutter, fighting like hell to hang on to control.

She groans, her muscles rippling around me as she does. "You can move."

"You sure?" I ask through gritted teeth.

"So sure," she insists, rolling her hips.

Blind pleasure blankets me in warmth. My body starts to sweat. I ease back and gently thrust forward, causing her to cry out, but there's no evidence of discomfort in her noise. That one sound is like a cup of gasoline thrown on a blazing inferno. My hips buck, moving within her at a slightly faster pace now. Her pussy is so tight, so wet, so perfect, and I'm not sure I'll ever get enough of her now. The match has been lit.

Ellie runs her fingertips up my back, her nails digging into my flesh. My mouth finds hers, our tongues tangling together as we both gasp for air. My hips start to move on their own, despite my best efforts to remain in control. Her legs shift and open farther before tightening around my lower back. The angle is pure fucking magic. That's the only way to describe this.

I feel her pussy ripple around me. I slow my pace and find her lust-filled eyes. "Are you going to come again, El?"

"Yes," she whispers. "So good," she groans as her nails dig deeper.

The pain causes my hips to flex, to fill her with a bit more force, but she doesn't seem to mind. In fact, she rocks her hips, meeting me thrust for thrust. At this point, there's no slowing down this freight train. It's hellbent on getting to its destination without a care in the world about what or who it destroys in the process.

I realize in this exact moment, what's getting wrecked is my heart.

Ellie cries out, and I swallow the sounds with my mouth. Her pussy squeezes the life out of me as she starts to come, waves of bliss fluttering around my cock, causing my balls to draw up tight. Before I even have a chance, my body is following her over the edge of oblivion, taking every ounce of pleasure it's offered.

Her name falls as a whisper from my lips as I release everything I have. Wave after wave of ecstasy courses through my veins as I shudder in relief. My body continues to move, long after the shock waves of pleasure start to subside. My kiss turns soft, my lips longing to keep our connection for as long as possible, and she seems in no hurry to break the kiss either.

Finally, when my body becomes too heavy for me to hold up any longer, I shift our positions. She releases her legs from behind my back as I move us both to our sides, facing each other. My cock, though getting softer by the second, still remains nuzzled in the warm, happy place he never wants to leave.

Ellie's face is pressed against my neck, her breathing labored and warm against my flesh. I wrap my arm around her waist, drawing her even closer, because I can't seem to get enough of her naked body against mine.

"TD?" she murmurs, her sated voice soft and sweet.

"Hmm?" I ask, running my hand gently up and down her back.

She pulls back and looks up, finding my gaze. "When can we do that again?"

A booming laugh rumbles my chest. "Well, as much as I love your enthusiasm, you probably need a little time to recoup. A warm bath would probably be beneficial to you, but there's only a shower stall in the bathroom."

She glides her hand up my arm. "I don't need a shower, unless you're in it with me."

My cock kicks in response. "That could probably be arranged...later. Maybe in the morning," I insist, allowing my hand to wander down to her bare ass. Her leg hitches over my own leg again, causing my cock to fall free from its favorite spot.

"You're probably right," she replies through a yawn. "The morning sounds perfect."

"Here," I say, carefully sliding up and off the couch without knocking her onto the floor. "I'll be right back. Stay here," I add, placing a kiss on her forehead before moving away.

Quickly, I head to the bathroom and discard the condom into the trash. Then, I retrieve a washcloth and clean myself up. When that task is completed, I grab a second cloth and wet it with warm water for Ellie before returning to the living room. I find her in the same spot I left her just a minute ago, except she turned and is now facing the fire. The faintest smile is stretched across her lips as she watches the flames dance in the darkness.

Suddenly, an idea hits me.

First, however, I need to take care of my woman.

I gently lift her leg and lightly brush the warm cloth across her sensitive area. She wiggles and takes the cloth from my hand, insisting on doing it herself. Usually, I might argue with her, but even in the darkened room, I can tell she's blushing. So, I don't draw attention to it for fear of embarrassing her further and turn my attention toward the bedroom. I quickly gather the pillows before retrieving the rest of the items I'm looking for from the hall closet.

Just as I round the corner for the living room, I find her standing in front of the couch, a confused look on her face. "I had a thought," I start, setting the bundle of bedding and pillows down on the floor.

First thing I do is unzip the sleeping bags and lay them on top of each other in the middle of the plush rug. Then, I grab the sheet and spread it on top of the sleeping bags, followed by the quilt and pillows. When our makeshift bed is made in front of the fire, I hold out my hand. "Do you need to use the restroom, or are you ready for bed now?"

She hitches her thumb toward the hallway. "I'd like to use the restroom."

When I nod, she disappears, closing the door to the bathroom softly behind her. I quickly move to the kitchen and start to make two mugs of hot cocoa. It's her favorite, which is why I brought all the stuff for our night in the cabin. While the milk is heating, I double-check the door locks, even though I know they're already secure. I will never risk her safety, and verifying the doors are secured are vital.

Just as I'm pouring the milk into the mugs of powder, I hear the bathroom door open. Moments later, she rounds the corner like the fucking goddess she is, her hair a little wild and wearing one of my T-shirts. Weird, because I didn't bring that shirt here.

Ellie notices and drops her eyes to the black shirt with the hardware store logo across the front. "Uhh, I might have borrowed this."

"That's fine," I assure her, stirring the first mug. "It looks way better on you anyway."

She blushes. "I don't know about that."

"I do. Where'd you get it, though? I don't recall packing it."

"Uhh, I might have taken it a few weeks ago," she states with another crimson blush.

I chuckle and set the spoon on the counter, carefully picking up both mugs. "Honey, you can have every last shirt I own if I get to see them on you at bedtime," I state with a wink.

We take our places in the middle of the floor, surrounded by the blankets and fire. I've never really considered myself a romantic, but I don't seem to mind digging down for it where she's concerned. Ellie deserves the flowers and the chocolates and the rom-com movies. She deserves the hand-holding and the all-night phone conversations and the hot chocolate in front of the fire. She deserves it all because she's worth it.

"Thank you for this," she says, taking a sip from her mug.

"You're welcome. I figured it would earn me a few brownie points I could cash in later," I tease, even though that's not the reason at all. I made it because it's one of her favorites. It's that simple.

"I have a few ideas about that," she says softly, avoiding my gaze.

Taking a drink of my own hot cocoa, I set the mug on the coffee table and give her my full attention. "Well, don't hold out on me now. Let's hear these ideas."

Clearing her throat, she sets her mug beside mine and shifts a little closer. I slide my leg around her body, pulling her back against my chest and wrapping my arms around her waist. "Well, I rather enjoyed your...mouth work earlier. I was hoping we might be able to do that again soon."

"Done," I reply immediately, lowering my mouth to kiss against her neck. "I'll eat your pussy every day for the rest of your life if that's what you want."

She shivers in my arms.

"What else?"

"Well, I thought I'd return the favor."

My cock is suddenly very happy to hear this and starting to get thick in anticipation. "That can definitely be arranged, El. In fact, I look forward to that day very much."

Glancing over her shoulder, she meets my gaze. "Like now?" she asks, but it's instantly followed by a yawn.

Realizing it's getting late and knowing I want to let her rest before I get my hands—and mouth—on her again, I shift us both until we're lying down on the soft bedding. "Now, I think we sleep. I don't want to hurt you. There'll be plenty more opportunities for all that and more."

She yawns again, making me smile. "Let's talk about that more," she whispers, turning to face me. She buries her face into my neck and throws her arm and leg over my body. The most comfortable peace falls around me as I lie on the floor, holding Ellie in my arms.

This is what I've been craving all my life, and finally, at thirty-five years old, I feel like I have it all.

The girl.

Her son.

The life I've always pictured us having, if I was ever brave enough to take the chance.

Well, I finally did it, and now everything I've ever wanted is laid out in front of me. No, we're not anywhere near the declarations point of our relationship, but just knowing we're on the same track, possibly heading for the same destination, is all I need.

For now.

Everything else will fall into place.

It's those thoughts that keep me company as I slowly start to drift, Ellie snuggled against my side, and the sounds of her soft breathing lulling me into sleep.

Her mouth is warm and wet, her tongue the sweetest sin, as it glides from the base of my cock to the head. Her soft hand is wrapped around me, gently squeezing as it moves up my shaft. Part of me needs to open my eyes, to watch her work me over, but I'm too afraid it'll be a dream if I do.

The tip of her tongue swirls around the tip of my dick before she lowers her mouth around it, sucking it into the confines of her mouth as far as she can go. A groan slips from my lips as she opens around me, drawing me to the back of her throat. Ellie gags a bit but doesn't stop her assault on my cock. She readjusts her position and goes back for more.

My eyes open and lock on her mouth as my hand moves to her head. I thread my fingers into her hair, holding it back as much as I can so nothing obstructs this delicious view. All I can do is stare in awe as she sucks my cock like a fucking champion, twisting her hand, swirling her tongue, and adding the right amount of suction to make me lose my mind.

She's the perfect storm, and I don't think I can ever get enough of her.

Ellie runs her tongue down my shaft and across my balls. My hand instantly tightens as the pleasure races through my body. "Fuck, El," I murmur, trying to remember to breathe.

She hums, sending pure bliss vibrating through me. The combination of her mouth on my nuts and her hand twisting as she jacks my cock has me ready to blow after only a few minutes.

"I'm getting close," I warn, holding her hair up and rocking my hips.

She lifts her head long enough to reply, "I know. Come in my mouth."

This is the moment I die.

Physically, I'm still here, but mentally, I die and go to heaven.

Ellie returns her fantastic mouth to my cock and continues to suck. My balls draw up tight and that familiar tingle starts at the base of my spine. I feel my cock tighten to the point of pain as she doubles her efforts to make me come. It works, of course, because moments later, I explode, shots of cum hitting her throat and coating her tongue.

I find myself gasping for air as I float back down to the ground, and when I'm finally able to open my heavy eyes again, Ellie seems awfully pleased with herself. Her green eyes sparkle and there's a wide smile on her swollen lips. Suddenly, all I want to do is kiss the hell out of her.

"Come here," I say, reaching my hands toward her and pulling her on top of me.

She comes willingly, her mouth descending to mine as her arms slide around my neck. I have no idea how long we lie naked kissing, but by the time we break the kiss, I still want more. My body craves hers like no other, and I know now I've gotten a taste of her, I'll never get enough.

"So, about that shower," she murmurs as my lips brush down the column of her neck.

"Yes. Definitely."

Giggling, she straddles my lap, her wet pussy glistening in the morning light filtering through the window. As she sits up, I link our fingers together and smile up at her. "I, uh, I had a really great time last night," she says, blushing.

"Me too, El. I want more nights like that. I know we won't be able to get away to a cabin, but I'm hoping we can figure out a way to spend evenings and maybe nights together moving forward."

"I'd like that."

"Me too. I think Brody is old enough to understand you may spend the night at my place or vice versa, but I'll let you take the lead on that with him."

"You're right, he knows our relationship has progressed, and he seems very supportive. I may have to have a conversation with him soon about that part, despite how awkward that might be," she replies with an embarrassed chuckle.

"Well, you don't have to go into details, El. I'm sure he's old enough to figure it out without them," I quip, squeezing her hands.

She rolls her eyes dramatically. "I will *not* be going into any details, Thomas Dexter. It was hard enough having the birds and the bees conversation back when he was twelve. The last thing I want to do is have it again, especially when talking about you and me."

"I can help with that conversation if you would like," I offer.

"No, it's fine. I want to see how things are going with Morgan and him too. They seem to be doing well."

"They are," I agree.

She nods and moves her hips, coating my cock with her wetness and causing it to start to get hard again. "I have to work tonight, but maybe I can talk to him after practice one night this week."

"Sounds good, and the offer still stands if you want my help or me to be with you."

She shimmies her hips, ensuring I'm completely hard and ready to go once more. "I'll let you know," she replies a little breathlessly.

"Good," I tell her, sitting up, releasing her hands, and wrapping my arms around her waist. "Now, about that shower…"

CHAPTER
Twenty one

Ellie

I pull the stuffed shells from the oven and set them on top of the stove just as the bottom door opens and closes, followed by my son's heavy footfalls. "Hey, Mom," he greets as he enters our apartment, securing the top door before setting his football bag down on the floor.

"Hi, Brody. How was school?"

He turns and gives me a, "Good. I have that big English exam on Friday. Why do they do tests on Fridays? Fridays are for football."

I can't help but giggle as I start to dish up his plate. "Yes, but better than on Monday and having to spend your whole weekend studying, right?"

He seems to consider that before replying, "I guess you're right. A few nights of studying throughout the week is better than spending my Saturday and Sunday with my nose in a book."

"See?" Placing the first plate on the table, I return to the stove and scoop only two shells this time for me.

"What's up with Coach? I mean TD?" Brody asks, placing water on the table for us to drink before having a seat.

"What do you mean?"

"He had some lame excuse about needing to water his lawn tonight instead of having dinner with us," he states, rolling his eyes.

I can't help but laugh, but I'm not sure if it's the fact Brody clearly knew it was an excuse or because of the silliness of it. "You don't think people water their lawn in October?"

He pins me with a look that lets me know he's not buying it. "Two nights after it rained? In Wisconsin in October? Come on, Mom."

Smiling, I take my seat and start cutting up my pasta. "You're right, it was an excuse. He wanted to give us an opportunity to talk."

Brody looks up, his fork going still in the air. "About what? Is everything okay?"

"Yes, everything is fine," I quickly reassure. "Things have been going very well, actually."

My son smiles at me, suddenly looking so youthful and happy. "Good. Coach is awesome."

"He really is," I reply, knowing this is the perfect segue into the conversation I need to have. "That's sort of what I wanted to discuss with you." I scoop up a bite of the marinara covered cheesy noodle and take a small bite. "We're having a great time together, and our relationship is moving forward. We're not rushing anything, but we definitely enjoy each other's company, and well, I wanted to make sure you were still okay with that."

"I'm more than okay, Mom. TD is the closest thing I have to a dad."

His words seem to shock the both of us. It's as if he didn't really mean to say that aloud.

"Brode, about that," I start, but he holds up his hands, cutting me off.

"I didn't mean anything bad by it. I know he's not my dad and I'm not trying to say he is, but we've all been pretty close my whole life. He, Logan, and Gabe have all been there for me, but TD even more so, probably because he's my football coach too. They're all cool and I like hanging out with them. TD teaches me a lot of stuff, like fishing and camping. He taught me how to play football and pretends to help me with my homework when I don't really need it."

That comment makes my eyes water as a lump forms in my throat.

"So, if you're asking if I'm okay with you and him getting even closer, I am. I love you, Mom, and want you to be happy. It's a bonus that it's him you're dating. I'm not going to be around forever, you know. Soon, I'll be going off to college, and if I know you're here with him, then I won't worry about you nearly as much."

A single tear slides down my cheek. "I don't think I'll ever stop worrying about you, whether you're living under the same roof or not."

He gives me a cheeky grin. "I know. It's part of the Mom code." He scoops up a huge forkful of dinner and slowly chews.

"So, you'd be okay if, maybe every once in a while, I spend a Saturday night at TD's house? I know you're plenty old enough to be here by yourself."

He shrugs. "It's cool. And if he wanted to stay here sometime, totally all right by me."

I take a deep breath, letting it out slowly. This conversation went as well as I'd hoped. "Okay, good to know. How are things with Morgan?"

His smile is wide and instantaneous. "Great. We're talking about going to the movies in Hudson Saturday night for that new scary movie coming out."

"Eww, I'll pass," I mumble, shivering at the thought of watching something terrifying.

Brody chuckles. "I figured. Anyway, I'm going to ask her to the winter dance. She had mentioned something about dress shopping soon, so I wanted to ask her before she went."

"That's great. I think you two will have a lot of fun," I reply, choking on the fact my baby boy is preparing for all his lasts. Last football game this Friday, last winter dance, prom, and eventually, graduation. As crazy as the years have been, they've definitely gone by fast.

We continue eating in relative silence, mostly because my brain is stuck on something else he said. He referred to college, but has yet to disclose what those plans may be. Oh, we've discussed several post-high school careers over the years, but he hasn't told me which way he's leaning. His goal for senior year was to make sure he had the right amount of elective classes, as well as any necessary general education ones needed for either a two-year community college or four-year university. It's still October, so I know his long-term decisions don't need to be finalized right now, but I'd love to know which way he's leaning.

"So, can I ask you something else?"

"Of course," he replies, finishing off his dinner.

"You mentioned college. Have you made any decisions about that?" My heart is hammering in my chest with nervousness as I await his answer.

"Umm, yeah, I think I have." There's a mix of confidence and apprehension in his words that sets me on edge.

"All right," I state softly, pushing my plate away. There's no way I'll be able to eat what's left of my food at this point.

Brody sits up straight and looks me in the eye. "I want to enroll in community college and earn my associate of applied science degree in criminal justice."

My mind spins as I repeat those words in my head. *Criminal justice?*

"I've been doing a lot of thinking," he starts, taking a deep breath, "and watching. I want to help people, like TD." He quickly holds up his hands. "Before you freak out, I know there are a lot of risks. I watch the news and hear all the stories, Mom. It's a scary world out there, and not just with policework. Teachers are worried about arming themselves in classrooms and businesses are being robbed in the middle of the day. But I just keep going back to the fact that I know I can do a lot of good in this world by becoming a police officer. I want to be the man children know they can go to when they need help, who listens to the people around him and does everything in his power to make it right. I think I can be a good officer, Mom, just like TD. I want to try."

My throat is closed, and I can't draw oxygen into my lungs. There are tears in my eyes as I sit here, truly listening to his words, to the passion behind them. My heart is not ready for this next phase in his life, but I know he's going to do amazing things in this world, and I will always be there to support him.

Clearing the emotion from my throat, for several long seconds, all I can do is nod. When I finally find my voice, I whisper, "I'm so dang proud of you, Brody Daniels. You are, without a doubt, the best person I've ever known."

He smiles and reaches for my hand. "I've had great role models, Mom. You, TD, and the rest of the gang. Even Logan and Hallie with their obsessive bickering back and forth. Oh, by the way, I'm pretty sure they'll end up together."

A bark of laughter flies from my mouth. "I don't know about that. They'd probably kill each other after one night," I retort, even though I secretly agree with him.

He shrugs. "Maybe, maybe not. The point is I've been watching you all my entire life, and I'm excited to take these next steps because I know I've had your support and love."

I'm moving. Before I even realize I'm up and around the small table, I'm there, throwing my arms around his neck and crying into his shoulder. My son doesn't say a word, just holds me and lets me shed my tears. They're a mixture of happiness, relief, worry, and sorrow for all the hardships we've had to endure throughout this life, but knowing he's become this incredible person despite being raised by a single mom has my heart bursting with love and pride.

"I love you so much, Brody."

"Love you too, Mom."

After a few minutes, I finally release my hold on him and pull away, wiping away the remnants of tears with a sigh. "You're going to make an excellent police officer one day."

"Thanks," he replies with that boyish, goofy grin I love.

I keep myself busy cleaning up the leftovers and washing the dirty dishes while Brody goes to take a shower. The entire time, my heart bursts with pride and love for the human I created by accident all those years ago. He may not have been planned, but I'm not exaggerating when I say he's the best thing to ever happen to me. My greatest joy.

I can't wait to see what's in store for him in the future.

"Hey, where's Gabe?" I ask, setting a bundle of silverware down on the table in front of Blair.

"He's on his way. He had to finish up with a patient and sent me ahead to get a booth. You know how Saul's meatloaf days are," she replies.

"Oh, I'm aware," I state with a chuckle. His bacon-wrapped meatloaf and mashed potatoes special is one of the biggest draws on the menu. "What do you guys want to drink?"

"Just iced water for both of us."

"Coming right up. Do you want me to go ahead and put in your orders for the special? I can watch for Gabe and bring them out when he arrives," I offer, knowing it'll get busy very quickly as the noon hour hits and the specials will go quickly.

"That would be amazing. Thank you."

"I'll be right back with your waters," I tell her, jotting down their order on my pad and taking it back to the kitchen. As I'm filling two glasses, I hear the bell over the door chime, signaling the arrival of another customer. "Welcome," I holler, spotting Mrs. Duggan and her friend from out of town, who always get together on Wednesdays at lunch to visit.

The friends wave their greeting and find their favorite booth by the window, while I add two glasses of unsweetened iced tea to my tray. I stop by my new table first and drop off their teas. "The special today, ladies?"

"Of course, dear. We've been looking forward to it all week," Mrs. Duggan announces pleasantly.

"Coming right up," I tell them before heading for Blair's table. "Two waters," I announce, placing them on the table.

"Gabe's on his way. He just left the office," she informs me. Their office is just down the block, which means he'll be here in a minute or two. "I know you're busy, but I haven't seen you since the game. How'd Saturday night go?" she asks, referring to my overnight cabin stay with TD.

I feel the familiar blush settle in my cheeks. "It was…amazing," I whisper, causing her to squeal in delight.

"I knew it!"

"Shhh, keep it down, will ya?" I tease.

"Sorry, but Hallie and I totally called it. We both knew it would be explosive," she murmurs quietly so any patron nearby can't overhear.

"Well, it was." My face is hot, but I refuse to cover it in embarrassment.

"Yay," she sings, clapping her hands together. "So what now? Big plans this weekend?"

"Uhh, he might be spending the night tonight," I mutter, ignoring the bell over the door for fear everyone in the room will see my embarrassment.

"Really? That's big," she concludes.

"It is. I talked to Brody Monday night, and he's okay with it, so we thought we'd give it a try. I might stay at his place Saturday night."

"Wow, big steps for you two. Love it," she states. "Just make sure he's wearing a raincoat, okay? Not that I don't think you two wouldn't make beautiful babies, but apparently, there's something in the water lately. We've had six pregnancy confirmations in the last month."

"Six?" I ask, my eyes wide. That seems like a really high number for our small town of three thousand.

"Don't you be number seven," she quips.

"Seven what?"

I startle as Gabe slides into the booth across from Blair.

"Number seven baby confirmation," she says before sipping her water.

He looks my way and smiles. "Ahh, that. Yeah, we've had a bit of an influx lately. Apparently, it has been a very busy fall," he adds with a wink.

"Oh my gosh, but wouldn't TD and Ellie make the cutest babies? Seriously, with your green eyes and his complexion and dark hair, those would be some seriously adorable kids."

My heart starts to pound, and I'm certain if the diner wasn't getting louder by the second with the lunch rush, everyone in the room would be able to hear it beat.

"Can Hallie and I throw you the baby shower?"

My mouth falls open. "What? Stop it! I'm not pregnant," I insist, praying no one in the vicinity overhears.

"I know, but if you were, we could throw your shower, right?"

My eyes roll widely. "Enough," I grumble. "I'm gonna go grab your lunches."

Blair and Gabe start chatting as I walk away, pausing to take a drink order for a new table that just arrived. However, the damage has been done. I can't stop wondering what it would be like to have a child with TD. I'm certain he'd be my partner in every way, from the first onset of the pregnancy through the growing and caring for stages. He'd be there for bedtimes and meals and disciplining. He'd take photos and teach him or her how to throw a football in the backyard. He'd be there for every moment, a true partner in every way.

In all these years, I never pictured myself having another baby. Dating wasn't easy with a young child, and the few times I did manage to go on dates, I definitely wasn't thinking about long-term and the potential for more babies. But now I can't stop thinking about it.

With TD.

He'd be an incredible father, and that baby would be the luckiest child in the world.

Does he want kids?

It's way too soon to ask those questions, but at the same time, neither of us is getting any younger. We're thirty-five, which means I'd be considered high risk for any future children I have, and I'm not sure I want to risk that. My son is nearly grown. Do I want to start over again with the diapers and sleepless nights part of parenthood?

I shake my head and grab four plates of meatloaf, loading them onto my tray. I'm getting way ahead of myself here. TD and I have only been dating about six weeks. The possibility of babies shouldn't even be on my radar.

But it is.

Now that the seed has been planted, it's rooting and growing in my head.

The fact is I *would* like to have more babies, and the more I think about the future, the more I see TD in it. After all, he's been right by my side the entire time. Since I was seventeen, alone, pregnant, and terrified, he's been my rock, my constant.

My best friend.

And now, all these years later, my lover.

I hope we're on the same page about the future, because I'm not sure I could go back to mere friends at this point. Somewhere, over the last many weeks, it grew into more. My feelings for him are so deep, they're embedded in my soul and written on my heart. I've fallen in love with him without even knowing it.

Now I just have to figure out how to tell him.

Will he reciprocate, or will my confession leave him running for the hills?

God, that's a terrifying thought.

It didn't end so well for me the last time I told someone life-changing news. I was painted as a whore, the proverbial letter A stitched on my sweater for the world to see. I lost my family but gained a bigger support system in the friends I was surrounded with.

I take a deep breath.

Now isn't the time to worry about all that. We're dating and having a lot of fun. I don't need to think about the future and whether or not TD might want to have kids someday.

What I need to do now is push those thoughts aside and worry about them when the need arises.

Ha! Do I not know anything about myself?

I'll be dwelling on this forever.

CHAPTER
Twenty Two

TD

"Honey, we're home," Brody announces as we enter the apartment. The scent of meat permeates the air, causing my stomach to growl.

"Hi, guys," Ellie greets once we're inside the kitchen. "Dinner's ready," she adds, as she keeps her eyes focused on the food in front of her.

"Smells amazing, El," I say, dropping my bag onto the floor by the wall and approaching where she stands at the stove. My hands wrap around her hips as my mouth grazes across her neck. "You smell amazing too," I whisper, my lips gently tickling her skin and causing goosebumps to erupt.

A throat clears behind us, reminding me we're not alone.

Yet.

"How was practice?" she asks, a little flustered as I reach around her and take the pot of pulled pork and placing it on the table. Brody finishes setting the table and retrieving drinks, and we sit down together to eat.

"It was good," Brody replies, and I sit quietly as he tells his mom about his day. I can't get over how *right* the entire exchange feels. Sitting at the dinner table, discussing the day, practice, work, and everything in between. It's comfortable, as if we've been doing this sort of thing all along. And in a way, we have, but more frequently now. In fact, I'm here for dinner more nights than I'm not, and now that we're dating, I don't have to leave after the meal.

In fact, tonight will be the first evening I don't go home. I'm spending the night, holding her in my arms while she sleeps. Brody knows. She told me all about her conversation with him Monday evening, and while I wanted nothing more than to stay last night, we decided Wednesday would be best. She's not on the schedule tomorrow, which means she doesn't have to get up at four to open the diner.

As we progress through dinner, I can tell there's something on her mind. She's smiling and listening to the conversation around her, but there's a hint of concern in her eyes. A touch of worry mixed with contemplation. Something is bothering her, and I intend to find out what. I just have to go about it very carefully so I don't freak her out. Ellie has always worn her heart on her sleeve. In fact, it's one of the things I love most about her. She's passionate and emotional, and when she feels things, she feels them deeply.

Brody hops up and immediately starts clearing off the dinner table. I reach for Ellie's hand and slide my fingers around hers while we watch him work. Usually, Ellie will tell him to shower and start his homework, but the teenager wasn't having it tonight. He insisted on cleaning up the dinner mess, and when he started to fill the sink to wash, I got up to help him dry and put away.

Turns out, we make a great team—on and off the field.

"All right, I'm going to shower and get to work on my homework," he says, grabbing his sports bag from the spot near the door and throwing it over his shoulder. He pauses and stares down at my own bag. I know he saw me bring it up, but he has yet to say anything about it. When we arrived and were walking toward the steps, I wondered if I should say something, but opted to just let it ride. Now, his eye is on it, so we'll see what transpires.

Brody doesn't say a word, just heads for the walkway separating the kitchen from the living room. Before he rounds the corner and heads for his bedroom, he pauses and looks back. "Morgan and I are planning a video chat to work on Civics together. I'll have my noise-cancelling headphones on all night. You know, in case you're worried about that." Then, he winks, and just like that, he's gone, the sound of his laughter echoing down the hall as he retreats.

"Did he just say what I think he said?" she asks, her mouth hanging open in shock.

Snickering, I nod. "Uhh, yeah, El, he did."

"Oh my God, how embarrassing," she mutters, dropping her face into her hands.

I move in her direction and pull her into my arms. "He's seventeen, honey. He knows what happens behind closed doors," I reason, kissing her forehead.

"Yeah, but he's not supposed to draw attention to the fact he knows. He's my baby boy."

Smiling, I reply, "Yes, but he's seventeen. You probably don't want to think about the things he's doing himself."

Ellie's jaw falls, a look of horror etched on every inch of her beautiful face. "No, I don't want to think about that at all."

With my arms wrapped around her shoulders, I hug her against my chest. "I assure you he doesn't want to think about it either. He was teasing us since he saw my bag. He was acknowledging it and letting us know he's okay with me spending the night."

She sighs and presses her face into my chest. "Still embarrassing. These walls are so thin."

"They are, but that's not something we have to stress about. Wanna go watch some TV and snuggle?" I suggest, hoping it'll help get her mind off her son's reference to us being together tonight.

"Sure," she says, taking my offered hand and walking to the couch.

The living room is small, but comfortable as we sit together on the sofa. There's also a recliner chair, coffee table, and a bookshelf with some of their favorite books and photos beneath the TV. Ellie grabs the remote, while I kick my feet up and get cozy, her curled against my side.

We spend the next hour and a half watching a mindless show she enjoys, but it doesn't bother me. In fact, I love it. Listening to the sound of her giggles is the best noise in the world, right after the sound she makes when she's coming.

When she yawns just after nine, I take that as our cue to shut off the television. "Ready for bed, El?"

"Yeah. I don't have to get up as early tomorrow, but I'll still be wide awake by six." That's what she considers sleeping in. I can tell something's still on her mind, and I want to find out what it is. Maybe I can help her with whatever is weighing on her mind.

I flip off the TV and toss the remote onto the couch. "I'll go make sure the doors are locked, while you get ready," I suggest.

While I move to the kitchen and down the stairs, I hear her knock on Brody's door and they have a conversation. After ensuring both the bottom door and the top one are secure, I grab my overnight bag and make my way toward her bedroom.

When I reach the short hallway, Brody's standing in his doorway dressed in a pair of comfortable lounge pants and a T-shirt. "You get everything locked up?" he asks, his eyes dropping to my bag once more.

"I did," I confirm. "You okay with this?" I find myself asking, knowing if he wasn't, I'd apologize to Ellie and take off. No way do I want to cause Brody any uneasiness in his own home, especially with me spending the night with his mom.

"Yeah," he insists rapidly. "Of course, TD. I, uh, think it's cool you're here."

"Okay," I reply. "If at any time you're not cool with it, will you tell me?"

He nods. "Of course, but I'm pretty sure that's not going to happen. She's not the only one who loves having you around."

A small smile hits my lips, and I reach out and give his shoulder a squeeze. "Night, Brode. See you in the morning."

He returns the grin and stands up tall. "You making eggs and bacon for breakfast?"

"If you help me," I reply.

"See you at seven," he states before stepping back and gently shutting his door.

Slipping inside Ellie's bedroom, I find her nervously twisting her hands together in the middle of the room. She's wearing flannel pajama pants and a matching button-down top, and even though she looks warm and cozy, my cock takes notice of the way the material hangs across her bare tits. "Let me get ready, okay?"

She nods quickly, moving to her bed and pulling the warm comforter down to climb beneath. I exit the room once more and go to the bathroom in the hall. I quickly brush my teeth and use the head, knowing I need to get back to her and find out what's eating at her. I pray she's not second-guessing me staying tonight, but if she is, we'll deal with it together.

When I've completed those tasks, I return to her room, closing the door tightly behind me. She's lying on one side of her bed, an empty pillow waiting for me. I toe off my athletic shoes and socks, followed by my long-sleeved T-shirt. I leave my black joggers on, not knowing what to expect from our conversation, even though I'd much rather take those off too, especially since I tend to sleep on the hot side.

Finally, I climb into her bed and draw her close. Her arms reach for me the same way mine reach for her, and she instantly throws her leg over mine. Her toes are like icicles against my foot, but I don't mind. "Tell me what's wrong, El," I encourage quietly.

She exhales loudly but doesn't say a word for nearly a full minute. Eventually, I feel her tense before she looks up at me and asks, "Do you want to have kids?"

A flash of shock crosses her wide eyes, as if she can't believe she just blurted that out.

"Wait, no. You don't have to answer that. I shouldn't have asked."

I pull her down to my chest once more and run my fingers through her hair. "You have every right to ask me any question you want."

"But we haven't been dating that long," she counters, tapping her fingers nervously against my bare skin.

"No, but we've been friends forever, El. And to answer your question, yeah. I've always thought I'd have them at some point, but I guess I've never really found the person I wanted to get serious enough with to have that discussion."

When she tenses against me, I realize that didn't come out the way I intended for it, so I quickly add, "Until now. You're the first person I've ever really considered a future with. If that means kids, then great. If not, I'd be okay. Do you know why?"

"Why?" she asks, her voice crackly and raw.

"Because as long as I have you and Brody, I'll be set." That seems to make her relax a little as she returns to her snuggled position at my side. "What about you? Do you want more kids?"

Exhaling, her warm breath tickles my chest as her fingers dance across my skin. "I never thought about it before. I mean, I was always too busy and tired raising Brody, and it's not like I was dating anyone."

"What happened to make you think about it?" I ask gently.

"Blair. She and Gabe stopped by for lunch earlier and she said something about us having cute babies. It just made me realize I've never really thought about having more kids."

"That's fair. Your son is seventeen and a senior in high school," I reason, even though I suddenly really, *really* feel this overwhelming urge to convince her to have babies with me. Lots of babies.

"He is," she says, turning her head and placing a kiss on my chest. That one little touch makes my cock jump in my pants as excitement rushes through my veins. "I just, well, I wouldn't want to be the reason you don't have kids, if that's what you're looking for in life."

We're moving before I even register what I'm doing. She's beneath me, pinned to the mattress, my body hovering over hers. "El, you're the reason my life feels complete for the first time. Whether kids are in our future or not doesn't matter. Having you by my side is all that does. When our relationship grows more, we'll get a bit more comfortable having those long-term discussions, but just so you know, what I see when I look at my future is you. That's it. You and Brody. So kids or no kids, marriage or no marriage, as long as you're by my side, my life will be complete."

I almost tell her right here and now how much I love her, but I can tell she already feels a bit overwhelmed. Relationships haven't exactly worked out for her in the past, the few she's taken the chance on, and I know I need to ease into the whole love declaration thing. Not because I don't feel it, but because I do.

I love her.

Probably always have.

I damn sure know I always will.

When she's ready to hear those words, I'll scream them from the mountaintops.

Until then, I'll show her in other ways.

Her legs wrap around my waist, and even though we're both wearing sleep pants, I know she can feel my steel cock pressed between us. "I don't want to freak you out, but I think I do want all of that. Someday."

I brush my lips across hers. "Nothing about that freaks me out, El. In fact, it makes me want to fuck you bare in the off chance of putting a baby in your belly," I confess, saying words I should have probably kept to myself.

She shivers, her nails digging into my back. "I want that, TD," she whispers her sweet confession, rocking her hips against my cock. "Someday. When we're ready."

I claim her lips in a bruising kiss, demanding she open for my tongue. She does so willingly, giving as good as she takes. I reach between us, my hand sliding past the waistband of her pants and finding her slick, wet pussy. "You're not wearing panties," I whisper unnecessarily.

"I'm not." Ellie reaches into my own pants and cups my erection in her palm. "You are."

"I wasn't sure what our plan was tonight. I'm fine with just holding you all night. I don't want you to be uncomfortable, knowing Brody is nearby and the walls are thin."

She gives me a saucy grin as she squeezes my cock and gently twists her hand. "You're just going to have to make sure I'm quiet, Thomas."

My mouth slams down on hers, our tongues tangle, and all I can think about is getting her naked and beneath me. Moisture seeps from the head of my cock as I get up and hastily remove her pants. My fingers move rapidly to release the buttons on her shirt, the comfortable flannel falling open and exposing her mouthwatering tits. I lower my mouth, latching on to one perfect nipple, sucking it greedily into my mouth. Ellie whimpers, arching her back and pressing her tits closer. Her fingers grasp at the waistband of my joggers, pushing them over my hips and down my ass. I don't even want to take the time to remove them, honestly. I just want to be buried deep inside her.

"Condom. Drawer," Ellie whispers, her hand blindly reaching toward her bedside table.

I glance to my left, realizing I'm going to have to release her nipple in order to reach the drawer, so I do it quickly, pulling a condom out of the new box stashed inside, ripping open the foil packet, and sliding it over my dick. When I'm covered in the protection, I take my place between her thighs and line myself up at her entrance. I try to keep my composure, but the moment the head of my cock is wrapped in her tight, wet pussy, all bets are off. I thrust forward, filling her completely.

And the bed squeaks loudly as it hits the wall.

We both pause, our eyes wide with shock and humor. "Oh my God," she murmurs, covering her mouth with her hand.

"Yeah, that's not going to work, El," I quip, glancing around the room. "Come here."

Much to my dick's dismay, I pull out and stand up beside the bed, kicking off my joggers and reaching for her hand to help her down. Once both feet are planted on the ground, I reach around to her ass, grip her tightly, and lift. Her legs automatically wrap around me, her pussy once again aligning perfectly where I ache for her.

I give my hips a gentle thrust, my cock once again wrapped in her wet heat. Holding her up, I walk toward the outer wall, away from the door and where her son sleeps. When I press her back against the cool drywall, she gasps and bites back her groan of pleasure.

"You can't hold me up, TD. I'll break you," she whispers.

"I can and I will, El," I state, rocking my hips and filling her completely. Using the wall as leverage, I gently pump in and out of her body and kiss her sweet lips. She holds on tightly, pressing her tits against my chest and silently gasping for air. "I can feel your pussy tightening around me, honey. Are you getting close?"

She whimpers in response, sucking my tongue into her mouth. That one little action causes my hips to buck wildly, thrusting and filling her repeatedly, and racing toward the finish line. Her pussy starts to choke me, rippling around my shaft in sweet pleasure as her release grabs hold. My arms burn as I continue to lift and lower her onto my cock, but there's no way I'm stopping. My arms could fall off my body afterward for all I care. All I can feel right now is her orgasm squeezing my cock, which triggers my own need to come.

"Fuck," I mumble, locking my lips against hers to keep us both from crying out.

I come hard, filling the condom as she starts to come down from the high of her own release. When my legs are jelly and my arms cry for mercy, I walk toward the bed and gently lower her onto the bedding. "I'll get dressed and go grab a washcloth in a minute," I tell her, climbing onto the bed and needing a minute to catch my breath.

"No way," she whispers, curling into my side and reaching for the blankets. "I want you to stay right here, in bed with me."

No place I'd rather be.

Knowing I'll need to get up soon and dispose of the condom, I slip my arm beneath her neck and draw her close. She fits so damn perfectly against me, curling into my side as if she were a piece of me. I sigh in contentment as she starts to relax, my body wanting nothing more than to fall into a deep sleep, but I hold on to consciousness. Must. Get. Rid. Of. Condom.

Just when I think she has drifted off to sleep, I turn, ready to slip out of bed. She reaches for me, her delicate fingers grasping at my arm. "Don't go."

"I need to take care of the condom," I insist, rolling her to the side and kissing her forehead.

"'Kay. But come right back," she murmurs, her eyes closed as she burrows into the warm bedding.

I don't know how long I stand beside her bed and watch her sleep, but it's quite a while. Even after I dispose of the used protection and slip back beneath the covers, sleep doesn't find me. I lie here, memorizing the way she sleeps, the sounds she makes, and the way she makes me feel.

Contentment and love don't even come close to what I feel for this woman.

She's rooted deep into my soul, and I hope she never leaves.

I want her there—right beside me—forever.

CHAPTER Twenty Three

Ellie

I can't believe we're here.

Senior night.

It's Brody's last regular season home game, and it's hitting me hard. He's played football since freshman year, plus the summer flag football program ran through the park district, and it's difficult to comprehend it's coming to an end.

Well, not completely. The Panthers earned a post-season playoff spot and will find out Sunday evening when and where they play next. Until that time, we will focus on tonight's game against the Cooper Vikings.

I'm bundled up to the point of discomfort, but the temperatures are hovering around the upper forties right now and will continue to drop as the night progresses. My layers are wearing layers, and I'm wrapped in a thick blanket as the stands start to fill. The fans are all sporting their versions of warmth as we prepare to sit and cheer on our team for the next few hours.

My eyes scan the field and lock on Brody. He's wearing cold weather gear under his uniform but says he doesn't get that cold on the field. Between the running and adrenaline, he claims the temperature doesn't bother him until after the game.

"Hey," Hallie says, sliding onto the bleachers beside me. "My nipples are so hard I fear I might have some sort of permanent damage from the cold."

A throat clears right behind her, and I giggle when I see Logan standing there, having heard her comment about her nipples. "I could help warm them up for you," he offers, having a seat directly behind where she sits.

"I'd rather cut them off," she chirps back, wrapping a blanket around her entire body. "Aren't you cold?" she asks, glancing back.

"Nope. This is perfect football weather," he replies. Logan's wearing a pair of jeans, his work boots, and a brown winter Carhartt jacket with the lumberyard logo across the breast.

"Nothing about this is perfect. Football should be June through August," she states through chattering teeth, curling the blanket around her neck.

"Brody appreciates you coming to support him," I add.

My friend looks my way with a soft smile on her face. "I wouldn't miss this night for him. What did you bring?" she asks, glancing down at the bag between my legs.

"Ava made it for me," I tell her, referring to another friend, who is one of the craftiest ladies I know.

"Oh my goodness, that's so cool," she says when I pull the ball from the bag. She made me a treat bouquet with all of Brody's favorites sticking out of the top of a football used as a vase.

"She did such a great job, and she refused to take any additional money for her time." I bought all the goodies and Ava put it together for me, doing a much better job than I could have done.

"Of course she did," Hallie replies as Gabe and Blair head our way.

First thing I notice is the drink carrier in Blair's hands, steam billowing from the lids. "We come bringing warmth," she announces as Gabe places a blanket down on the bleachers. "I brought one for each of you," she adds, handing over a gourmet hot chocolate from Molly's.

"Does mine have bourbon in it?" Logan quips, taking one of the offered insulated cups.

"No, but it does have salted caramel in it," she replies as she hands the last cup to Gabe. She sits down beside him and he wraps the blanket around her legs and back, cocooning them together.

It makes me miss TD, wishing we were sharing body heat beneath my blanket, and my eyes instantly seek him out. He's standing on the sidelines, talking to the quarterback before the coin toss. As if feeling my eyes on him, he looks my way and gives me a smile that suddenly warms my entire body from head to toe. There's a promise written on those lips, one that lets me know he'll be using them later tonight when we're alone.

"He is so smitten," Hallie sings beside me.

"No one says smitten anymore," Logan chastises.

She rolls her eyes but doesn't come back with an equally pointed jab. "You two are the cutest ever."

"I agree," Blair says, still curled up into Gabe's side.

We all turn our attention to the field, as TD, Brody, and the other captains walk toward the center for the coin toss. I try to take in every moment, knowing this is his big night and possibly his final home game of his high school football career. The stands are packed as the Panthers prepare to receive the ball to start the game.

By the time we're nearing the end of the first half, my voice is hoarse from cheering and I'm a little numb from the cold, but our team is up fourteen to seven. "Would the parents of the senior football players, cheerleaders, and band members please make your way to the west end of the bleachers for senior night recognitions."

I reach for the bag at my feet. "That's my cue," I say, standing up and leaving my blanket on my seat. The chill seeps through my clothes and causes goosebumps. "Do you think it would be bad if I took my blanket?" I ask with a chuckle, not entirely kidding.

"No one would say a word," Hallie assures me, and even though I consider taking it, I opt to leave it behind.

I make my way down the bleachers and toward the west end, along with other parents of Brody's classmates. I look around, finding moms and dads all huddled together, and a wave of sadness washes over me. It's not the first time I've wished Brody's father was part of his life, and I'm certain it won't be the last. Nights like tonight are the times I resent his absence. Not because I wasn't capable of taking care of him by myself all these years, but simply because Brody was cheated. He should have both parents standing with him, supporting him during his final home game. There should be two people telling him how proud we are of him, not just me.

The buzzer sounds, startling me and signaling the end of the half. Mr. Wilken, the athletic director, gets parents lined up in alphabetical order by sport as we await our kids to join us for the introductions. When they start heading our way, I spot Brody immediately and smile the moment he grins at me.

As he takes off his helmet and joins me at my side, he pulls me into a hug. "Did you see my catch to start the second quarter? It was a little overthrown, but I was able to reel it in."

"It was an amazing catch," I confirm proudly.

"What's that?" he asks, pointing down at the goodies in my hand.

"It's a treat bouquet," I tell him as the line starts to move forward. The cheerleaders are introduced first, followed by the members of the marching band.

"It's all of my favorites," he realizes before hugging me a second time. I have to blink rapidly to keep the tears at bay. My emotions are already choking me, but now that he keeps showing his appreciation with hugs, he has me on the verge of a total meltdown.

"Brody Daniels, son of Ellie Daniels," the announcer calls, and even though I hear the words, my legs don't seem to want to cooperate. My heart is so happy and proud, yet I also know this chapter of life is coming to an end.

"It's all right, Mom. I've got you," he whispers, offering me his arm and gently leading me out onto the track. Suddenly, the support I'm offering my child on his possible final home game does a one-eighty, and he's the one assisting me. I suppose that says a lot about our relationship. We've held each other up and kept each other moving for the last seventeen years, whether he realizes it or not.

The crowd cheers for us as we walk along the track, following the line of others being honored tonight. I spot the football team standing along the track, holding out their hands and high-fiving their fellow classmates and teammates as they pass. Brody accepts a plaque from the principal before holding out his hand and being greeted by the rest of the team.

When we near the end of the line, I spot a familiar face standing amongst the coaches. His smile is wide and as equally proud as the one I wear on my face. As we approach, Brody releases my arm and throws his around TD's neck. TD returns the gesture, hugging my boy tightly to his chest and tapping his pads a few times before releasing him. That's when Brody reaches for TD's arm and pulls him out of the line, right beside him.

Realization hits me square in the heart, and I can see the moment it hits TD too.

Brody links his arm back through mine and keeps the other one on TD before taking a step forward. TD looks my way, confusion and worry etched on his gorgeous face. He understands what my son is doing and seeks my approval. All I can do is nod and give him a watery smile. The tears I've been fighting start to fall. My son doesn't just have me, but my friends too. They've been part of his life since birth, and he's including the man who has been the biggest father figure in his life on this important night.

I couldn't be prouder of the man he is becoming.

Taking a step forward, I turn my attention back to the bleachers. I spot Hallie standing up, taking photos, so I pause for a moment and point her out to Brody. He turns to face the stands and pulls me to his side. TD goes to take a step back, but my son stops him in his tracks. "I want you beside me too, TD. Family isn't always blood. Family is the people who step up and refuse to walk away."

I don't care that I'll look horrible, a crying mess in all the photos, I'll cherish this moment—this night—for the rest of my life.

TD's eyes turn glassy as he places his right hand on Brody's shoulder and steps up beside him. We take a quick photo together, and even though we're ushered along, his words are forever etched in my heart, and as I glance over at TD, I can tell they're written on his too.

We pause long enough to take a second photo for the school photographer before moving to where the rest of the honorees are lined up. Once everyone has been announced, Brody turns to TD. "Shall we get to the locker room and get the team ready for the second half?"

TD just smiles. "Yes, Brode, we shall."

Brody turns to me, that boyish grin I've always loved on his face. "Thanks, Mom, for the gift. I love you," he tells me before wrapping his sweaty arms around me and hugging me tightly.

"Love you more than you'll ever know, Brody," I whisper, my voice hoarse and dry.

He pulls back and meets my gaze. "I do know, Mom." Then he turns to TD and holds out his hand. "Thanks for walking with us. It felt right to have you there. You've been by my side since I was little."

TD grins as he reaches for my son's hand, but I can see the battle in his eyes to keep his emotions in check. "Honored to be included, and just so you know, there's no place I'd rather be."

Cue. The. Waterworks.

My heart is so full, it might actually burst in my chest. Watching their exchange just cements my feelings for this man. I'm completely smitten. So in love with him, I can't understand why I didn't risk it all years ago. All these years we could have been more than just friends. A wave of sadness washes over me as I think about that point, but I refuse to let it get me down.

Tonight is about Brody, and there's no time to rehash my mistakes and fears.

"See you after the game, Mom," Brody says, taking a step back to head to the locker room.

"Me too," TD adds, leaning in and kissing me on the lips.

Right there.

In the middle of the track.

In front of everyone.

My cheeks are suddenly really warm as he pulls back and grins. With a wink, he jogs off with my son so they can prepare for the second half of the football game. I want to cover my face, hide my embarrassment at the very public display of affection. However, as I turn around and notice all the other parents slowly making their way off the track, barely anyone is paying any attention to me. And if they are, so what? TD and I are in a relationship, and do you know what? I'm proud of it.

Smiling, I follow behind the others as we make our way toward the gate. As I pass the end of the bleachers, I glance up and almost gasp. Sitting in the crowd is Helena and Allen Davidson.

Brody's biological grandparents on his father's side.

My heart starts to pound in my chest as I force myself to take one step forward, followed by another. I pass the entrance to the bleachers, opting to walk all the way around to the other side so I don't have to pass where they sit.

I've seen the Davidsons over the years, but never at something pertaining to Brody. They rarely come into the diner, and when they do, they ask to be seated in someone else's section if I'm working. I've run into them on occasion at the grocery store or other public places, but they quickly turn away. I haven't spoken a single word to either of them in eighteen years. Not since they called me names and refused to even consider their precious son, Rusty, was the father of my unborn baby. He, of course, proclaimed it wasn't true, and they believed him.

My heart still aches over the betrayal.

Not because I still have feelings for him, but for other reasons all surrounding my son. We were fairly new in our relationship, just barely seventeen and eighteen ourselves. We were at the beginning of our senior year of high school, and I thought what we had was love. I gave him my virginity.

He gave me a child.

Then, when I realized later I was pregnant, he broke up with me. He told me it wasn't his, told everyone who'd listen I'd been cheating on him the entire time we dated. Not only was I dealing with my own parents refusing to accept the fact their unwed teenage daughter was with child, but the father of said baby proclaimed me a whore and refused to step up.

That's when Fran stepped in. She took a scared, crying young woman during her senior year of high school and gave her a place to stay in the old apartment above the diner. She gave me a job and stability. When my own parents shunned me for even considering keeping a baby out of wedlock, the sweet older woman stepped forward and helped me.

Brody's completely right.

Blood doesn't make someone family.

I make my way back to the bleachers where my friends are. The night doesn't seem nearly as cold as it did before. Maybe that's because of the extra layer of worry I'm suddenly carrying around me. I don't understand why Helena and Allen are here. They made their feelings about me and my son very clear, even after I tried to be the bigger person and invite them to Brody's first birthday. They sent me a letter telling me they'd get a lawyer involved if I contacted them again.

So I didn't.

Ever.

Nor did I reach out to their son. I tried throughout my pregnancy to offer for him to be involved, but he made his stance perfectly clear. He wanted no part of being a father and was willing to lie to everyone so he didn't have to man up and help take care of his responsibilities. After graduation, me walking that stage looking like I was about to pop, Rusty went off to a fancy college on a golf scholarship. If he's ever come back, I wasn't aware. We never ran into each other, nor have any of my friends so much as breathed his name. I have no idea where he wound up in this world, and I'm okay with that.

"What's wrong?" Hallie asks as soon as I return to my seat.

"Nothing. Where'd everyone go?" I ask, noting Logan, Blair, and Gage are gone.

"Restroom breaks and snacks," she informs me.

I nibble on my bottom lip, watching the marching band perform a snippet of their show during the remainder of halftime.

"I got some great pics," Hallie states, pulling up her phone and showing me the pictures she took. I have to agree. She captured some beautiful photos. Brody and me walking onto the track, smiling at each other, one of him slapping hands with teammates as we walked by, and one of him hugging TD. Even though the photo is from a distance, you can't miss the look of love written all over my face.

"You did. Thank you," I tell my friend.

She pulls me into a hug. "You're welcome." Sliding back, she meets my gaze. "What's wrong? Is it Brody and the emotions of senior night?"

I take a deep breath, knowing I can't lie to her. "I saw Helena and Allen in the stands."

Her eyes widen and she looks around. "Seriously?"

"Yeah, when I was walking off the track. They're sitting on the far east side," I tell her.

"Are they here for Brody? I didn't think they'd come to any games before," she says, almost absently.

"They haven't."

"I wonder why they'd be here now."

I shrug in reply, my eyes now focused on the field where both teams are returning and starting to stretch and warm up. My friends return, and even though Blair tries to share her popcorn with me, my stomach is in knots. Throughout the entire rest of the game, I'm unable to relax and just enjoy the moment, simply because my mind is spinning and I keep trying to steal glances toward the opposite end of the bleachers.

Finally, with a final score of thirty-five to seventeen, the game ends with the Panthers on top. I manage to take photos with my phone, including of their team celebration in the middle of the field. The stands start to clear out, so we all slowly make our way down to the ground to wait for Brody. "Do you all have time to hang around for a few minutes? I'd love to get a picture of you all with Brody."

"Of course," Hallie replies.

"We'd be honored," Logan adds, while Gabe and Blair nod.

I pull out my phone, ready to take the photo when the time arrives, and catch movement just off to my left. Standing not too far away from me are Helena and Allen. Helena's gaze catches mine, and the moment she realizes who I am, her eyes narrow into little slits. My heart starts to gallop in my chest as my mind spins every scenario as to why they're here and hanging around near the players' locker room.

I've never told Brody about them. He knows his biological father and family wanted nothing to do with my pregnancy, but I've never told him their name. I'm sure he could have easily found out in a small town like Pine Village, and if he were to ask me for more details, I'd tell him, but this is not how I wanted to do it.

Are they here to meet him?

I know I need to be prepared if that's the case. I'd much prefer to do this somewhere other than the football field, surrounded by the entire town. "Excuse me a second," I say quietly to my friends before walking straight to where Rusty's parents stand. They're with Fiona and Harry Zimmerman, friends of theirs for decades, as well as another couple I've seen around town for years, but don't personally know.

"Helena," I say politely when I approach.

Her head whips around as her wide, shocked eyes stare back at me. "What do you want?"

"A word?" I ask, again as civilly as I possibly can.

"I have nothing to say to you," she snaps, lifting her jaw and looking away.

"You don't?" I ask, confused once more. Why are they here? "I thought with it being senior night and you here—"

"You think we're here for you and your *kid*?" she demands loudly. "You tried ruining our son's life!" she yells, most likely catching the attention of anyone nearby.

"I'm sorry, I didn't—"

"It's Fiona and Harry's granddaughter's senior night, so we're here to watch her play in the band." Allen just stands to the side, barely paying me any attention.

My heart seems to crack and bleed right here on the gravel walkway. They're not here for Brody. As much as that gives me relief, it makes me incredibly sad at the same time. "Oh."

Helena starts to laugh, but it lacks any humor. "You're still playing this farse, I see. Telling the world my son is the father of your child, even after all these years. Well, you've always been nothing but a liar. A calculated storyteller, trying to ruin my boy's life by claiming he's the father. Once a liar, always a liar I see."

My cheeks burn with mortification, and all I want to do is turn and run. Run away from the people who continue to spit venom at me, when my only crime was believing the guy I was dating when he said we didn't need to use a condom.

"Don't you call my mom a liar."

My stomach drops into my shoes as I spin around and stare wide-eyed at my son. My very angry son.

"Excuse me, young man, but you don't talk to adults like that," Helena demands, hands on her hips and a very unpleased look on her face.

"Maybe you should take your own advice then," he argues, stepping up beside me. "I know this woman better than anyone else on the planet, and I assure you, she's not a liar. The fact you'd think that says more about you than it does her, actually."

Helena's cheeks darken the same way her son's would back in school when he'd get upset. "Listen here, you—" she starts, but is cut off.

"No, you listen to me. You have no right to disrespect my mom like this. I don't care what you think you know about her. You're wrong, and I won't stand here and let you call her names."

Tears burn my eyes as I realize we've drawn a crowd. If it were possible to disappear forever, I'd choose to do it right now. I hate the scrutiny, the judgment in their eyes as they watch the exchange. On top of that, we're at the school, surrounded by families and my son's teammates, and there's no escaping this scene. I wouldn't be surprised if cell phones are pointed at us, documenting the entire ordeal.

I reach out and place my hand on Brody's arm. "Let's go, Brody," I say softly, begging with my eyes to let it go.

That's when I feel another presence step up beside me, a protective hand on my lower back. As if this moment can't get any worse, now TD is here to witness my mortification.

"No, hold up, Brode. I have something to say too."

CHAPTER *twenty four*

TD

The moment I saw Ellie standing over by Helena Davidson, the hairs on the back of my neck stood on end.

The moment I heard Brody defending his mom, I saw red.

Not at him, of course, but at the audacity of Rusty fucking Davidson and his parents.

The woman staring back at me now is shooting daggers from her cold eyes, and if I were any lesser of a man, I might back down a little bit. I can see why her husband is standing back, not getting involved in the exchange. He's been well trained over decades of marriage to stay back and remain silent, letting Helena wear the pants in the relationship. But that's not who I am, so I won't let this woman walk away without at least hearing what I have to say first.

Ellie turns, refusing to meet my gaze. There are tears swimming in her eyes, which pisses me off even more. At times, she's been through hell over the last eighteen years, no thanks to this woman and her son. They denied her any help where Brody was concerned and called her a liar for the entire town to hear. "Let's just go, please," she whispers, her beautiful green eyes cast down in embarrassment.

Oh, fuck no.

"In a minute, El," I reply gently, keeping my hand on her hip when she tries to pull away. She's looking to run, this I'm certain. Ellie's always been the people pleaser and having all this attention directed her way—especially for confrontation—is the last thing she wants. In fact, she's searching for her escape route right now.

With my hand on her side, I give my attention back to Helena. "I was hoping you could pass along a message to Rusty for me, Mrs. Davidson."

That seems to stump her for a moment. "Excuse me?"

I fling my arm around Ellie's shoulder and draw her close. I feel how tense she is, and I know I'll help release that stress later, but for now, I have a statement to make. A very public one. "If you could tell him thank you for me, I'd appreciate it."

"Thank you?" she asks, her eyes narrowing into little slits once more.

"Absolutely. Since he was stupid enough to walk away from Ellie all those years ago when she needed him the most and tell vicious lies about her, I watched her bring this remarkable boy into the world and raise him in a loving, supportive home. I got to see every birthday and teach him to ride his bike and throw a football. Because your son was so fucking stupid, I found exactly what I was looking for in both Ellie and Brody." I turn and hold Ellie's gaze as I add, "I fell in love with them, and someday, if I'm lucky, I'll get to spend the rest of my life showing them just how amazing they are and how much they mean to me."

I hear Ellie gasp, watch as her mouth falls open.

"My son is a dentist in Milwaukee. He's married to a former model and has two beautiful children, created out of love," the woman retorts. "She's just a waitress," she adds with a smirk.

"Yeah, she is, and a damn good one," I reply proudly, smiling down at her as I catch her gaze once more. Turning back to Helena, I continue, "So, please tell him thank you for me. His loss was my gain, and I'm not about to let something this precious ever slip through my fingers."

Now, I turn to Brody, holding his smiling green eyes. "I know I'm not the man who helped create you, but you're *my* son, Brode. You've always been my boy. If you need a father in your life, let it be me. I promise I'll always be there, ready to support and love you."

Brody grins that crooked smile. "You already are that man. That's why I never sought out the Davidsons when I learned who my father really is."

A strangled noise comes from Ellie's throat again. "You knew?" she asks, glancing his way.

Brody shrugs and gives her a sheepish look. "Yeah, well, it's a small town."

"Oh my God," Ellie whispers, closing her eyes as her cheeks turn a delectable shade of pink.

"I'm not going to stand here and listen to this any longer. Come on, Allen," Helena demands, turning her back to us and starting to walk away, her husband tucking tail and following behind her without saying a word. Her friends seem shocked and just stand there, not knowing what to do or say.

I hold up my hand and wave. "Have fun spending the rest of your life knowing deep down, your asshole of a child lied to you and refused to take care of his responsibilities. Oh, and by the way, your precious son has been having an affair with his dental hygienist for years and has at least two other kids he's secretly supporting. Enjoy your night!"

They both seem to pause, but only for a brief moment. They continue walking away, Helena yelling at Allen the second they're out of earshot, and I'm not sure if I'm more relieved or ashamed of them. They are truly despicable people who have no idea what they're missing.

The rest of the audience who gathered around slowly starts to dissipate, but my attention is solely on Ellie. "Hi," I whisper, reaching down and linking our fingers together. Those green eyes I absolutely love fill with tears once more. "Don't cry, El. I can't handle tears," I add, reaching up with my thumb and wiping away droplets.

She sniffles, her nose pink and cold from the temperature. "I can't help it," she mutters, making me chuckle.

"I know. Your soft, kind heart is one of the things I love most about you."

Her eyes widen, almost comically, as she looks up at me. My fingers slip beneath her stocking cap and into her hair, those soft strands like silk against my skin. "You said it again."

The corners of my mouth curl upward and the urge to kiss her silly is so strong, I have to fight not to do it, but first, there's something I need to make sure she knows. "I did, because it's true. I love you," I declare, chuckling when realization hits me upside the head like a two-by-four. "I'm pretty sure I've always loved you, since we were dumb kids in high school."

Ellie closes her eyes for a moment, the faintest grin on her lips. When she reopens them, there's a fierceness revving to life, a fire dancing in those green orbs that makes my heart want to burst from my chest. Her cheeks are red, and not just from the cold. "I love you too, Thomas Dexter."

A small growl erupts from my throat at her use of my given name as I draw her closer to my chest. The sound of her laughter is the balm I didn't even realize my soul needed. "You'll pay for that later."

She giggles the sweetest sound. "I hope so."

After holding her to my chest for a minute, I pull back. "I want to be your everything, sweetheart. I want to be the person you talk to about life, the one you share all your hopes and dreams with, the one you depend on to help you through the good days and the bad. I want it all. With you."

She blushes once more. "You are pretty dependable."

"Fuck yes I am, El. If you ever need me, I'm right here. Always."

"I know you are. When I look back at my past, I realize you've always been there. For me, and for Brody. I just wish we wouldn't have wasted so many years when we could have been together."

I shrug and angle my mouth toward hers. "We can't change that, but we can make up for it now."

When my lips brush hers, there's an electrical charge that races through my veins. Her mouth opens for mine, granting my tongue entrance to savor and taste.

A throat clears loudly behind me. "Uhh, guys? I can no longer feel my toes or fingers. Mind making out later?"

Ellie peels her lips from mine and turns to the left. I do the same, finding our friends standing there, smiling. "Well, this is awkward," she mumbles, turning and burying her face in my sweatshirt.

"Nah, they knew this was coming, and better be prepared to see it more often, because I plan to kiss you all the time, El," I tell her.

"Like, all the time, all the time? Because if so, I might reconsider my stance on you dating my mom, Coach," Brody chimes in, making everyone laugh.

Ellie heads his way and pulls him into a hug. "I'm sorry to ruin your senior night."

"You didn't," he quickly reassures her, glancing around him. "I have all the people I love here with me. Everything else is just noise."

She squeezes him hard. "I know. I just wish that confrontation wouldn't have happened here. Or at all," she mutters.

"It needed to happen," Blair adds. "They needed to know they've been wrong about you this whole time."

Ellie turns my way. "By the way, how did you know all that stuff about Rusty? About the affair and kids and stuff."

I run my hands over the back of my neck, not wanting to out my friend. Fortunately, he takes care of that for me, sharing how I knew those details about Rusty.

"He told me," Logan announces. "Last summer, when I was in Milwaukee for a convention, I ran into him at a restaurant. He invited me to have drinks with him, and even though I didn't want to, I couldn't exactly lie to his face to get out of it."

"Yes, you could!" Hallie demands. "You kick him in the balls and walk away."

Logan rolls his eyes. "Anyway, after only one beer, he started telling me all about his fancy life, bragging about everything, including the fact he's been banging his dental hygienist for years and they share two small kids."

"What a loser." I turn and realize this statement came from Brody. "Seriously, Mom. I'm glad he's not part of my life."

"If he wanted to be, I would have allowed it," she quickly adds. "I tried to include him. Him and his parents, but they refused."

"I know," he replies with a shrug. "It doesn't matter, really." He looks my way. "I got the better part of the deal anyway."

My heart.

Fuck, I love that boy.

"Let's take some pictures before we all freeze to death," Gabe announces, making everyone laugh.

We spend the next fifteen minutes taking dozens of photos with all the people close to Brody. I take a few on my own phone of just Ellie and her boy, and happily save the ones of the three of us together Hallie took and sent. The close-up of us was quickly set as my phone background image.

"Mom, is it okay if I take Morgan by Miss Molly's Ice Cream to see the gang?"

"Of course," Ellie replies. "Have fun and be safe."

Brody walks over and gives her a quick hug. "I'll be home by curfew. Love you. Thank you, all, for coming tonight. Means the world to me that you were here."

Gabe, Blair, Logan, and Hallie all say their goodbyes to him and head for their vehicles. Before Brody and Morgan take off, he walks over to where I stand. I prepare for a handshake or something, but not the big hug I'm given. I return the gesture, gently squeezing back and giving a firm pat on his upper back.

"I know we're guys and all, but I hope it's okay I hug you every now and again," Brody says quietly.

"It's more than all right, Brode. You can hug me whenever you want."

He nods and releases me. "Cool." He shifts on his feet, something I know he does when he gets a little nervous. "Also, I wanted you to know I love you too. I know I haven't said it before, but I've always secretly wished you would have been my dad. Even if that never officially happens, I've looked up to you as if you were since I was a little boy."

My throat closes. Seriously, how the fuck am I supposed to breathe after that?

"I've always considered you my boy, Brody, and always will."

He nods and squeezes my shoulder before turning his attention to Morgan. I watch as he takes her hand and leads her toward the car, a wave of pride washing over me so strong I'm not sure I'll ever feel anything but that where he's concerned. "I know I've said this before, but you've raised an amazing kid, El."

She slips her arm around mine and cuddles into my side. "*We've* done an amazing job. I was never alone, even if, at times, it felt like I was."

I wrap my own arms around her. "Never alone moving forward either."

She sighs and rests her head against my chest. "We should probably head out too. I think we're the last ones here."

"It's okay. I know the coach," I quip, earning a chuckle. "But you are correct. We should head back to your place. We can do a little snuggling while we wait for the boy to get home. If I'm lucky, I'll slide into second base again tonight," I add, wiggling my eyebrows suggestively.

"I was hoping for a home run, myself," she replies, taking my hand. I grab her bag along the way, as well as her blanket, and lead her toward my truck.

She slides into the passenger seat of my truck, and I quickly turn over the engine and fire up the heater. As I'm pulling out of the lot, I turn toward her apartment, wondering how quickly I can talk her and Brody into moving in with me. Now probably isn't the right time, but I'm hoping I can convince her sooner rather than later. I'd much rather fall asleep beside her every night and wake to her beautiful face in the morning. I guess, until that day comes, I'll just plan to stay at her place as much as she'll let me.

When we reach her apartment, I follow behind, carrying her bag and blanket, as we head up the stairs. The moment we're inside the warm space, she slips off her winter coat and hangs it on the back of a kitchen chair. I'm wearing a crewneck sweatshirt with a thermal long-sleeved shirt beneath it, and thanks to the adrenaline of the game, I was plenty warm. Now, I'm a little heated in other ways. All I want to do is strip off that thick sweater, her jeans—with probably leggings beneath them for extra warmth—and the four pairs of thermal socks she's got on in those boots.

"You know, we don't have much time before Brody gets home. Second base might be all we achieve tonight," I tell her, pulling her into my arms.

"Are you kidding? We've got all night, Thomas Dexter. I'm not letting you leave anytime soon," she coos, sliding her fingers up my arms and wrapping them around my neck. I try to ignore the fact they're like little ice cubes against my skin.

"No? You asking me to stay the night with you, Ellie Daniels?" My cock is already hard and ready to go.

"I am. We'll have to be quiet, though."

I walk her backward until her ass is pressed against the wall. "You're in luck. Quiet is one of my specialties. We just have to stay out of your squeaky bed."

She giggles. "I'd say wall sex is one of your specialties, and I might like another demonstration."

"Done." I plaster my mouth to hers, deepening the kiss immediately and slowly moving her toward the bedroom. "First one'll be quick. Second one, I'm taking my time and savoring you all night, love."

She whimpers, rolling her head to the side and giving me access to her neck. "That sounds good to me."

The moment we cross the threshold into her bedroom and lock the door behind us, I release my belt buckle and grab for the button and zipper on my fly. We both undress in record time and I have a condom in place within seconds, I lift her into my arms and press her back against the wall. Slowly, I lower her onto my cock, trying not to explode right here and now at the feel of her pussy gripping me. Only when she's completely seated do I exhale the breath I was holding. Ellie runs her hands through my hair and holds on tight.

"All night, El. All fucking night."

Then, I start to move, determined to show the woman I love just how much she means to me.

Not just for the night, but for the rest of our lives.

That's literally my main goal from this point forward.

Something she'll be able to count on from here on out.

I'm dependable like that.

EPILOGUE
epilogue

TD

7 months later

"I've been waiting months for this," Brody says from his lawn chair across the fire, as he finishes off his third hot dog of the night.

"Me too," I confirm, sitting back in my chair and just watching him. "I'm just glad the snow finally melted and the weather is starting to warm up."

It's early May, and even though the cold winter weather has been lingering, Brody and I decided to get our first camping trip under our belt for the season. For me, it's not just about hanging out and camping with him though. I have an important question I want to ask him where his mom is concerned, and I felt this was the best way to go about it.

Brody and Ellie have been living with me for the last two months. I asked her on Valentine's Day to move in with me and after discussing it over with her son, they agreed. So, the first weekend in March, I officially moved the two people I love most in the world into my house, and it's been the best two months ever. Just as expected, falling asleep with her in my arms every night and waking in the morning the same way is a dream come true.

Now, I just have to take a step toward the rest of that dream.

When he's finished his food, I quickly clean up what little mess we made and take the condiments into the cabin. We agreed to camp tonight but decided to forego the tent and wait for warmer weather to enjoy that aspect of it. Tonight we'll be sleeping inside, on regular mattresses, in a temperature-controlled environment.

After making sure everything is put away, I grab the small box from my bag and head back outside to the fire. I take my seat once more, finding it harder to get comfortable. My nerves have me worked up. Honestly, you'd think I was about to ask his mom to marry me, not have a simple conversation with him about the prospect.

Just as I go to open my mouth to start the conversation, he asks, "Can I say something?"

"Sure," I reply, my heart thundering like a snare drum in my chest.

"I think you should marry my mom."

A flashback to the time last fall he said almost the exact same thing, except referring to me dating her, dances through my mind. I can't help but smile. "Yeah?"

He nods. "Hear me out," he starts, adjusting himself in his seat to face me head-on. "You know how amazing she is, right? I mean, you wouldn't have asked her to move in if you didn't, and she's happier than I've ever seen her when she's with you. Like crazy-happy, TD. It's sometimes sickening the way you two are always kissing and stuff, but that's beside the point. The point is," he says, taking a deep breath and holding my gaze. "I'd love for you to marry her."

I grin back at the most remarkable young man to set foot in my life. "I think you're right."

He seems a little shocked for a moment, as if he was prepared to spend more time convincing me. "You do?"

"Yep. Do you remember when I told you I regretted not asking that girl out back in high school? Well, I refuse to have any more regrets where that woman is concerned. I want to marry her, and that's actually what I wanted to talk to you about tonight. I have a ring, and I'd love your blessing to give it to your mom."

Brody jumps up. "Yes, you've got it." He walks around the fire and throws his arms around me just as I stand up to meet him.

I hug him back, something we tend to do often. I don't care that we're both guys. If my boy wants a hug, he gets a hug, and it doesn't matter what age he is.

When he releases his hold, I pull the small box out of my pocket and hand it to him. He carefully opens the lid and smiles down at the small solitaire diamond nestled in the blue velvet. "Cool."

"I went with something classic and timeless, like her."

"She's gonna love it," Brody assures me.

"Yeah, okay. Good." I take the ring box back and slip it into my pocket once more.

"When are you going to give it to her?"

I shrug, reclaiming my chair around the fire. "I'm not sure yet."

Suddenly, as if an idea hits him, he reaches for his phone. "Tonight," he says, firing off a series of text messages that causes his phone to chime repeatedly.

"Tonight?" I ask, suddenly feeling a little overwhelmed and panicky.

He looks over at me. "Yeah. Why not?"

"I..." but no words come out. He's right. Why not tonight?

"She's on her way," he says with a wide smile as he drops his phone onto his lap.

I release another long breath, my mind spinning. "I wasn't planning on this tonight. It's our guys' camping night."

"I know, but I think this'll be better. Besides, you can't tell me you haven't missed her the whole time we've been here. Plus, we'll get another night soon when the weather actually lets us camp outside in the tent again. That'll be guys only."

Smiling, I nod in agreement.

"So, how are you going to ask her?"

"I don't know yet," I reply with a laugh. I've thought of the moment I'd ask Ellie to be my wife but have never given one thought as to what I'd actually say.

"Do you trust me?" Brody asks with a grin.

"Of course."

He reaches out his hand. "Then let me have the ring and follow my lead."

Reaching into my pocket, I pull out the box again, and walk it over to where he sits. I don't know what he has planned, but I know I can trust him with this important moment. He's as much a part of this as Ellie or me, and it feels fitting to have him take the lead on my proposal.

It's the three of us against the world.

We're a team.

Now and forever.

Ellie

I pull down the dirt path that leads to Logan's cabin. I can't help but wonder why their sudden change of plans with the insistence I come out and stay with them. I was just starting to fill the bathtub and lighting a few scented candles. I had my book all ready to go. But then the text came from Brody, insisting I pack a bag and come out and camp with them. I was going to tell him no, to enjoy the one-on-one time with TD, but he begged for me to come and make it a party of three.

Plus, they're staying in the cabin, which means I won't have to sleep in a tent surrounded by bugs.

When I reach the clearing, I find both TD and Brody around a small fire. I park my car and climb out, both men rushing toward me. Brody grabs my bag, while TD plasters his lips to mine, kissing me breathlessly the way he always seems to do.

"Good evening," he whispers, his warm breath tickling my cool face.

"Hi."

"Come on, Mom. Let's go inside where it's warm."

I shake my head and look up at TD. "I was a little surprised to be getting an invite to boys' camping night."

He shrugs, not giving anything away. "Maybe he missed you?"

I snort a laugh. "Right. An almost eighteen-year-old boy misses his mommy the first camping trip of the season? I doubt it," I state. Brody's birthday is next month. He'll be continuing to work through the summer at the grocery store before starting college in the fall for his criminal justice degree.

TD shrugs again as we reach the front door to the cabin. He holds it open, allowing me to step inside first. The fireplace is roaring, the warmth of the fire wrapping around me and soothing my cool skin. There are also flameless candles sitting on the mantle, as well as the end tables. I remember Logan replacing them not too long ago, making sure he keeps those and lanterns stocked up in case of power outages.

"Can you have a seat? There's something I wanted to talk to you about," Brody says after returning from the hallway, most likely from placing my overnight bag in the master bedroom.

I take a seat on the couch, perching at the edge of the cushion. There's a fresh wave of nervousness sweeping through me, as I wait to find out what's going on.

TD sits beside me and entwines our fingers together. It's both comforting and creates extra insecurities, as it makes me think something bad is about to happen.

"Okay, so I'll get right to the point of why I wanted you to come out here, Mom. I've been doing some thinking lately. I know I'm about to turn eighteen and graduate, and maybe it doesn't really matter much in the grand scheme of things, but I've been thinking about my last name."

My heart? It stops beating in my chest.

"What?" I ask, my mind flashing to Rusty and the fact I didn't put him down on the birth certificate all those years ago. Does he want to change his name to Davidson?

"Breathe, El," TD whispers, lightly stroking the top of my hand with his thumb.

"Don't freak out, Mom."

I nod, but it's hard to *not* freak out right now. Not with my son wanting to talk about changing his last name.

"Anyway, I've been doing a lot of thinking over the last few months. My last name means everything to me. It's a link to you. You've been my rock my entire life, and even though you never wanted me to see it, I know we struggled at times. A lot. But at the end of the day, I was always proud to be Brody Daniels, and I still am.

"But there's another last name I wouldn't mind having now. It's one that means just as much to me as Daniels does and signifies a new beginning."

He walks toward me and hands me a small box.

With shaking hands, I reach up and take it from him. I don't open it because I'm still trying to process what in the world is happening right now.

TD reaches over and takes the box, slowly lifting the lid. Inside is the most beautiful diamond ring I've ever seen. A small gasp spills from my lips as I gaze down at it. It's in that moment, I realize TD had moved. He's kneeling in front of me, taking the ring between his two fingers and placing it at the tip of my finger.

"El, I have been in love with you my entire adult life. You're my best friend, my person. Every day I'm with you is better than the last, and all I want to do is create new memories with you." He glances over to Brody. "I brought this ring with me this weekend so I could ask Brody for your hand in marriage. He told me yes right away. Actually, he told me first that I should marry you," he adds with a chuckle.

"He didn't know I was going to talk about my last name. I wanted you both here when I broached the subject, and let's be honest, this felt like the right time to do it. When you marry TD, you'll become a Dexter. I want to be a Dexter too, because that's my dad's last name."

I lose it, crying tears of joy as two sets of arms wrap around me. They don't say anything, just let me absorb this moment and their words. When I finally feel like I can talk, I pull back a little and wipe away the wetness marring my face. "So, I guess there's only one question left, huh?"

TD laughs and replaces the ring at the edge of my finger. "Ellie Daniels, will you complete my life and become my wife?"

I nod instantly. With a sniffle, I whisper, "Yes."

The ring is placed on my finger, and I'm pulled into the strong, secure arms of the man I love. He kisses me soundly, his hands gliding along my jaw, fingers dancing into my hair. "I love you so much, Ellie."

"I love you too, TD," I murmur against his lips.

"Best day ever," Brody says with a smile over by the fireplace. "I know you guys are gonna want to celebrate and all, but if we can refrain from that until we're back at the house, where my bedroom is on the opposite side of yours, I'd appreciate it."

TD barks out a laugh and takes my hand. He leads me over to where my son stands and pulls him into a hug. "Just so you know, you can have whatever last name you want, but if you decide to choose mine, there's nothing in this world that'd be a bigger honor. You're my son without the name, but calling you Brody Dexter would be at the top of the list, right along with hearing your mom say yes."

He grins back at him. "Thanks, Dad."

I instantly start sobbing once more. I've never heard my son say that word in that context before, and hearing it now is almost too much for my overflowing heart to bear. Nothing can top this moment, this life we're creating.

TD squeezes my hand and leads me over to the couch once more. I can't help but steal a glance or two down at my ring, a ring I never thought I'd ever wear. My life has always revolved around raising my son, and now I realize how much better it is with TD by my side. We're a team, the two of us, and we have our whole lives ahead of us.

Brody plops down on the other side and pulls out his phone, already making a list. "Come on, Mom. We have a wedding to plan."

BOOKS ALSO BY lacey black

Rivers Edge series
Trust Me, Rivers Edge book 1 (Maddox and Avery) – FREE at all retailers
Fight Me, Rivers Edge book 2 (Jake and Erin)
Expect Me, Rivers Edge book 3 (Travis and Josselyn)
Promise Me: A Novella, Rivers Edge book 3.5 (Jase and Holly)
Protect Me, Rivers Edge book 4 (Nate and Lia)
Boss Me, Rivers Edge book 5 (Will and Carmen)
Trust Us: A Rivers Edge Christmas Novella (Maddox and Avery)
    ~ This novella was originally part of the Christmas Miracles Anthology
BOX SET – contains all 5 novels, 2 novellas, and a BONUS short story
With Me, A Rivers Edge Christmas Novella (Brooklyn and Becker)

Bound Together series
Submerged, Bound Together book 1 (Blake and Carly)
Profited, Bound Together book 2 (Reid and Dani)
Entwined, Bound Together book 3 (Luke and Sidney)

Summer Sisters series
My Kinda Kisses, Summer Sisters book 1 (Jaime and Ryan)
My Kinda Night, Summer Sisters book 2 (Payton and Dean)

My Kinda Song, Summer Sisters book 3 (Abby and Levi)
My Kinda Mess, Summer Sisters book 4 (Lexi and Linkin)
My Kinda Player, Summer Sisters book 5 (AJ and Sawyer)
My Kinda Player, Summer Sisters book 6 (Meghan and Nick)
My Kinda Wedding, A Summer Sisters Novella book 7 (Meghan and Nick)

Rockland Falls series
Love and Pancakes, Rockland Falls book 1
Love and Lingerie, Rockland Falls book 2
Love and Landscape, Rockland Falls book 3
Love and Neckties, Rockland Falls book 4

Standalone
Music Notes, a sexy contemporary romance standalone
A Place To Call Home, a Memorial Day novella
Exes and Ho Ho Ho's, a sexy contemporary romance standalone novella
Pants on Fire
Double Dog Dare You
Grip
Bachelor Swap, A Bachelor Tower Series Novel
Perfect Kiss, Mason Creek Series book 9
Waiting For Love, The Love Vixen Series book 11
Quarterback Keeper, a surprise baby novella
Kissing A Stranger, book 4 in the multi-author The Kissing Games series

Burgers and Brew Crüe Series
Kickstart My Heart, book 1
Don't Go Away Mad, book 2
Same Ol' Situation, book 3
Wild Side, book 4
What's It Gonna Take, book 5

Home Sweet Home, book 6
Too Young to Fall in Love, book 7
Without You, book 8
Time for Change, book 9
You're All I Need, book 10

Pine Village Series
Pretty Remarkable, a free prequel short story
Pretty Incredible, book 1
Pretty Dependable, book 2
Pretty Drunk, book 3
Pretty Relentless, book 4
Pretty Wild, book 5
Pretty Desperate, book 6

Snowflake Falls
Merry Little Mix-Up, book 1
Merry Little Sugar Rush, book 2

Co-Written with *NYT Bestselling* Author, Kaylee Ryan
It's Not Over, Fair Lakes book 1
Just Getting Started, Fair Lakes book 2
Can't Get Enough, Fair Lakes book 3
Fair Lakes Box Set
Boy Trouble
Home To You, a second chance novella
Beneath the Fallen Stars
Tell Me A Story
Royal – Writing as Rebel Shaw
Crying Shame – Writing as Rebel Shaw

ABOUT lacey black

USA Today Bestselling Author Lacey Black is a Midwestern girl with a passion for reading, writing, and shopping. She carries her e-reader with her everywhere she goes so she never misses an opportunity to read a few pages. Always looking for a happily ever after, Lacey is passionate about contemporary romance novels and enjoys it further when you mix in a little suspense. She resides in a small town in Illinois with her husband, two children, adorable black lab puppy, crazy cat, and three rowdy chickens.

Website: www.laceyblackbooks.com
Email: laceyblackwrites@gmail.com
Facebook: https://www.facebook.com/authorlaceyblack
Instagram: https://www.instagram.com/laceyblackwrites/
Bookbub: https://www.bookbub.com/authors/lacey-black
Amazon: https://www.amazon.com/Lacey-Black/e/B00MW2UGZI
Twitter: https://twitter.com/AuthLaceyBlack
Goodreads:
https://www.goodreads.com/author/show/8414783.Lacey_Black

Sign up for my newsletter so you don't miss a single sale, reveal, or release!
http://www.laceyblackbooks.com/newsletter

www.ingramcontent.com/pod-product-compliance
Lightning Source LLC
Chambersburg PA
CBHW060627260626
47161CB00008B/2817